CALLER ID

FROM THE AWARD WINNING AUTHOR OF
WRONG NUMBER

RACHELLE J. CHRISTENSEN

CALLER ID

FROM THE AWARD WINNING AUTHOR OF
WRONG NUMBER

RACHELLE J. CHRISTENSEN

SWEETWATER BOOKS
An imprint of Cedar Fort, Inc.
Springville, Utah

ISBN 13: 978-1-59955-990-2

Published by Sweetwater Books, an imprint of Cedar Fort, Inc.
2373 W. 700 S., Springville, UT, 84663
Distributed by Cedar Fort, Inc., www.cedarfort.com

LIBRARY OF CONGRESS CATALOGING-IN-PUBLICATION DATA

Christensen, R. J. (Rachelle J.), 1978-, author.
  Caller ID / Rachelle J. Christensen.
     pages cm
  Summary: Courtney Beckham, a twenty-three-year-old daughter of a rich and highly successful land developer, is abducted in the mountains near her home and held for ransom.
  Includes bibliographical references and index.
  ISBN 978-1-59955-990-2 (alk. paper)
  1. Kidnapping--Utah--Fiction. 2. Drug traffic--Utah--Fiction. I. Title.
  PS3603.H743C35 2012
  813'.6--dc23

                           2011046221

Cover design by Angela D. Olsen
Cover design © 2012 by Lyle Mortimer
Edited by Kelley Konzak

Printed in the United States of America

10 9 8 7 6 5 4 3 2 1

Printed on acid-free paper

To Patrick and Necia Jolley—For sharp eyes, giving hearts, and endless encouragement. Thank you.

And to Grandma RaNae, with love.

PRAISE FOR CALLER ID

"Fans of award-winning author Rachelle Christensen will be standing in line for her latest release, *Caller ID*. With tension, action, danger, and definite hints of romance, this book represents everything we love to read."

—Tristi Pinkston, author of the Secret Sisters Mysteries

"Rachelle Christensen does it again! *Caller ID* is a real page turner with a resourceful protagonist you'll root for."

—Heather Justesen, author of *Family by Design*

"Christensen weaves a fast-paced, witty tale that is impossible to put down. Special Agent Jason Edwards makes a hunky agent-in-shining armor that would be difficult for any girl to resist, even the privileged Courtney Beckham. A 2012 must read!"

—Nichole Giles, author of *The Sharp Edge of the Knife*

PRAISE FOR WRONG NUMBER

"I give Rachelle Christensen ten-plus out of ten for her debut novel and look forward to reading more of her work. *Wrong Number* is beautifully written, fast paced, and full of cliff hangers that make it impossible to put down. . . . I recommend this book for all readers who enjoy mind-wrinkling suspense, well sprinkled with mystery and clean romance."

—Anne Bradshaw, author of Famous Family Nights

"Rachelle Christensen has penned an exciting novel that will hook readers from the accidental discovery of a dead body to the thrilling and unexpected climax, with lots of twists and turns along the way. Don't expect to get a lot of sleep with this one. If the thrills of the chase don't get you, the thrills of the heart will. An excellent debut. I'll be looking for more by this author."

—Jeffrey S Savage, author of the Shandra Covington mystery series and the Farworld fantasy series

ACKNOWLEDGMENTS

I'M GRATEFUL for the opportunity I've had to fulfill my dreams of becoming a published author. I couldn't have achieved this goal without my publisher—thank you to everyone at Cedar Fort for the incredible work you do. A special thanks to my editors, Angie Workman and Kelley Konzak, for their impeccable skills, and to Angela Olsen and the fantastic graphic design team for another great cover.

I'm lucky to have an arsenal of wonderful writing friends who have helped me with this book from the earliest stages to the final draft. Thank you to Nichole Giles, Cindy Beck, Connie Hall, Patrick and Necia Jolley, Heather Justesen, and Tristi Pinkston.

I had many questions when it came to the law enforcement action in this novel. Lieutenant Gary Giles, Greg Knapp, Jeremy Leonard, and Alan Lisonbee provided great information on the workings of the FBI, DEA, and local police forces. Their insight was invaluable and any mistakes in these areas are my own. Thank you again for your time and service to our country.

Thanks to all of the great writers of LDStorymakers and Authors Incognito for their incredible resource of knowledge and experience.

Writing can be quite discouraging at times with the many revisions and rejections involved. I am so thankful to have the most supportive husband and family in the world. Thank you, Steve, for being my sounding board, for laughing at me when I talk to myself, and for encouraging me every step of the way. My parents and siblings are my biggest fans and it means so much to me to have their love and support.

Thanks to each of my four children for their enthusiasm in my writing and for sharing my love of reading. Thank you for being patient with me when I need "just one more minute" on the computer. I feel so blessed to be a part of such a loving family. I'm thankful for the talents the Lord has given me and the opportunities to keep trying each day to be better.

1

THE FLESH of the apple broke with a satisfying crunch as Courtney bit off another juicy mouthful. She tossed the core in the garbage and then bent to tighten the laces of her running shoes. Her cell phone beeped, and she checked the text that had just come through from her father.

They still haven't found the murderer. Are you running with Sean today?

Courtney shook her head. Even though she was twenty-three and able to take care of herself, Eric Beckham hadn't ceased worrying about his only daughter. She typed in a reply:

Yes. Running with Sean. Don't worry.

Courtney hurried out the front door and unlocked her car. She'd left work a half hour early to pick up office supplies and barely had time to change into her running shorts before it was time to meet Sean.

She slid into her Mini Cooper and revved the engine, heading up Big Cottonwood Canyon. She loved her bright yellow convertible, but the heat waves rolling through the rugged Utah mountains known as the Wasatch Front had Courtney turning up the AC and keeping the top closed.

Fifteen minutes later, Courtney parked off the side of a dirt road and glanced at her watch. It was half past six—Sean should've been here by now. The dry heat assaulted her as soon as she opened the door of her car. She stepped out and adjusted her sunglasses, then stretched her arms over her head. Courtney pulled her long, dark hair into a ponytail, then she walked around the back of her car and lifted the trunk to grab an extra water bottle from the arsenal she stored there.

"Hey, babe."

Courtney whirled around and ran right into a white shirt emblazoned with a red U. "Sean, you scared me!"

He chuckled and embraced her. "Hello to you too. Why are you so jumpy?"

"I didn't see your car—you surprised me."

"I'm parked right there past that stand of trees." He pointed to the back end of his dark green SUV.

Courtney squinted. "I can barely see it. You did that on purpose."

Sean smiled. "I'm here, aren't I?" He rubbed her arms. "You okay now?"

"I'm sorry. You know my dad doesn't want me running in this canyon or doing anything alone in this area. Ever since that guy was murdered last year, he thinks it's too dangerous."

"The marathon runner." Sean ran a hand through his wavy brown hair. "I remember that. Did they ever catch the guy who shot him?"

"No, but I'm sure the victim was involved in something bad. Normal people don't get murdered in the mountains while they're out for a run."

"Probably what that poor guy thought," Sean said.

"Now you sound like my dad."

"No, I don't. I'm not worried. That guy didn't have a two-hundred-sixty-pound tight end running with him." He flexed his arms over his head and grinned.

Courtney rolled her eyes.

"I just love it when you give me that look." Sean nuzzled her neck, leaving kisses along her jawline.

"I didn't give you a look," she murmured before he covered her mouth with his. She relaxed into his embrace and breathed in the tangy scent of his cologne. Her fingers brushed the coarse brown hair at the nape of his neck.

Sean Whitmore played football for the University of Utah, and the tight end position could be taken literally when it came to his body. Sculpted biceps and triceps kept the short sleeves of his shirt taut, and he spent a lot of time in the weight room to keep them that way.

Between kisses, Courtney inhaled and tipped her head back. "We'd better get started. Didn't you say you wanted to run six miles today?"

"Did I say that? I think I'd rather do something else. It's way too hot. You're way too hot." He leaned in for another kiss.

"I'm not letting you off that easy. It'll be cooler the higher we run up the trail. You'd better drink some of this." She untangled herself before Sean could kiss her again and pulled another water bottle from her trunk.

Closing the trunk, Courtney leaned against the car and drank the lukewarm water, gazing out at the city of Cottonwood Heights below her. She glanced at Sean and felt a nervous flutter in her stomach. He wasn't satisfied with just kissing anymore. Courtney had hoped he would be different than the other guys she'd dated. Her mother had advised her to tell Sean about the incident with Felix so he would understand why she needed to take things slow, but every time she thought about confiding in Sean, she felt the old anxiety taking over.

Instead of dealing with her problem, she'd adopted a carefree, flirty attitude to cover her nerves. It was easier that way. Everyone thought things were fine, and as long as she was careful, she could handle herself. When Courtney finished off the water, she tossed the bottle in her car and locked the doors.

Sean had walked to the edge of the tree line. He pulled his shirt over his head and tossed it into his SUV. "Ice cream tonight?"

Courtney lowered her eyes and sidled up next to him. His bare chest felt warm under the sun's rays. "If you can keep up with me." She gave him a quick peck on the cheek and dashed toward the trailhead. Sean grumbled, and she laughed when she heard him sprinting to catch up.

The run felt invigorating, even though the air was still dry with the July heat. The dark green branches of the fir trees stretched over the trail, shading them from the worst of the sun. They ran a full loop just shy of six miles and ended back at the side of the road next to Sean's SUV.

"Thanks, Court," Sean said. "You know how to push the limits." He pulled her close and kissed her.

"So do you," she said. "You may be good-looking, but your sweat still smells like a guy." She pointed at the sheen of perspiration on his chest and wrinkled her nose.

Sean laughed. "We're going to have to do this again, but the first home game is only a month away. Coach said the new assistant is gonna kick our butts with his practice schedule, so I'll be spending my time on the field."

"Am I going to have to find a new running partner?"

"You're going to have to find a new running route. Hey, maybe you can run around the practice field to help motivate me."

"I think that'd be more dangerous than running in the mountains with a murderer on the loose."

Sean put his arm around her waist, pulling her close. "This season is gonna be the best, thanks to my own personal cheerleader."

Courtney closed her eyes and felt his lips against hers. A thrill tingled up her spine as Sean murmured, "You're so beautiful." His hands felt warm against her tank top, and he hooked a finger under her shoulder strap and pulled it down her arm.

She swatted his hand away. "Don't stretch out my shirt. This is one of my favorites."

"C'mon, Court," Sean said. He kissed her again and trailed his fingers across her back.

Courtney stepped out of his grasp. "I'd better get going. I have a few things to finish up tonight for my dad."

Sean groaned. "Why do you always do this to me?"

"What? You know my rules."

Sean pressed his lips into a tight line and blew out a breath. "You're a tease."

"No, I'm not." Courtney felt her face flush with anger.

"Yes, you are." Sean's face was only inches from hers. "You always want to be the center of attention. You want everyone to notice you."

She stepped back. "What? Where's this coming from?"

"I used to like it. We'd walk into a room, and every guy would look up and think, '*Man, that is one fine chick. That guy is so lucky.*' And I was good with that because I figured they knew you were with me—you were mine." Sean blew out a breath. "But now I know you just want to play. You're never gonna get serious."

Courtney looked up at the cloudless sky above them and shook her head. "Well, I'm sorry if I'm not interested in your idea of getting serious."

"It's all a game to you, isn't it?" Sean said. "You're just having fun, right?"

"I was having fun, but it's not just a game." She rubbed the back of her neck and wished there was an easy way to explain her fears to Sean. "I've enjoyed spending time with you."

Sean swore. "What's it been? Almost two months? And you're still teasing me." He clenched his fists until his knuckles turned white. "And given the chance, you'd probably make out with half the guys in that room I was just talking about."

"You are a self-absorbed, first-rate jerk. You're mad at me because I'm willing to kiss a few guys but not sleep with them?" Courtney narrowed her eyes. "What are you saying?"

"I'm saying I'm tired of wasting my time with you." Sean pushed past her and yanked the door of his SUV open.

Courtney bit her lip to keep it from trembling. "I'm sorry you feel that way." The old hurt welled up inside her chest, but she didn't want Sean to see how he'd affected her. She headed for her car with her head held high. "Good luck with football. I hope you get your trash kicked."

Sean peeled out onto the road, kicking up dirt and gravel as Courtney walked away. She waited for the dust to settle before pushing the button to retract the hood of her convertible.

On the way home, Courtney refused to let herself cry. She'd seen the warning signs—a split with Sean was inevitable. Blinking rapidly kept the tears at bay—she didn't want her mom to see her with red, puffy eyes. Sean's words had cut her to the core. He hadn't taken the time to see past her façade. She wasn't just a pretty face or a tease. Clenching the steering wheel, she pressed down on the gas pedal. Men. They were all the same. They didn't want to get to know her—they just wanted action.

Courtney swallowed the lump in her throat and swiped the moisture from her eyes. She didn't want to get serious with anyone yet. There were reasons for that. She wanted to make some changes in her life, but it was hard when everyone expected her to act a certain way. If only she could find a guy who made her feel safe enough to open up, safe enough to be loved.

If the right guy was out there, Courtney definitely hadn't found him, and she was tired of looking. Finishing college topped her list, and most of her concentration lately had been on preparing for her final semester in the fall. She wanted to enjoy this time in her life, and that didn't include what Sean had in mind. Past experiences had given her a taste of caution when it came to getting serious with a guy.

With a sigh, Courtney pushed thoughts of Sean from her mind and tried to enjoy the drive. It was still eighty degrees, but as she coasted down the road bordered by pine trees and scrub oak, the breeze felt good on her skin. It took her less than fifteen minutes to drive through the forested area toward her parents' sprawling estate nestled in Big Cottonwood Canyon.

The paved driveway seemed to sweat under the oppressive heat as she approached the massive gates to her home. She pushed the button on her remote and the gate swung open so she could speed through. She didn't bother to park in the garage and flinched when her tires squealed as she turned sharp in front of the house.

Courtney punched in the code to open the front door and called out, "Mom, are you here?" Her own voice echoed against the high ceilings of the entryway. She traipsed into the oversized kitchen and dining room. It wasn't a surprise to find no one at home. For a moment, Courtney longed for the chance to talk to her mom about her boyfriend problems, but she pushed the thought aside. Maybe it was better this way. She wasn't in the mood for a lecture.

A bark and a jingle preceded the family dog, Pepper. Courtney bent to scratch the cocker spaniel's ears, and Pepper rolled onto his back. "Okay, you silly dog." She rubbed his tummy. The quiet of the house allowed her a moment to relax. She dropped chunks of ice into a glass of water. They clanked together and immediately began shrinking. She gulped the ice water and refilled her glass.

Her cell phone rang, and Pepper yipped and jumped up on Courtney as she answered the call. She smiled when her dad's picture popped up on the caller ID. People often told Courtney that she took after her father. Eric Beckham was a handsome man. At forty-nine, his black hair still fell thick above his brow line. Courtney had the same dark hazel eyes and high cheekbones, but she'd inherited her mother's small, lithe figure. "Hey, Dad. Aren't you at dinner?"

"Yes. Why didn't you answer your cell earlier? We've had some things come up at the office, and I wonder if you could cover for Mandy in the morning." His questions spilled out so quickly, Courtney wasn't sure which to answer first.

"I was running with Sean, remember?" She pulled the elastic from her hair and shook out the midnight strands. "I can cover for Mandy." Courtney didn't want to mention that she and Sean were history because then she'd have to hear the lecture about how she wouldn't have so many relationship problems if she would just date someone her father recommended for once.

"Have you seen your mother?" Eric's voice sounded terse.

"Nope. She's probably out with Heidi." Courtney untied her running shoes and wriggled her toes.

"Hmm. Well, I'll see you in the morning."

She straightened and climbed the stairs to her room. "Aren't you coming home tonight?"

Eric cleared his throat. "No, I have too many things at the office to finish up. I'd better let you go, Sweets."

"G'night."

As Courtney walked down the hall to her room, she glanced toward the master bedroom. Lately, her father had been sleeping at the office a few times a week, and her mother seemed to plan her nights out to coincide with his work schedule. It left Courtney with a quiet house to relax in, but she didn't like the uneasy feeling she had when she thought about her parents' marriage.

She swiped a strand of hair from her forehead and grabbed her cotton pajama shorts. A cool shower would feel good right about now. Her phone vibrated, and she unlocked the screen to view the incoming text. It was from Sean.

I'm sorry about tonight. Can I make it up to you? I'll pick you up tomorrow at six. Wear something nice.

She brushed the keypad with her fingers, trying to decide how to reply. Part of her wanted to tell him where he could go tomorrow at six. But she knew Sean was persistent. If she refused now, he'd call her the rest of the night—maybe even show up at the house—and she wasn't in the mood to fight with him.

Courtney frowned. Dating was such a pain. It was supposed to be fun, but there was way too much drama involved. Well, maybe she'd give Sean a taste of his own medicine. She smiled and pushed the keys rapidly.

Will a little black dress work?

She reclined against her pillow and tried to quiet her inner conscience telling her not to tease. Her phone pinged, signaling a new message.

Yeah, you look smokin' in black.

Putting off the inevitable breakup wasn't a good idea. Courtney pursed her lips. She'd figure out a way to end it with Sean—but not tonight.

With a sigh, she rolled over on the bed and flipped on the TV. She'd programmed the DVR to record the news every night so she could watch the sports highlights and stay up with Sean and his ramblings about college football. What a waste of time. She pushed "play" and began fast-forwarding through the headline news. She stopped when a ticker stating "Breaking News" caught her attention.

She rewound and read the ticker at the bottom of the screen: *Man arrested believed to be involved with last summer's murder in Big Cottonwood Canyon.*

So they finally found him. Courtney couldn't stop the smile from spreading across her face. She thought about all the times her dad had discouraged her from going horseback riding in the mountains near their property because of the murder. From the looks of things, the case was closed. It was time for a horseback ride.

2

THE DJ on Courtney's favorite pop station announced that it was six minutes past eight as she pulled into the parking lot the next morning. Courtney cringed. Late again. She dashed into the office, hoping she could sneak past the receptionist who also acted as her dad's personal assistant. When she rounded the corner, she saw Sandra, the efficient secretary, in front of the computer and no one there to distract her from Courtney's arrival. Courtney pasted on a smile.

"Hi, Sandra. Is my dad in a meeting?"

"Hello, Courtney." Sandra raised a finely penciled brow and pointed at one of the green lights on the phone system. "He's supposed to be leaving to meet with a contractor soon, but his line is still busy, so I think you can catch him."

"Thanks. I'll hurry."

Heads lifted as Courtney walked through the office. As the only child of Salt Lake Valley's largest and wealthiest developer, Courtney was privileged, but she'd worked hard to prove that she was more than a spoiled rich girl.

Awards and framed photos of Eric Beckham's buildings plastered the hallway. Courtney straightened her shoulders as she approached her father's office. She turned the knob slowly, inching the door open so she could see if he was busy.

"Natalie, I told you never to call this number."

Courtney flinched when she heard her father speak.

"You know why. I'm hanging up now."

Her father's voice, tenor with a bit of gravel, had always been easy to identify—especially when he was angry, which was how he sounded right now. She kept the door open just a crack. Eric leaned against the desk with the phone to his ear.

"No, we'll work it out later."

He hung up the phone and pushed a hand through his coarse black hair. Courtney knocked once as he turned toward his desk. He looked up as she entered.

"Hi, Daddy."

The angry slant of his eyebrows relaxed, and he smiled. "Hey, Court." Eric glanced at the clock. "I'm about to leave for a meeting. Did you need something?"

Courtney nodded and leaned against the leather chairs flanking the desk. "Mom mentioned you're thinking of selling the house in Park City."

Eric's mouth turned down, and he shook his head. "That woman can't keep a secret."

"It's okay, Daddy. I was just wondering if you'd hold off until September." Courtney squeezed the back of the chair and kept eye contact with her father. "My friends and I had planned a retreat there to kick off our senior year."

There was a knock at the door. Sandra opened it and stepped inside. "Eric, your clients are waiting."

"I'll be right there."

Sandra closed the door, and Eric grabbed a pile of papers off his desk. "I'll see what I can do." He patted Courtney's back. "We'll still have the condo, you know."

Courtney frowned. "It's not nearly as big."

"But it's the location that matters, right?" He grinned. "I have to go. Let's talk later."

"Thanks, Dad." Courtney moved to follow him out of the office but then hesitated. She was curious about the phone call she'd overheard. Who was Natalie? She glanced at the door. Her father had left it slightly ajar when he exited. She hurried to his desk and grabbed a pad of sticky notes and a pen. If Sandra returned, she wanted to look busy.

Her finger hesitated over the caller ID button. She looked at the doorway once more and pushed the button. The screen flickered, and she watched the words *Tropical Resources* move slowly across, followed by the number. Courtney didn't recognize the area code, which meant it was out of state.

She furrowed her brow, thinking of the accounts she'd worked on. All their subcontractors and suppliers were either in the state of Utah or in a handful of states in the surrounding region—maybe her dad was looking into other avenues for suppliers. Courtney recalled the anger she'd overheard in his voice. Why was he so upset?

Her cell phone jangled with an incoming text message. Courtney sucked in a breath and backed away from her father's desk. She read the text from Sean.

Can't wait to see that little black dress tonight.

Courtney responded as she exited her father's office.

Sorry, won't be able to make it. I'm working for my dad today.

She'd had to cancel on Sean before, so he probably wouldn't think too much of it. Maybe it'd give her time to come up with a way to let him down easy. Courtney glanced back at her father's office and then mentally tamped down her curiosity. The line of filing cabinets she passed on her way out of the office reminded her that she had plenty to keep her busy at Beckham Development without worrying about random phone calls.

At the end of the hall, there was a small waiting area with two upholstered chairs and a glass-topped coffee table. A pile of framed photos stacked haphazardly on the table caught her eye, and she stepped closer. Courtney reached out to pull the first frame off the stack.

Her fingers stilled as the fluorescent light cast a glare on the photo. Her throat tightened, and she glanced nervously around before focusing on the smiling face of the handsome young man. Felix Haran. The blood pulsing through her veins caused a throbbing near her temple. Her eyes flicked to the engraved brass square under his photo: *Employee of the Month*.

The photos must have been from a few years ago—probably

the same ones that had hung in the lounge upstairs she had care-fully avoided when Felix's picture first went up. The insides of her hands tingled as the frame pinched her skin. She hadn't realized how tightly she was gripping the picture. With another glance down the hall, she shoved the frame underneath some others in the stack. The whir of the air conditioner blew cool air on her back, and she wiped her sweaty palms on the sides of her pants.

He was gone. He couldn't hurt her anymore. Courtney heard footsteps and plastered a smile on her face. She wouldn't let him ruin another moment of her day. She rounded the corner and bumped into Corbin Whittier.

"Hey, Cobra. What's up?"

"I've been looking for you." The tattoo of a cobra on his forearm wriggled as he tensed and relaxed his muscles. "You'll be working with me today. Mandy's been assisting me on the Highland project."

"I'll be glad to help." Courtney's smile widened as she realized Cobra was saving her from filing duties with Sandra.

She followed Cobra into his office, and he motioned for her to close the door. His Rolex flashed under the fluorescent light—being Eric Beckham's right-hand man paid well. She pushed the door shut and turned toward him. He lifted his eyes to hers. "I asked your dad to have you cover for Mandy."

"Thanks. I'm so glad I don't have to stand in front of a filing cabinet all day." She set her purse on the floor and twisted her watch-band around her wrist. She mentally calmed the butterflies in her stomach—the crush she'd had on Cobra since he was first hired always left her feeling a bit flustered in his presence.

"I haven't seen much of you lately, Court." He clasped his hands in front of him, popping his knuckles. "You're lookin' great, by the way."

She followed his gaze to the mint green blouse and tan capris she wore.

"Are you busy this Saturday?"

Her cheeks lifted in a smile. "That depends if you're asking me for business or pleasure."

"Definitely pleasure."

Courtney had worked with Cobra before. He was thirty-one but often joked that he felt closer to her twenty-three years. She remembered when he'd told her why he'd chosen a cobra for his tattoo. "When I strike, it's for the kill."

"It's a good thing I was a snake charmer in a past life," she had responded.

"I don't think it was a past life," Cobra had said.

Courtney decided to sidestep his question for now. She rolled her shoulders back. "Do you want me to type up some documents?"

"Yeah, I need these files merged together." He pointed to his computer screen and patted the chair next to it. "Have a seat."

She walked around the sleek black desk and sat down. Several different documents were up on the screen. Cobra looked over her shoulder and motioned to three of the documents. "I'd like to merge this information into a spreadsheet. You're good with Excel. I was hoping you could create an expense tracker that's a little more sophisticated than what I've been using."

Courtney could feel his breath warming the back of her neck and fought the urge to turn and look at him. "Sure, that shouldn't take long."

"I'm still wondering if you're busy this Saturday."

"Tomorrow?" She swiveled in the chair to meet Cobra's gaze.

"Yeah, tomorrow afternoon some buddies and I are taking my boat out for a spin. Do you like wakeboarding?"

"I love it. It's been a while since I've been, though." Courtney thought about the horseback ride she wanted to take. She'd stopped by the stable and fed Tika some carrots this morning. Then she thought about Sean, and her face flushed—he thought they were still a couple, and she wasn't ready for a breakup fight to prove otherwise.

Cobra interrupted her thoughts. "Then come with me."

She flicked her hair over her shoulder. She thought of Felix's picture, and a nervous tremor ran through her. She opted not to tell Cobra about her impending breakup with Sean. "I'm seeing someone."

"Sure, I've heard. You're always seeing someone. It's the football player lately, isn't it?"

She raised her eyebrows. "How do you know?"

"I work with your dad, remember?" Cobra pulled his chair closer to Courtney. "And I might add that he approves of me." Cobra over-saw every new project from the planning stages to the building crews and worked closely with Eric. Courtney thought about her father's admonition to date more responsible men.

"But you're too old." She laughed when Cobra raised his eyebrows.

"And you're too young." He ran a hand over his shaved head. "I thought being in your twenties was all about having fun."

She thought of Sean's comment—it was cruel of him to say the things he did. If she kept busy enough, she wouldn't have to face him. Courtney smiled at Cobra. She didn't need to be scared of him. Maybe dating someone older would be a good idea. "Okay, what time?"

"I'll pick you up around two." Cobra put a hand on her knee and leaned toward her.

Someone knocked before Courtney could react to his closeness. Cobra smiled at her and headed for the door.

"I'll get going on this." Courtney motioned to the computer.

Sandra walked in as soon as Cobra opened the door. "Corbin," she said with a curt nod. She strode across the office toward Court-ney. "Your dad asked me to have you check your email as soon as you can."

"Thanks, I'll do it now." Courtney pulled up her email account as Sandra exited the office.

She glanced at Cobra. "I'll be just a minute."

He waved his hand. "No worries."

Courtney opened up the email her father had sent.

Sweets,

I'm planning a surprise getaway for Mom. We're leaving at six in the morning, and we'll be gone for three days. Have a good weekend and don't get in too much trouble.

Love you,
Dad

Courtney looked up to find Cobra watching her.

"What is it?"

"Nothing. My dad told me to have a good weekend since he's kidnapping my mom for a getaway."

Cobra grinned. "See, now you have to come boating. Daddy's orders."

She tossed a pencil in his direction and turned back to the computer screen. She typed a quick response telling her dad to have fun, and then she closed her account and focused on work. Cobra made phone calls while she spent the next two hours putting together the spreadsheet.

"Done," she said after color-coding the last expense tracker.

Cobra's office chair squeaked as he pulled it up behind her and leaned over her shoulder. "Show me."

Ignoring the increase in her heart rate, she highlighted a few of the features she'd created. "It's not that great."

"You're a whiz with this program." She felt his hand on her back. "Court, this is fantastic. Thanks so much."

She pushed her hair behind her ears. "Thanks."

"You've kind of surprised me this summer," Cobra said. "You're not just Daddy's little rich girl. You're a chip off the old block."

"Don't be fooled. I had to take a class in college to get these kinds of skills in Excel."

Cobra trailed his fingers along her arm. "Beautiful and smart."

She looked down at his forearm, at the snake tattoo imprinted with brown and gold, the red eyes staring up at her. It was hard to ignore the attraction she felt for Cobra, but her conflicted feelings over what had happened with Sean made her self-conscious about flirting. Maybe it was time to try a different approach. She shrugged out from under Cobra's touch and stood abruptly. "Do you need me to do anything else?"

Cobra stood as well and closed the distance between them with one step. "Yeah," he murmured. With a swift movement, he pulled her to him and crushed her lips in a fiery kiss. Courtney was stunned, frozen to the spot. She allowed her lips to soften as she wondered where the kiss was coming from. She'd worked with Cobra plenty of times before, and he'd never done more than flirt.

He moved back and pulled his bottom lip between his teeth. His blue eyes glimmered with desire, and he leaned toward her, slower this time. *So much for trying a different approach*, she thought.

Her cell phone beeped. She swallowed and pulled back. He held on, moving his hands down her sides. Her face felt hot, as if his lips had burned into her skin. She put a hand on his chest. "I—I have to think about this." She ducked her head and grabbed her cell phone. Her mom had just sent her a text. Before she opened it, she looked at Cobra. He smiled at her and squeezed her hand.

"You're not going to bail on me tomorrow, are you?"

She looked at his hand with uncertainty, wondering what path she'd just sprinted down. "No. If I don't want to do something, I won't do it."

"That's my girl." He brushed his lips against her cheek.

"I'd better go." She headed for the door, needing a reprieve from the electricity buzzing between them.

"I'll see you tomorrow then."

"Okay." She walked out of his office, opening the text her mom had sent.

Can you meet me for lunch? I haven't seen you much this week.

Courtney narrowed her eyes. Her mom wanted to spend time with her? Usually Chloe was too busy with her myriad spa appointments and volunteer committee lunch dates to make time for her only daughter. Courtney entered a quick reply.

Sorry, Dad wants me to finish up work before the weekend.

Courtney headed for the air vent in the hall and stood directly below it, letting the AC remove the flush from her cheeks as she thought of Cobra's kiss. Sure, she might flirt a little, but she'd never let a guy kiss her *before* dating him.

Her cell phone rang, and when Courtney saw it was her mother calling, she hurried to answer.

"Hi, Mom."

"It's pretty sad when a mother has to make an appointment to talk to her own daughter."

"I'm not the one who's never home," Courtney retorted.

"I know. We just keep missing each other," Chloe said. "So, are you doing anything with Sean tonight?"

Courtney walked outside so that someone in the office wouldn't overhear her conversation. A green ash tree offered some shade, and she stepped into the cool shadow. "Nope, and I won't be doing anything with him ever again."

"Oh, dear. Did you two break up?"

Courtney pulled a leaf off the tree and twirled it in her fingers. "Not yet, but as soon as I feel up to dealing with him, I will."

Chloe was sympathetic as Courtney explained about Sean's angry outburst when she wouldn't let him cross the line. "I liked Sean. He's smart and he's always been willing to help me study. We've had lots of fun times too." Courtney sighed. "Men are so confusing. Sometimes I wonder about that spark—when I'll feel it. You know, more than just physical attraction."

"You'll know," Chloe said. "It'll knock you down, and you won't be able to breathe right for days."

Courtney could almost hear her mom's smile through the phone. She wondered what had happened to the spark her parents must have felt at some point. Chloe murmured something, and Courtney could hear voices in the background. "Sorry we couldn't meet up, Mom."

"That's okay. What are your plans tomorrow?"

"I thought about taking Tika for a ride." Courtney kept her voice neutral. "I haven't been able to ride her as much this summer."

"Just as long as you don't go into the woods." Chloe's voice was rich and demanding. "You know your dad doesn't like it."

"But didn't you hear? They caught the guy."

Chloe tsked. "I did hear, and this morning they said it was a mistake. He's been cleared of all charges. Whoever killed that man is still running free."

"But Mom, that's like a freak thing. I'm sure he was involved in *something*."

"Court, you know how your dad feels. He wants to keep you safe."

"Okay, okay."

"See you later." Chloe ended the call, and Courtney stared at her cell phone for a moment. Tomorrow morning, her parents would be gone, and what they didn't know wouldn't hurt them.

3

COURTNEY SLEPT later than she'd planned. The absence of the usual morning sounds in the kitchen indicated that her dad had been successful in stealing her mother away for the weekend. It was eight o'clock. The sun had been up only a few hours. If she hurried, she could run Tika to the edge of the forest before it grew too hot. She put on a baseball cap and pulled her long ponytail through the back.

She ate a simple breakfast of grapefruit and whole wheat toast slathered with peanut butter. On her way out of the kitchen, she grabbed a water bottle and granola bar.

"C'mon, Pepper, let's go for a ride," Courtney called to the spaniel. He barked and followed close at her heels. When Pepper was still a puppy, Courtney had taken him for a horseback ride twice a week. He still loved to sit in front of her on the saddle, his tongue lolling to the side as they climbed the steep mountain trails of Big Cottonwood Canyon.

"Hi, Tika." The chestnut-colored mare flared her nostrils and snuffled at Courtney's hand. "We're going up the mountain today. You haven't gotten fat on me, have you?" Courtney rubbed the horse's sleek neck and checked her hooves.

Pulling the tack from the hooks in the stable, Courtney hummed as she approached Tika. The air held a stillness today, as if the rising sun had scorched the very breath from the insects. Not even a breeze rustled the leaves of the quaking aspens.

"We'd better hurry, Tika, before it gets too hot." By the time the ride was over, she'd definitely be ready for a cool dip in the lake.

Courtney felt a small thrill when she thought about Cobra. The black and green swimsuit she'd set out would accent the green flecks in her hazel eyes. Cobra would approve, and Courtney was pretty certain there would be more kissing by the day's end if she wasn't careful about it. She thought about the act she had mastered so well over the past few years and wondered what Cobra would think of her if he took the time to get to know the "real" Courtney Beckham.

Sean hadn't been able to see past the surface. Maybe she should have opened up sooner, given him a glimpse of what was inside her head. But something told her it wouldn't have made any difference. Sean had tried to call her last night, but she wasn't interested in hashing out a breakup, so she ignored his voice mail and subsequent texts.

Her mind was so focused on figuring out her dating dilemmas that her hands moved automatically to saddle Tika. The horse stood still, her flanks quivering with anticipation of the ride ahead.

Courtney led Tika out of the stable to the water trough near the edge of the field where the mare grazed. She turned the water on and let her horse take a long drink.

"Up, Pepper," Courtney called as she crouched down. The spaniel jumped into her arms, and Courtney lifted him onto the saddle. Pepper balanced himself as Courtney pulled herself up behind him. She clicked her tongue, and Tika began moving at a brisk trot.

"Easy," Courtney warned with a tug of the reins. "We don't want Pepper to fall off." She would hold the mare back until they reached the open field. Then the dog would have to jump down so that horse and rider could gallop at top speed.

Courtney hadn't told the ranch hand, Richie Halstrom, about her plans to ride because she didn't want to explain where she was headed. Her father had been adamant about staying out of the woods near their property. Her ponytail bobbed up and down with the horse's canter, and she smiled up at the sky. Her dad's overprotective nature had kept Courtney from enjoying a ride on her favorite mountain trail for over a year now. Sometimes a girl just needed some time to enjoy nature and try to find herself. Besides, Courtney was certain there was no danger in riding a few miles from home.

Thirty minutes later, she reined Tika to a halt and allowed Pepper to dismount. The spaniel yipped and dashed across the field. They loped across the open terrain, and Courtney loved the rush of air against her skin. Her shirt billowed out on the bit of breeze, and she heard Pepper bark in front of them. Courtney nudged Tika to the right as they drew closer to the edge of the field. The mare's fluid movements allowed Courtney to ride with ease. Galloping was still a workout for both of them, but Tika seemed to enjoy the exercise as much as her rider.

After fifteen minutes of hard riding, they came to a stop at the eastern edge of the field. Tika's flanks were hot, and sweaty lather clung to the reddish-brown hair on her legs. Courtney downed a full water bottle and tucked the empty container back in the saddle bag. She retrieved her cell phone from the bag and checked for text messages. There weren't any, so she slid the phone into the back pocket of her capris.

The quiet pressed in on them, and Courtney noted each trill of the black-capped chickadees and the crunching of dry weeds beneath horse hooves. Pepper snuffled through the brown grasses and then lifted his nose to the air. With a woof, he sprinted into the forest.

"Pepper!" Courtney sat up in the saddle and watched the dog disappear in the underbrush. "Come here!"

She urged Tika forward and stopped near a grove of quaking aspen trees. She listened, but the dog thrashed through the woods with no sign of returning. Courtney groaned and slid off the saddle. "C'mon, Tika." She grabbed the reins and led the horse to the edge of the clearing. Sliding the reins over Tika's head, Courtney looped them around a low-hanging branch. "You wait here, and I'll go get Pepper. I need to stretch my legs anyway."

Courtney ducked under the branch of a fir tree and walked in a crooked line, dodging tree roots to find her dog. Her legs ached from the ride, and her shirt clung to her back. She checked her watch. Almost eleven, and the sun had nearly risen to its peak. Time had gotten away from her. She was still a good forty-five minutes from home.

"Pepper! Come here, boy." Courtney stumbled when her toe caught on a rock. She scraped her arm against a tree as she fell on top of a bush. "Ouch! Pepper! I don't have time for this."

Clenching her jaw, she looked at the bright red scrape on her arm. Blood trickled down to her elbow. She sucked in a breath as the air hitting the wound increased the stinging sensation. Brown lines of dirt crisscrossed the scrape. Courtney stopped to get her bearings.

A creek ran diagonally through the mountains in this region. If she could locate it, she could wash her arm and probably find Pepper nearby. Courtney kept walking until she could hear the faint rush of the stream. She paused, listening for the jangle of Pepper's dog tags, but everything around her was eerily devoid of sound. Pepper must have spooked all the birds away.

Her throbbing arm kept pace with her footsteps crunching against small twigs and bits of dried leaves. She glanced at her watch again—she'd been hiking for fifteen minutes already. If she didn't find Pepper soon, she'd have to go back without him. Her brow felt sticky with sweat, and she wanted to take a quick shower before Cobra arrived.

The gurgle of the creek grew louder as she climbed higher along the rough path. Courtney noticed a clump of purple and white columbine growing near the water. She stepped over a fallen tree, pushed past a grove of scrub oak, and saw the water below. The creek ran slower this time of year as every living thing and bit of under-brush soaked up the water along the way. Courtney scrambled across the rocks lining the stream and knelt near the edge. Thrusting her arm into the current, she stiffened and then exhaled as the frigid liquid cascaded over the deep scratches. She cupped the water in her hands, drank a few mouthfuls, and then rose from her knees.

The path was uneven and rocky. Courtney moved carefully, the skittering of rocks accompanying each step. Her shoe caught on something, and she started at the strange sound the contact had created. She halted and listened, then glanced at her foot. A piece of black plastic tubing lay partly uncovered in the dirt. She nudged her toe against it, and it moved. The hollow ping of the plastic hose was what she had heard. She kicked at it, listening for the noise again.

This time her foot went underneath the tubing and snagged. She grunted and stumbled to her knees. It wasn't just a piece of hose, she realized as she examined the tubing in her hands. She pulled upward, and the tubing lifted from the underbrush surrounding the trees.

It was about a half-inch in diameter, easily hidden in the weeds and wildflowers off the trail. Courtney took a few steps, lifting the dirt-encrusted plastic as she went. She could feel the water rushing through it. It was connected to the stream. Courtney was certain this terrain was on the US Forest Service grounds. Why would they channel water from the creek?

She dropped the tubing to the ground but could see that it continued away from the stream. She walked through a bunch of quaking aspens, following the pipe for several yards into a small clearing. Her eyes widened as she took in her surroundings. Goose bumps scattered across her skin.

Thick plants pushed their pointy tips toward the sky. The drizzle of water in the undergrowth tickled her senses, and Courtney saw the end of the black tubing a few feet in front of her. The dark green plants were thriving in the rich soil, which was almost black with moisture.

Courtney thought of all the news reports she'd seen, the TV shows, and took a step back. The five-starred plants were foreign to this area. Marijuana. Someone must have planted it. Some of the plants stood at eye level to Courtney's five-foot-six frame. Just as she was contemplating that the plants must be nearly ready to harvest, she heard a twig snap behind her.

4

COURTNEY SPUN around. A man stood two paces from her. Fear ricocheted through her rib cage, and she bit back a scream.

"I—I lost my dog," she stammered as her heart raced with a surge of adrenaline. "Have you seen him?"

The man's dark skin glistened with sweat. He frowned and rubbed a hand over his black goatee. Then he shook his head and took a step forward.

"Pepper!" Courtney called. Her eyes swept to the left and right. "Pepper!"

She saw a flash of movement out of the corner of her eye and turned as something struck the side of her skull. Her teeth clattered together, and the ground rose up to meet her.

She screamed, but the impact of the fall knocked the wind out of her.

She lay heaving for a moment, head spinning and pain radiating through her skull. Her mind grasped at the surroundings, trying to focus.

Courtney's eyes flew open as someone yanked her arms from behind. The world spun as the man held her arms tight behind her back. He grunted and pulled Courtney to her feet. The sudden movement made her stomach roll, and she began dry heaving while still trying to suck in enough air to breathe. She tried to scream again, but her lungs couldn't seem to communicate with her brain.

Rough hands shook her, and she heard rapid Spanish. She struggled as her arms were tied behind her back. There were two men now, and they pushed her forward. Courtney realized how much trouble she was in and tried to think of something she could say to convince them to release her.

"Please. I won't tell anyone. I got lost. I don't even know where I am." They hauled her out of the clearing and back toward the creek, but then they turned and headed north through the woods. Courtney thrashed and screamed until they stuffed a dirty rag in her mouth.

Pepper came bounding up as they passed close to the creek bed. Courtney cried out against the rag and lurched forward. The man with the goatee barely caught her before she hit the ground. The other man pulled out a gunnysack and grabbed Pepper. He stuffed the dog in the bag and slung it over his shoulder.

They forced Courtney to keep walking, and she cringed as she heard Pepper yipping and whining inside the bag. With every passing second, Courtney grew more desperate. Where were they taking her? It had to be because she'd discovered the patch of marijuana. Would they kill her?

She felt tears prick her eyes as her father's stern voice echoed through her memory. He'd warned her about the danger in the mountains. A cry raked through her parched throat. The marathon runner killed last year. Were these men the murderers? Courtney shook her head. She couldn't believe that these men were behind it.

One of the men pulled a gun from his waistband, and Courtney stiffened. The lump on her head probably matched the handle of the gun. He clicked on a digital walkie-talkie and spoke again in his native language. Two years of high-school Spanish was enough for her to catch the words "chica" and "muerte," and she shuddered.

Fear washed over her, and she stopped walking, but the man beside her shoved her forward. The other man turned and waved his gun at her. She felt the blood draining from her face. They walked for several minutes, Courtney stumbling as the mountainside grew steeper. The men halted when they heard the sounds of an engine. Courtney felt a surge of hope, but when she noticed how calm her captors were, she knew the sound meant more trouble.

The noise of the engine grew louder, and Courtney saw an ATV with camouflage paint emerge on the trail above them. The man driving also had brown skin, and his jet-black hair was pulled back into a ponytail. He drove up beside them, and as Courtney scrutinized him, she saw his eyes widen with some kind of emotion. Hope flared in her chest again, and she cried out a muffled plea for help. He frowned and spoke in Spanish. She heard a name, Adán, and saw the man with the goatee step forward. The driver nodded at the men.

"Don't scream," he said as he pulled the rag from her mouth. Courtney coughed and spit out the foul taste of the dirty cloth. Her mouth felt like it was full of cotton balls, and she couldn't get her vocal chords to work.

"I'm going to take you for a little ride." He patted the seat behind him, and Courtney struggled to find her voice.

"Please, I'm lost. I was looking for my dog, and they hit me." She tried to move her hands, her shoulders burning from her arms hanging heavy behind her back.

"You saw too much," he said with a clipped Spanish accent.

"No, I was trying to find my dog," Courtney cried. "Please, I don't know what I did—why you're doing this to me. Please." Her eyes filled with tears as she watched the man shake his head.

"Get on the four-wheeler," he muttered.

Courtney lifted her shoulders. "I won't be able to stay on with my hands like this."

His eyes flicked over her, and he gave a command in Spanish. Adán yanked at her arms, and Courtney cried out. His rough actions freed her hands, but he rapidly pulled her arms in front of her and retied the nylon chord tight around her wrists. He pushed her closer to the ATV. Courtney turned to the other man, who held Pepper in the gunnysack.

"My dog," she whispered.

"Mátalo," said the man with the ponytail.

"No! Please, don't!" Courtney screamed when she recognized the command to kill in Spanish. The man on the ATV jumped off and slapped her.

"Shut up! Or I'll have him do it right now."

Courtney stopped—her cheek throbbing from the impact of his

25

brawny arm. Her vision clouded, and she struggled to focus. She heard a muffled yelp from Pepper. She turned and, with a scream of rage, rammed her body into the man holding the gunnysack.

He tripped and fell down, and Courtney couldn't keep from falling on top of him. The momentum carried her forward, and she rolled over and scrambled to her feet. Pepper wriggled from the sack and barked as Courtney stumbled toward him.

"Pepper, run!" Courtney screamed as she lunged forward. Pepper yelped and scampered around in a circle. Courtney's feet pushed against the uneven ground, and she broke into a run.

She only made it three steps before she felt the impact of someone colliding into her. Courtney hit the ground and continued trying to break free, struggling and screaming.

The driver cursed. "Do you want to die right here?" He shoved her face to the ground, and it felt like every particle of soil was a tiny blade, scratching her skin. She tasted dirt and blood in her mouth.

"Jesse," he growled and gave a command in Spanish. The other man smiled and replied. Courtney heard the name Ramiro, and she turned her head toward the driver. Jesse ran off in the direction Pepper had escaped.

Courtney watched him go and wondered if Pepper would make it back to Tika. Tika! They didn't know about her horse. Richie would come looking for her. Then she remembered her decision to call Richie when she got back from her ride to have him tend to Tika. The mare might not be missed until morning when Richie came by the stables. She groaned as the realization of her situation hit her full-force.

The driver stood and yanked Courtney up again. "You're coming with me, either dead or alive." He grinned and gripped her ponytail, pulling her to him. "I'd rather keep you alive. A lot more fun for everyone."

Courtney spat the dirt and blood from her mouth into his face. He recoiled and raised his hand. She ducked, but his open palm still connected with the side of her head. He cursed and dragged her toward the four-wheeler.

As he forced her onward, she remembered all the emails she'd read about kidnappers. She shuddered when she recalled watching an Oprah special about defending yourself, the news stories about never leaving the initial location with the kidnapper. She remembered the haunting statistics of what happened to women when a kidnapper took them to a second location. She couldn't remember exactly, but it seemed like most of them died. A panicky feeling threatened to overtake rational thought. She felt more afraid than she ever had in her life.

Courtney's wrists chafed against the ropes, her body was covered with abrasions, and her head hurt so bad she couldn't see straight. The man straddled the ATV. "Get on."

Courtney considered her options. If she tried to run, the risk that she would fall was too great because her hands were tied. She couldn't outrun Ramiro. Her eyes flicked to the gun he held nonchalantly, his fingers tickling the trigger.

"What are you going to do with me, Ramiro?"

The driver looked up. So she knew that was his name. He leered at her. "I'm not going to kill you if you cooperate."

The thought flashed through her head, *Would death be so much worse than what this man has planned?* Courtney struggled to keep the debilitating panic from overtaking her presence of mind. "Please, can't you let me go? I won't tell anyone."

"We'll see." Ramiro tapped the handgun as he lodged it in the waist of his jeans. "Don't try to run again, or I'll put you down right here. Now get on."

Adán stood behind her, his gun pointed in her direction. Courtney gulped back tears and climbed on. Ramiro shouted something to Adán as he gunned the engine, and they began the climb up the mountain.

Courtney squeezed her thighs against the seat, trying to stay balanced without leaning into Ramiro. Her legs already ached from the long horse ride, and soon her thighs were screaming for mercy. Fumbling with the ties on her hands did nothing to ease the pain of the rope burns on her wrists. Courtney thought about her parents, and disappointment washed over her. They had both warned her to stay out of the mountains, and she hadn't listened.

After riding for fifteen minutes, Ramiro looked back. "Hold on. We've got a steep climb ahead."

Courtney's head throbbed, her body felt like it had been rubbed down with sandpaper, and she felt disoriented. She tried to calculate how far she'd traveled from where she tied Tika to the tree. She turned her arm to look at her watch. It was already one fifteen in the afternoon. Cobra would be coming to pick her up in forty-five minutes. Would he look for her when she didn't show?

Her lips tingled when she thought of the way he'd kissed her. But then he'd asked, "You're not going to bail on me, are you?"

Fresh tears filled her eyes. Cobra wouldn't look for her—he'd probably be angry because she was a no-show.

She should've called him when Pepper ran off—then he wouldn't think she was ditching him. Her phone! Courtney could feel her cell phone in the back right pocket of her capris. She pulled at the rope on her hands and gritted her teeth.

Ramiro focused on the trail ahead of them as the motor of the four-wheeler rumbled, the all-terrain tires gripping the surface of the slope. Courtney sat up straight and reached her hands toward her right hip. The stretch in her left shoulder wasn't unpleasant, so she turned her body more, positioning her hands closer to her back pocket. Her fingers brushed the top of the pocket, and she moved forward and bumped into Ramiro.

He took his left hand and gripped her thigh, pulling her closer. "We're almost at the top." He patted her leg and then clutched the handlebar again.

Courtney pushed the tips of her fingers against the smooth surface of the phone, nudging it out of her pocket a centimeter at a time. They would probably search her and find her phone once they reached their destination. Now was her only chance.

Her arms ached, and she leaned farther into Ramiro to get a better angle on the phone. He turned his head to glance at Courtney, and she pulled her arms back in front of her.

"I feel like I'm going to fall off. I can't hold on to anything." She lifted her hands, bound tightly with rope.

Ramiro glared at her and gunned the engine. Courtney bounced in the seat and screamed. He laughed, and the sound sent chills of fear up her spine. She could feel her phone sticking out of her back pocket—the bumps had jostled it loose. As they crested the summit of the mountain, she forced her bound hands behind her again and grabbed the phone.

With careful movements, she pulled it from her pocket. Her fingers tensed, and she gripped the cell phone, bringing it in front of her. She held her breath as she unlocked the keys and pushed 9-1-1. The phone flashed when she pushed the "send" key, and she watched the words "Call Sending" float across the screen.

Her heart stuttered when the words changed to "Call Failed." She looked at the top of the screen and saw a phone with a red slash through it. No service.

Her lips trembled, and she moved her aching arms to her right side and worked on easing the phone back into her pocket. If she was lucky, there might be some way to get a call out later.

Ramiro shifted down to a lower gear, and Courtney's head jerked forward. A huge cabin stood about a hundred yards away. They hit a bump, and Courtney lost her grip on the phone. She turned to see it bounce off the path into the underbrush. The white and teal case glimmered in the sun, and Courtney prayed Ramiro wouldn't find it. She wanted to cry, but instead, she focused her attention forward as Ramiro parked the ATV in front of the cabin.

They must have crossed to the other side of the canyon. She knew there were cabins scattered throughout Big Cottonwood Canyon, but this one must be particularly isolated because only rough trails led up to it—trails only wide enough for an ATV.

"Welcome home," Ramiro said as his boots whipped over the side of the ATV and landed in the dirt. He pulled Courtney off and kept a firm hold on her arm.

A sick feeling rose in her stomach. Ramiro hadn't blindfolded her. He wasn't worried about her seeing the area. Her thoughts strayed to the reasons why he hadn't taken those precautions, and Courtney choked on her tears as she thought that twenty-three was too young to die.

They walked to the entrance of the two-story cabin. A deck ran along the west side, while the east side sat snug against the mountains. Ramiro paused by the front steps and looked at her with undisguised hunger in his eyes. Courtney turned her head away, trying to hide the tears running down her cheeks. He yanked on her arm, and she followed him inside.

Wildlife hung on every wall in the great room, giving her an ominous feeling about her future. Elk, deer, a bighorn sheep, and an antelope stared with glass eyes as Courtney and Ramiro walked farther into the room. Courtney gasped when they turned a corner and she saw a cougar crouched on a rock.

Ramiro laughed and tapped the glass case as they continued into the kitchen.

"What are you going to do with me?" Courtney asked again.

"You'll find out soon enough," Ramiro said. He pulled a glass from the cupboard and filled it with water. He took a long drink and held it in front of her. She lifted her hands to take it, but he pulled back and shook his head. Anger at being kidnapped surged through her. Ramiro was working hard to show his level of control, and Courtney detested him more with each passing second. She narrowed her eyes and pursed her lips, letting her hands drop in front of her. Ramiro held the glass and touched the cool cylinder to her mouth.

His fingers were brown, with lines of black soil embedded in every crease. She guessed him to be in his late twenties. The smooth, dark skin of his face was devoid of wrinkles. His mustache was neatly trimmed, and his thick hair was pulled back into a ponytail. She stared into the depths of his eyes and inhaled. She could still taste the dirt in her mouth, and her lips were so dry that they stuck together. Ramiro tipped the glass forward, and she gulped the water hungrily.

"More?" Ramiro asked as he shifted the empty glass back and forth.

"No, thanks." Courtney scanned the room for a back exit. Her nerves felt raw and her senses were frayed with the constant pressure of trying to figure out how to get away from Ramiro. Now was the time to carefully watch for a weakness in her captor that might lead to her escape.

He set the glass on the counter and took hold of her hands. Courtney winced. "Please, can you untie them? My wrists are raw."

Ramiro examined her wrists and took a step closer. "That depends on how you behave."

Courtney stiffened and backed away from him, but he still held her hands and closed the gap between them. She took another step back and felt the edge of the countertop. Ramiro's lips pulled back in a smirk, and she noticed stains on his teeth. He pressed his body against hers, and she thought about the decision she'd made as she rode behind him. He wouldn't take her without a fight.

"Don't." She turned her body and pushed her shoulder into his chest.

Ramiro grabbed hold of her arms and turned her to face him. He yanked her wrists, and Courtney winced again. "Remember what I said about behaving."

She swallowed hard as he leaned toward her. "I said, don't." She moved her leg, preparing to knee him in the groin, but he anticipated her and stepped to the side. With one fluid movement, he slung her over his shoulder and carried her from the kitchen. "Let me go!" Courtney screamed.

He shook her roughly in his arms. "You're testing my patience, bonita." He tightened his grip and climbed a massive staircase. By the time they reached the second floor, his forehead glistened with sweat from struggling to hold on to her.

The throbbing in her head had begun to subside after they got off the ATV, but now the pounding returned with renewed force. Courtney could see the ground floor below them as Ramiro turned to the right and carried her across an open game room with log railings on one side. He continued down a hallway and opened a bedroom door. He strode across the room and heaved her onto a king-size bed with a log frame.

"I think I'm going to throw up," Courtney said, lifting her head and doubling over.

Ramiro turned and grabbed a small wastebasket. He shoved it in front of her. "Go ahead."

Courtney squeezed her eyes shut and slumped back on the bed. "I'm serious. My head hurts from when that guy hit me with his gun."

"He hit you with his gun?"

She opened her eyes when she felt Ramiro's weight on the bed next to her. He crouched over her and touched her head. Courtney flinched.

"Just hold still. I want to look at your head, make sure you're okay."

The blood pulsed in her ears as he took off her baseball cap and pulled the elastic from her hair. He parted her dark locks and felt along her skull until she cried out.

"You've got a bump, but I think your hat kept the gun from breaking the skin." He rattled off something in Spanish that Courtney guessed were cuss words.

"You're so pretty." He hovered over her, his face inches from hers. "What were you doing in the woods today?" His fingers trailed along her cheek, and Courtney fought back the urge to flee.

A million thoughts cascaded through her mind with the force of a river rapid. She tried to focus, but her thoughts were punctuated with fear. Then she held onto an idea before it could be carried away in the stream of anxiety. They didn't know about her horse. Her only hope was that Tika would be found and lead someone in her direction before it was too late.

"My dog ran off, and I was trying to find him." Courtney watched his face for a reaction.

The black pupils in Ramiro's eyes nearly blended into his dark irises. "And what did you see?" He leaned forward slightly so that his body rested against hers. Courtney squirmed, and he reached his arm across her and squeezed her shoulder. "What did you see?"

Courtney bit her lip, trying to think of an answer that would appease him. "I saw the creek, and I walked around for about twenty minutes. I got lost."

Ramiro shifted his weight on top of her. "That's a lie. Tell me what you saw."

Courtney turned her head and cried. "I was lost. Those men attacked me. I didn't do anything. I didn't see anything." She kept her head turned and squeezed her eyes shut. She felt tears trickle across the bridge of her nose and heard the soft plops as they landed on the bedspread beneath her.

"Don't cry." Ramiro gently turned her to face him, but Courtney shook her head.

"Why won't you believe me?" She opened her eyes. "Why did you want to kill my dog?"

She could feel his hot breath on her cheek, and she picked up on a smell that unearthed a memory from her high school calculus class. The class was held after lunch, and every day, her friend Bruce would come in late, smelling just like Ramiro. Slightly sweet with a strange bit of spice that Courtney found out was the scent of marijuana.

Ramiro closed the distance between their lips, and a new fear crept into Courtney's heart. If he was high, her chances of reasoning with him would be severely diminished. She wondered what her best line of defense was. She kept her lips frozen in place, and he stopped and looked at her.

"Kiss me," he commanded.

She remained unresponsive, so he moved his mouth across the curve of her neck. He opened the light cotton button-up shirt she'd worn over her tank top and ran his hand up and down her side. Then he stopped. "Tell me what you saw. We'll have some fun, and I'll let you go."

Courtney's eyes filled with moisture. She didn't believe he would let her go, but maybe telling him something would keep him from getting angry. "Okay." Her voice trembled. "I saw a tent. I wondered who would be camping in that area."

"What else?" He kissed her jawline.

"That's all. I swear." She shifted her body away from his groping hands.

Ramiro hesitated and looked at her with a warning in his eyes. He crouched on the bed, and Courtney wriggled underneath him, waiting for just the right moment. When he lowered his head, she slammed her knee between his legs.

Ramiro howled and rolled off her, sucking air between his teeth. Courtney lunged forward, but he grabbed his gun and held it to her head, cursing as he pushed the barrel against her skull.

"Wait!" Courtney cried. She thought of something that might stall Ramiro and hoped it would work. "My father. He has a lot of money—he wouldn't bat an eye at a million-dollar ransom."

Ramiro grabbed her throat. "Quit playing with me. I'm tired of your games."

"It's not a game." Courtney's voice rasped.

He released her throat, but she could feel the cold steel of the gun pressing against her temple. "What's your name, and how can you prove your father is rich?"

Courtney licked her lips and tried to decide if she should tell the man her name. If he hadn't heard of her father, how could she prove to him she was telling the truth?

"Did you hear me? I said, 'Who are you?'" He nudged her head with the gun.

Her father was well-known throughout the valley as the richest developer in northern Utah—maybe his money could keep her alive. She made a decision. "My name is Courtney Beckham, and my father is Eric Beckham, the multimillion-dollar developer. Please, I know he'd pay anything."

Ramiro's eyes widened, and he jerked the gun from her head. "I should've known."

"What?" Courtney watched his face flit with different emotions. "Do you know who my father is?"

He rubbed his fingers over his mustache. "I've heard of him." He slid off the bed, and Courtney noticed he moved awkwardly from the impact to his groin. He glared at her. "You say he could pay a million?"

"He would pull that much together to save me," Courtney said. It was true, and she knew her parents could pay more, but Courtney didn't offer up that information. She held her breath, waiting for Ramiro to respond.

"I guess I've got some planning to do." He waved the gun. "Adán and Jesse will be here soon. Stay in this room and don't try anything stupid. Next time, they won't just hit you with a gun." He motioned toward the window. "Two stories straight down to a concrete patio. I'll let you rest, but I'm not through with you."

"My father will want to talk to me. If you do anything to me, I'll tell him, and he'll hunt you down and kill you."

Ramiro's eyes narrowed, and he opened his mouth as if to speak. Instead, he slid his gun into his waistband and tapped it. "If you want to stay alive, don't move."

Courtney sat up on the bed. "If you know anything about Eric Beckham, know this—he has ample resources, and he loves his only child. He'll fight to the death for me."

Ramiro left the room, and Courtney could hear him pounding down the stairs. Barely a minute later, she heard him returning. An aching fear overcame her as he tromped back in the bedroom. He tossed an apple and a bag of crackers toward her. "Remember what I said."

Courtney lowered her head, and tears filled her eyes. She watched the red hue of the apple blur as moisture streaked down her cheeks. She heard the door click shut, and she fell back onto the bed, her chest heaving with sobs. Every bone in her body ached, but at least Ramiro was gone. Fear like nothing else she'd ever experienced overwhelmed her senses. She pulled the comforter over her and cried until her throat was sore. The aching in her head hurt worse than ever, and she closed her eyes, trying to calm herself. She took deep breaths and pressed her hands to her temples. After several minutes, the throbbing began to subside, and Courtney drifted into a restless sleep.

5

"HONCHO, WE'VE got a problem." Ramiro spoke evenly into his cell phone.

"What now?" the man he referred to as Honcho replied in a gruff voice.

"Some girl wandered into the southeast crop." Ramiro heard a sharp intake of breath and a curse.

"Was it a hiker?" Honcho asked. "What did you do with her?"

"Adán and Jesse grabbed her, and I brought her back to the cabin. I was going to have a little fun with her, but then she told me her name." Ramiro paused. "I think you'll be interested in this one. Her name is Courtney Beckham."

"What? You kidnapped Courtney?" the man bellowed into the phone.

"The guys didn't know it was her, but she saw the crop," Ramiro said.

"Are you sure?"

"She said she saw the tent and is acting like she didn't see the plants, but they're as tall as me—she saw them."

The man cursed again. "Find her horse. She had to be riding to get up that far. She probably had a dog with her too."

"She did. I sent Adán after it," Ramiro said.

"His name's Pepper. Call him and he'll come around. Shoot him and ride the horse north to the other side of the canyon. Leave her to graze and take the dog into the woods. Smear some of his blood on

36

a piece of Courtney's shirt and leave it there."

"We're going to have to get that crop harvested now," Ramiro said.

"You'll have to work fast before someone comes looking for her," Honcho said. "How close is the crop?"

"I'd say at least another week, and even then, it'd be pushing it," Ramiro said.

There was silence on the phone for a moment, then the man grunted in frustration. "You're going to have to hold her there. I'll take care of the ransom note. We'll give it a week, clear out all the evidence, and then negotiate a ransom and return."

Ramiro shook his head. "It won't be easy to keep her here. She's feisty."

"Keep her tied up. Give her a few bruises. Scare her enough that she won't want to leave."

Ramiro snorted. "She's already pretty banged up. She put up a fight when the guys took her."

"You're going to have to get rid of Adán and Jesse."

"I'm not disposing of any more bodies. It's too risky."

"Then we'll have them deported." The man cleared his throat. "Send them into the city tomorrow to get supplies. I'll have someone there to apprehend them."

Ramiro paced back and forth between the mounted animals in the cabin. "I can't send them tomorrow. I'm going to need at least four more guys first. A couple to help guard the girl, and two more to guard the crop."

"Okay. Keep them busy, and I'll have your men up there by Monday. You can see about doing a partial harvest. And, Ramiro, keep your hands off her."

As soon as Ramiro hung up, he picked up his radio and barked out instructions to the men. They'd have to find the horse and ride it almost five miles away from the grove, but first they had to get some of Courtney's clothes. He glared at the phone and thought of Honcho's warning. With careful steps, he ascended the stairs and licked his lips.

Courtney hadn't slept long when she felt movement beside her. The backs of her eyes ached, and she tried to recall why her face felt raw. She came fully awake when she felt Ramiro's mustache tickle the side of her ear.

She held still and allowed the fog to clear from her mind, trying to think of how to get rid of the scumbag. Then his arm tightened around her waist.

Courtney stiffened and launched her head backward, ramming it into Ramiro's face. She cried out with the impact but kept moving as Ramiro moaned. Rolling off the side of the bed, Courtney dropped her head between her knees and tried to keep the room from spinning.

Ramiro howled and cursed as she crawled across the floor to the bathroom. She grabbed onto the door frame and pulled herself up. Stumbling into the bathroom, she tried to shut the door and screamed when she saw Ramiro running for her. His face had blood smeared across it, and his nose kept a steady stream of crimson dripping onto his shirt.

Ramiro grabbed the door frame before she could close the door and then yanked Courtney's arm.

"Stop it!" she screamed as he dragged her back into the bedroom.

"I'm gonna kill you!" He clenched his fist. As he pulled back, Courtney shielded her face with her arms, allowing them to take the brunt of the impact. She turned to run back toward the bathroom. Ramiro grabbed for her and caught hold of her sleeve.

She heard the fibers of her long-sleeved shirt tearing in his hand, and she cried out as he pulled her back. With a burst of energy, she jerked forward, and before he could react, she dashed into the bathroom, slammed the door, and locked it.

"Open the door!" Ramiro bellowed as he banged his fists against the wood. He rattled the door handle. "If I have to, I'll shoot through this door."

"Go right ahead. Let's see how much ransom money you can get with a dead body," Courtney yelled back. "I told you my father will want to talk to me before he pays anything."

Ramiro stopped banging on the door. "I need a piece of your shirt."

"Why?" Courtney glanced down at her shirt, noticing the ragged tear on her sleeve from their struggle.

"Just give it to me." Ramiro banged on the door so loudly that Courtney jumped.

"My hands are still tied. I can't get it off."

"Come out here and I'll help you." He jiggled the doorknob.

Courtney twisted her arms and tried to think how she could get her shirt off without Ramiro's help. Then she heard another sound coming from outside. The familiar rumble of an ATV skidding to a stop and Ramiro swearing as he moved away from the door gave Courtney a glimmer of hope.

The bathroom had one tiny window, but it was between the shower and the toilet, and all Courtney could do was stand on her tiptoes and look out. The window was on the back side of the cabin facing the woods. She saw the forest spreading before her, the evergreen trees holding their dark green branches wide, hiding the secrets she had stumbled upon.

Courtney crept closer to the door and listened. Ramiro must have left the room. The bathroom had a long vanity with built-in drawers and cupboards. She pulled all three drawers open to block the door, then pawed through the drawers for something sharp enough to cut the cords that still bound her hands.

She cried out with relief when she found an old disposable razor. She broke it apart and held the blade carefully in her fingers. They trembled as she sawed through the rope. Within a few minutes, she successfully cut through one strand and was able to pull her right hand free. She loosened the knots around her left hand and tossed the rope in the garbage can.

Every movement of her wrists made her want to cry out, but she shrugged out of the shirt she had worn over her tank top. She glanced at the dainty blue flowers dotting the fabric and thought of the many times she'd worn it on sun-drenched horse rides to protect her skin from burning. She didn't know why Ramiro wanted her shirt, but she wasn't going to risk having him break down the door. With a hard swallow, she stuffed the shirt underneath the door.

Courtney turned on the sink and plunged her hands into the icy cold water. Grabbing a washcloth, she ran it under the cool water and pressed it to her aching head. She looked in the mirror, and her eyes widened.

Several scratches covered her cheek, and the right side of her face looked swollen. Her usually sleek, dark hair was tangled and matted, and there were dirt smudges across her brow. Scrubbing her face with the washcloth helped, and she rinsed her mouth with the cool water to try to ease the hunger gnawing at her senses. She wished she'd eaten the apple and crackers from earlier.

She leaned against the bathroom wall and slid down to the floor, resting her head on her knees. She was trapped and being hunted by a wild animal. Ramiro was crazy, and Courtney swore to herself if he touched her again, she'd do her best to kill him or die trying.

6

RAMIRO MOVED down the hallway and looked out the picture windows in the front of the cabin. His back stiffened when he saw Adán and Jesse. He watched them unload a bundle of marijuana from the back of the four-wheeler. He needed to get Courtney under control before they came in.

He headed back to the bedroom. As he approached the bathroom door, he heard movement and watched as Courtney's shirt emerged beneath the door. He frowned, chewing on the corner of his lip, then reached down and snatched the shirt with a grunt.

He mopped the blood from his face with Courtney's shirt as he headed down the stairs. Adán and Jesse tromped through the door, speaking rapidly, but they fell silent when they noticed Ramiro.

"What happened?" Adán asked in his native tongue.

Ramiro looked at the shirt in his hand, covered with blood. "I had to get her shirt." He smiled. "She didn't like it."

The men laughed.

"Did you kill the dog?"

Jesse shook his head. "We haven't found him."

Ramiro scrunched the shirt tighter. "He might've gone back to the house. His name is Pepper. Call for him and he'll come. Shoot him. The girl was riding a horse. You need to find it and move it north of the house about five miles, in the clearing. Plant the dog near the horse." Ramiro thrust the shirt at them. "Hurry. If we don't get the horse moved in time, someone could find the crop."

The men turned to go, and Ramiro took a step after them.

"Honcho is sending more men to help harvest the crop early. If we do this right, we'll all come into a lot of money."

"Maybe he should send someone to help guard la chica." Adán laughed. "Looks like you're having some trouble."

"Get out of here." Ramiro scowled. He walked back into the kitchen and ducked his head under the faucet. His nose wasn't broken, but it throbbed painfully. Courtney was a spitfire, but their altercation proved worth it because the blood all over her shirt was just what he needed. When someone found her ripped and bloodied shirt miles away from here, they'd go looking for a body first. Anything to keep them away from the marijuana crop.

Courtney lifted her head when she heard male voices downstairs. Her shoulders sagged; they were speaking Spanish. The men from the marijuana grove must have returned. She wondered if they'd found Pepper. And what about Tika? What would they do to her horse if they found her? For the thousandth time, she wished she'd listened to her father and not gone riding in the woods.

Ramiro seemed in no rush to send out a ransom. Her only hope now would be for someone to notice her missing. At least Richie would go looking for Tika when he didn't find her. Courtney lifted her head and felt fresh tears spring to her eyes. On the weekends, she fed Tika at night, so Richie wouldn't come by until Sunday morning. Because she hadn't called to tell him about her ride, he would have no reason to come earlier.

She covered her mouth to push back the fear rising up her throat. No one would even wonder where she was until tomorrow morning. A terrible thought weighed on her heart. Maybe they wouldn't wonder where she was at all. Richie would only wonder where Tika was. She thought of all the times she'd gone riding and left Tika tied up at the stable waiting for Richie to come and groom her so that she could hurry off to another date. She thought of how she'd looped Tika's reins around a sapling. It wouldn't take much to get them loose, and if Tika did succeed, she'd head back for the stable.

Courtney rubbed her hands over her forehead. Her mom and dad wouldn't be back until late Monday night. She would have to do her best to convince Ramiro to contact her father about a ransom. She shuddered. What did he have planned for her in the meantime?

Her legs grew tired, and she stretched out on the bathroom rug and closed her eyes, willing her head to stop aching. A door banged shut downstairs, and the window rattled with the vibration. About ten minutes later, she heard someone walking across the bedroom floor.

"Courtney, I've got some food for you." Ramiro's voice sounded muffled, and she wondered if it had anything to do with his nose. She kept perfectly still, trying to control the tremors of fear racing through her body.

"C'mon. I don't want to break down the door." His weight rested against the wood, and it creaked. He pounded on the door. "Fine, but you're going to have to come out eventually so we can call your parents."

Courtney sat up. "When are you going to call them?"

"We'll let them miss you first. Get a little nervous." She could almost hear the smile in Ramiro's voice. "When your father's sweating, that's when we'll call."

Courtney swallowed and let her head fall to her chest.

"When will your parents start to get worried?" Ramiro asked. "What are you, twenty-one? Twenty-two? Do you stay out late often?"

Courtney didn't want to tell him that her parents wouldn't know she was gone until Monday. It wasn't out of the ordinary for her to miss her parents for days at a time with their busy schedules—especially on weeks when she didn't make it into the office. She at least tried to text her mom occasionally, but she had to admit the mother/daughter relationship wasn't as strong as it should've been.

She recalled the last time she'd seen her mom. They'd met for lunch over a week ago, and then her mom had tried to meet up with her again Friday. It was somewhat unusual, if she considered how difficult it'd been to spend time with her parents. The undercurrent of hostile emotions she'd sensed between her mom and dad had made it hard to be around them.

A tap on the door alerted her that she hadn't answered Ramiro's question. "I have a pretty busy schedule—we all do."

"And when will your parents be concerned?"

She focused on the door, wondering how far to stretch the truth. "I think they'll be pretty concerned by tomorrow morning. We always have Sunday brunch together."

"Good—we'll wait until Tuesday. By then they should be desperate."

"What? But why?" Courtney stood and approached the door. "Please, my dad will need time to get resources together."

Ramiro tapped the door. "I'm leaving your food, but I won't be far. When I come back, you better be out of this bathroom, or I'll break down the door."

Courtney didn't answer. She pressed her ear to the wood and listened to Ramiro's retreating footsteps.

The last thing she'd eaten was a piece of toast and a grapefruit before her morning ride. Back then, she was thinking about her date with Cobra and wondering how to end things with Sean. She had been absorbed with the fun waiting for her on Cobra's boat, not considering the dozens of ways her life could end.

She waited, stomach growling incessantly, for ten minutes. When the hands on her watch pointed to the eight, she carefully closed the three drawers she'd opened and put her hand on the doorknob. She strained her ears for any movement, but the room was devoid of sound. Fighting the rising panic, she pulled the door open.

A paper plate lay at her feet with crackers, cheese, pickles, and some Oreo cookies. Definitely not the gourmet meal she could've had at a restaurant last night with Sean, but she was so hungry, she didn't care. Courtney watched the doorway to the hall as she took small bites of the food. She grabbed the apple from where she'd left it earlier on the bedside table and ate it along with the crackers.

She glanced back at the bathroom. Ramiro had told her he'd break down the door, and she believed him. It was probably best not to make him angry, but she needed some way to protect herself from his advances.

She cringed when she thought of how Ramiro had tried to kiss her. She wondered how long she would be able to fend him off.

The food settling in her stomach reminded her of how tired she was. The constant rush of adrenaline had left her feeling like a rag doll. She considered pulling a few blankets into the bathroom and trying to get some sleep, but before she could act on the thought, Ramiro returned.

Courtney immediately stood and moved toward the bathroom.

"Just stay where you are. I'm not going to hurt you." His accent emphasized the word "stay," and Courtney scowled and folded her arms.

"I don't want you to touch me. Ever. Again."

Ramiro walked closer to her and stopped inches from her face. He smiled and grabbed her wrists. Courtney winced as pain shot up her arms.

"I see you've been busy."

She yanked her hands away and tightened them in fists, every cell in her body wanting to punch him.

"Did you like your dinner?" His nose looked puffy, and Courtney hoped it hurt as much as her head.

"Thank you," she mumbled.

Ramiro laughed. "I came to tell you that unless you want me to sleep with you in that bed, you'd better not set one toe outside this room."

Courtney stepped back against the wall.

He rubbed his mustache with his fingers. "I'll be right outside your door, and Adán and Jesse will be downstairs."

A new fear bubbled up in her chest. "Please, don't let them hurt me."

He leaned forward, resting his arm on the wall. "No one's going to hurt you, but I wish you'd be nicer to me."

"No, Ramiro." Courtney stepped to the side to create more distance between them. "You'd have to kill me, and then you wouldn't get any ransom money."

His nostrils flared, and she could see his mind working behind the cruel darkness of his eyes. With a huff, he pushed off the wall and folded his arms. "If you want to stay alive, you won't give me any trouble."

Courtney nodded.

"Stay put." Ramiro jerked a thumb at the bed as he headed out.

She didn't move until he had closed the bedroom door. His boots thunked against the hardwood stairs, and she strained to hear his steps across the main floor. Courtney crept toward the door and examined the knob—there wasn't a lock.

Exhaustion rode along every one of her tattered nerves, but she couldn't fall asleep unless she knew she wouldn't be surprised by Ramiro or his men. Her eyes focused on a decorative straight-backed chair at the foot of the bed.

Cautiously, she lifted the chair and carried it across the room. Tremors ran through her body as she positioned it against the door. She tipped the chair back until it was secure against the knob. She listened and took a deep breath. Ramiro might be angry about the chair, but at least she'd have a warning if he was thinking of climbing into bed with her again.

Courtney returned to the bathroom and drank several gulps of water from the faucet. Walking back into the bedroom, she peeked out the window and noticed how dark the night had fallen outside. She glanced at her watch. It was almost nine thirty—still early for her schedule, but Courtney felt as if her eyelids were sagging. She turned off the bedside lamp and listened for the sound of her captors.

The men must not have returned yet, or maybe they had to stay in the tent and guard their precious crop in the woods. Courtney crawled into the bed and laid her aching head on the pillow. She kept listening for Ramiro, but even though she was afraid to close her eyes, she drifted into the unconscious realm of sleep.

When she awoke, the beams of sunlight shining into the room indicated it was late in the day. Sunday was normally a quiet day spent at home, and Courtney wished she was in her own bedroom, safe under her embroidered quilt. She turned her head toward the door and gasped.

Ramiro sat in the chair, leaning his head against the wall, watching her with a half smile. "So the princess is awake?" He stood and rotated his head in a slow circle, stretching out some imaginary kink in his neck. Courtney untangled herself from the sheets and almost fell out of the bed in her haste to put her feet on the floor.

"You're a pretty sound sleeper, no? You thought a chair could keep me out of your room?"

"No, I just wanted to know if someone came in," Courtney said.

Ramiro chuckled. "I was careful not to make much noise." He had crossed the room as he spoke, and now he reached out his hand. His fingertips grazed Courtney's cheek as she turned her head. "You think you're pretty smart?"

Courtney glared at him. Ramiro slapped her face, moving so suddenly she couldn't react. "It's not so smart to keep causing trouble."

Tears spilled onto her throbbing cheek, and Courtney slid to the floor, covering her face with her hands. She felt the toe of Ramiro's boot nudge her side. "There's food by the door. Eat, but don't clean yourself up. I'm going to take a picture, and you can help me send it to your padre's cell phone."

"When?" Courtney lifted her head.

Ramiro stared at her. "Not yet, but I want a picture before those scratches start to heal."

7

RICHIE HALSTROM whistled as he approached the Beckham stables. Courtney used to take Tika out every Sunday for a ride after brunch, so he arrived early to feed the horses. But lately, she'd been too busy chasing boys—according to her father—to bother much with riding. Richie thought it probably had more to do with Eric's strict rule that Courtney no longer ride near the mountains.

"Tika," he called. "How's my lazy mare doing?" Richie's voice trailed off when he saw the empty stall where Tika usually greeted him. With a glance, he could see that the tack was gone, so a rider had taken her out. But he'd noticed the horse trailer parked on his way in, so horse and rider had to be close by. Why hadn't Courtney called him?

Maybe she planned on taking care of her horse for once. Richie busied himself cleaning the stalls and grooming the two other horses stabled there. Nearly an hour had passed, and the late July heat would settle into the valley soon. Richie shaded his eyes and looked out across the fields. He couldn't see any sign of Tika.

He walked to the edge of the pasture as he dialed Courtney's cell, ending the call when her voice message greeted him. Crouching, he put his finger in the groove of a hoofprint in the dirt. He took a few steps closer to the water trough and stooped again. Courtney must have filled it for Tika recently.

He could see where the trough had overflowed, as usual, and the dirt had turned into a temporary bit of moist earth. He traced the outlines of Tika's horseshoe, and the dirt crumbled against his finger. The hoofprint was deep because Tika had stepped in the mud, but now it was dry. As he stood, he noticed paw prints dried in the mud as well.

"Pepper!" he called. He walked near the house and whistled long and loud. "Pepper, here boy. Pepper!" He waited a few minutes, but the friendly little dog didn't come. He always came when Richie called, usually bounding through his automatic doggy door built into the side entrance to the house. Richie called one more time. He listened for the sound of the electronic door sliding open, but still nothing. He dialed the house number and both cell numbers Eric had given him with no luck. Richie narrowed his eyes. The sun was climbing higher over the mountains. Where were they?

He hurried to the stables and straddled the ATV parked in back. He turned the key, and the engine roared to life as he urged it outside. Richie sped across the pasture toward the mountains. After twenty minutes of driving, he still couldn't see any sign of Tika, Pepper, or a rider, be it Courtney or another member of the Beckham clan. He drove back to the house and banged on the door again, called for Pepper, and tried phoning Eric.

As he zoomed back down the driveway, he decided to head south to the mouth of Big Cottonwood Canyon. It was a long ride, but Courtney had taken Tika there a few times over the past year when Eric terminated their normal riding course.

Eric and Chloe must be out of town—he could usually reach Eric on his cell. Richie kept the four-wheeler at forty miles per hour as he traveled the five-mile stretch, then he shifted down to navigate the rocky terrain.

He switched to first gear as the engine grumbled along the path. Then he turned off the power and looked around the clearing. The stillness of the morning sent an eerie chill through him. He tramped through the underbrush and walked around a thicket of bushes.

He heard Tika whinny before he saw her, and he jogged to a thatch of quaking aspens. Richie quickened his pace when he saw Tika tied to a tree securely with a lead rope, the reins hanging loose over her head.

"Oh, no," Richie murmured when he saw the stiff, dried hair

on Tika's legs. She'd been ridden hard, but not recently. He checked the saddle bags and found an empty water bottle and a granola bar. The rider had to be Courtney—she was always munching on those health bars after a long ride.

"Courtney, are you hurt?" He walked a few paces into the trees. "Court, it's Richie. Can you hear me? Pepper?" The scrub oak grew in bunches surrounding the sparse trees, and Richie surveyed the ground as he walked. He walked for twenty yards and veered right, then began to circle back, continuing to call for Courtney and whistle for Pepper.

He sucked in a breath to sound a shrill whistle for the dog, but the notes lodged in his throat when he noticed something in the grass. Pepper lay motionless on the ground, ten feet ahead. Richie cried out and lunged forward. The black and white spaniel's once silky hair was covered in blood. He examined the dog to see what had caused Pepper's death. "No, no, no!" Richie felt a wave of fear come over him as he looked around the clearing once more. He pulled out his phone and dialed 9-1-1. Pepper had been shot twice, and there was no sign of Courtney.

Eric stood on the balcony of his condo in Park City and looked out at the stunning view of the mountains that defined the city. He and Chloe had just finished a late brunch, and Eric was struggling to keep his mind from straying to the mounds of work he'd left at the office yesterday. His cell phone rang, and he glanced at Chloe before answering. "I'll keep it short."

Chloe sighed but waved her hand. "I'll go get ready."

Eric glanced at the caller ID and hesitated. He didn't recognize the number, but he accepted the call before it went to his messaging service. "Eric Beckham speaking."

"This is Detective Gardner with the Cottonwood Heights Police Department. Are you the Eric Beckham who lives on Legacy Drive?"

"Yes. What's this about?"

"Where are you, sir?"

Eric frowned. "My wife and I are in Park City. Is there a problem?"

"I'm afraid I have some bad news." The detective hesitated. "Your daughter, Courtney, has been reported missing."

"Courtney?" Eric asked. "She's not missing. She's probably at her boyfriend's."

"Well, sir, I'd like to meet with you. We're concerned because your ranch hand, Richie Halstrom, found her horse and dog almost five miles from your home. I'm afraid the dog had been shot to death."

Eric gasped. "My wife and I can be there in an hour. Did Richie know Courtney was going riding this morning?"

"Richie says he never heard from your daughter. He thinks she may have gone riding yesterday, and the horse has been tied up in the canyon since then."

"What are you saying?" Eric leaned against the arm of the sofa, ignoring the startled looks from his wife. He struggled to hear over his pulsing heartbeat reverberating in his ears.

"We're searching the area right now." Detective Gardner cleared his throat. "If you could make some phone calls and see if you can find out what your daughter had planned for this weekend, it would be a big help."

"I'll do it right now."

"Thank you. I'll meet you at your house."

Eric ended the call and turned to his wife. "That was the police. Courtney went riding, and they found Tika in the canyon, but no sign of Court."

Chloe's face paled, but then she shook her head. "She can't be far. Remember how she likes to ride Tika and then go for a jog?" She gave her husband a hopeful look.

Eric pulled his wife into his arms. "They found Pepper. He'd been shot."

"What? But why would someone kill Pepper?" Chloe clung to his shirt and looked to Eric for answers. Tears appeared in the corners of her eyes, and Eric could feel her arms trembling.

"I don't know. We need to get home. I need you to get Sean's number and find out what he and Court's plans were for the weekend. Richie thinks she went riding yesterday."

Chloe cried out and covered her mouth. Tears spilled onto her cheeks. "They think she's been missing since yesterday?"

"C'mon. We need to hurry. Let's not think the worst. Like you said, she likes to go running. Maybe she fell—sprained her ankle or something."

Chloe wiped a hand across her face and opened her suitcase. She grabbed her makeup and clothes and threw them inside. She zipped up the suitcase and choked back a sob. "I'm ready. Let's leave now."

Eric drove too fast on his way out of Park City, his fingers digging into the leather cover on his steering wheel as he tried to quash feelings of panic over his daughter. Chloe kept dialing the phone, trying to reach Courtney's friends. She had to call four of them to find Sean's phone number. Her shoulders slumped after she spoke with him.

"Sean said Court canceled their dinner date Friday night. When I talked to her on Friday, she mentioned they'd had a fight and she didn't want to see him again. But Sean didn't say anything about it. He seemed upset she hadn't returned any of his phone calls or texts."

Eric pushed on the gas pedal. "Richie's out there searching with the police. I called a few of the neighbors, and no one saw anything." It had been a futile attempt because the nearest neighbor was over a quarter of a mile away, but Eric needed to stay busy to keep his mind from going into a panic.

"I'll see who else I can call," Chloe said.

Eric gripped the steering wheel until his fingers turned white. "She's gonna be okay. We'll find her."

8

DETECTIVE GARDNER arrived at the Beckham residence ten minutes after Eric and Chloe got home. Eric watched him approach with trepidation. The tension level in the house ratcheted up another notch. Eric noticed the detective kept his face devoid of emotion as he climbed the front steps, and sweat glistened on his brow. "Mind if I come inside for a drink?"

After draining a glass of lemonade, he cleared his throat. "Could we sit for a minute?"

Chloe tensed but sat on the edge of the sofa. Her jade-colored sundress stood out against her platinum blonde hair. Eric noticed the tremor in her hands and gripped them in his own. He faced the detective. "I want to get out there and help look."

Detective Gardner pursed his lips. He was balding, and the top of his head was shiny with perspiration. "I know you do, but this case just took a bad turn."

Eric straightened. "What did you find?"

Chloe whimpered and leaned in to Eric.

"I think we found your daughter's shirt. I'll need you to identify it, but there's a lot of blood on it."

"Please, no," Chloe whispered.

"But you only found her shirt? She could be out there some-where—injured." Eric stood.

"We've got teams searching on a grid, and this is the only thing they've come up with. We're still looking, but we haven't found any sign of other vehicles or animals in the area." Gardner mopped his brow. "Why don't you come outside and take a look at the clothing."

Chloe rose slowly from the sofa.

"It's okay, Mrs. Beckham." Gardner motioned for her to sit. "We can just have your husband take a look, if you'd like."

"I'm afraid he might not recognize it. Courtney has a lot of clothes."

Gardner nodded. "Good point."

They followed him out to the police cruiser and waited as he removed a sealed bag. Chloe recognized the white top dotted with blue flowers immediately. "That's hers." Her eyes widened at the dark red smear of blood across the back of the shirt. Several drops of dried blood followed the edge of the ripped fabric. Chloe sank onto the front steps. "She usually wore it when she went riding." Her hands trembled as she covered her eyes. "This can't be real. She has to be out there somewhere."

Eric sat next to his wife and put his arm around her. "We'll find her. She's tough." He rubbed at his eyes and cleared his throat.

"I'm sorry, but I need to ask you some questions." Gardner put the bag away and sat next to Chloe. "Do you know anyone that would want to harm your daughter?"

Chloe looked up and wiped the tears trickling down her cheeks. "Court? I don't think she's ever had an enemy. She's so fun-loving and cheerful."

"Yeah, Court has always been the life of the party. Everyone wants to be her friend," Eric added.

"What about boyfriends?" Gardner asked.

"She's dating a football player right now, but it's only been a month or two," Chloe said. "She mentioned they had a fight the other night and that she wanted to break up."

Gardner perked up. "What night was that?"

"I think it was Thursday night." Chloe rubbed her forehead. "Yes, that's right, because she told me about it on Friday over the phone."

"Did she seem upset about it?"

"More disappointed. To be honest, I wasn't sure if she really would break up with him," Chloe said. "She was more upset with the male population in general. She said she just wanted to have fun, but they always wanted more."

"Would her current boyfriend be angry about this?"

"I don't know. I only met Sean once, and it was in passing," Chloe said.

"Do you know his last name?" Gardner held his pen above his notebook.

"Whitmore. I got his number from one of Court's friends and called him on our way home. He hasn't heard from her, and she usually answers his texts."

Gardner jotted down the information and then turned his gaze to Eric. "Mr. Beckham, you said Courtney works at your office. Did she have any close friends there?"

Eric shook his head. "She only worked ten hours a week doing odd jobs for the other employees. They all know her, but I wouldn't say she was particularly close with anyone."

"I'd like you both to think about other boyfriends she's had and anyone who might have a motivation to do her harm." Gardner flipped a page in his notebook. "And I'd like a list of her girlfriends and how to reach them, if you have that available."

"I can get that easily enough from my personal assistant," Eric said. "Sandra helped put together a surprise birthday party for Courtney and sent out invitations."

"What about enemies, Mr. Beckham?"

Eric looked at Gardner and bit the inside of his cheek. "Detective, I'm in development, and unfortunately, that means that I probably have twice as many enemies as I think I do."

Gardner chuckled. "Understood, but why don't you give me the rundown on anyone you suspect would go to the lengths of foul play to get back at you."

"I try to let the water go under the bridge, so I'll probably have to consult some of my records to see who was delinquent in their accounts." Eric tapped his foot on the bottom step. "A few names come to mind, but I can't see any of them wanting to hurt my family."

"Well, whatever you can think of that might help. We're

following all leads right now." Gardner tucked his pen and notebook into his pocket.

"What is being done to try to find my daughter?" Eric asked.

"We've got a search and rescue team out there now. All indicators are that she's been missing since yesterday. If that's the case and she's injured, she could be unconscious and unable to hear people calling for her."

"If she's unconscious, won't it be near impossible to find her in the woods?" Chloe asked.

Gardner fiddled with his pen. He hesitated and then looked at Eric and Chloe. "We're planning to double back over the area and widen the search. We're hoping to bring out the dogs soon, so we'll need some recently worn clothing or other personal effects for them to acquire Courtney's scent."

Eric lifted his head. "How big of a radius can you cover?"

"If we get enough volunteers, we can cover a three-mile radius by tomorrow evening," Gardner said.

"What if we don't find her by tonight?" Chloe stood and looked at the mountains that lined their property.

"We will, honey." Eric gripped her hand and sent a pleading look at Detective Gardner.

9

RAMIRO ANSWERED the phone on the first ring. "Yo, Honcho."

"Change of plans. I want you to put the ransom in tonight."

"Tonight? Why?" Ramiro asked.

Honcho cleared his throat. "The less you know, the better. Just follow my instructions."

"Okay. Are you watching the family?" Ramiro tapped his fingers lightly on the countertop.

"Don't worry about that. Just do your job, and I'll do mine."

Ramiro flinched at the anger in his boss's voice.

"Once you put the ransom in, you won't be able to call me at this number. I bought a new cell phone. Don't try to contact me unless it's an emergency. I'll call you."

"Whatever you say, Honcho." Ramiro listened as his ruthless boss gave him detailed instructions, then ended the call.

Courtney knew she'd slept too long, but her body called for more. Unconscious to the dangers surrounding her, sleep was the only time she felt safe. Ramiro hadn't tried to touch her again, possibly because she'd run into the bathroom and pretended to throw up when he came into the room earlier. She'd flushed the toilet as he approached and splashed her face with water, putting on quite a show of being sick.

She looked toward the window and processed the meager ideas she had thought of to aid her escape. When Ramiro delivered the ransom message, Courtney wanted to hint to her father where she was. If he knew she was only miles from home, he could save her.

"Time to send a picture to Daddy," Ramiro said as he entered the room.

Courtney sat up. "You have to let me talk to him. He'll want proof I'm alive."

"We're sending a picture message. I'm going to take your picture and then you're going to say, 'Daddy, please help me. Do what they say.'"

Courtney felt her lip trembling. Her plan was failing, and she didn't have a back-up. Frustration tinged with fear seeped through her veins, and she struggled to compose herself. "Please, let me talk to him."

"Why? So you can try to give away your location? I don't think so." Ramiro held up his phone. "Look at me."

Courtney raised her head and waited for him to take a picture of her bruised and battered face. Ramiro pointed at her. "Now, say the words." He pushed a button on the phone and held it over her.

She took a ragged breath and said, "Daddy, please get me out of here. Do what they say."

Ramiro pushed another button and nodded. "Nice touch. Now write your dad's cell phone number on this paper." He tossed a pencil and paper at her.

He waited while Courtney scribbled down the number, then he grabbed the page and put the phone in his pocket. "Don't get your hopes up. They won't be able to trace this message. When they try to track it, they'll be in for a wild goose chase."

He closed the door, and Courtney fell back against the pillows and let a sob break free from her chest. Something had happened. It was only Sunday night, and Ramiro had decided to contact her parents. Maybe someone had discovered her missing and they were searching for her. She held onto the shard of hope the thought gave her.

She gritted her teeth, struggling to find courage to survive another encounter with Ramiro. Focusing on hopeful things was the only way to keep from completely breaking down. She remembered seeing search parties on the news—people banded together, walking through the woods hand in hand and calling out the name of the missing person. She squeezed her eyes tight and felt another tear trickle down her face. If they were searching, there was a chance someone would start checking all the cabins in the area.

A few more tears spilled out when she realized that Ramiro would never let her be found alive without the ransom money. She had to figure out a way to escape.

10

A S ERIC searched the woods, he cried Courtney's name until he was hoarse. After the sun went down and they were tripping over the underbrush, Detective Gardner convinced him to take Chloe home. "I don't want us to miss something in the dark. It's best if you continue phoning everyone you know who can help find Courtney."

"I just don't want to think of her being out here alone another night," Chloe said.

"We're communicating with the FBI, and we've put out an alert," Gardner said. "We should have plenty of help by morning."

Eric finally relented and drove home. He changed out of his dirty clothes and took a shower.

"Here, you need to eat something." Chloe handed him a sandwich.

He took a bite and chewed slowly. "You need to eat too."

"I had a yogurt," Chloe said. "I've contacted most of Court's friends, and none of them talked to her in the past three days. I can't find anyone who knew what her plans were."

Eric put his arm around Chloe. "She worked at the office on Friday. I'll call Sandra again and see if she knows anything."

Eric left a couple of messages for Sandra, and he paced the room while Chloe looked through the address book to ask people to join the search in the morning. His phone vibrated, and he pushed a button to see who was texting him.

When he saw an announcement for an incoming picture message float across his screen, he froze. Eric opened the message and gasped when he heard a familiar voice. He fell to his knees beside Chloe and played the message again.

Chloe shrieked when she saw the picture of Courtney's face, covered in abrasions. Her daughter's voice repeated, "Daddy, please get me . . ."

"She's been kidnapped," Eric cried. He showed Chloe the accompanying text message:

We have Courtney. Prepare ten million dollars ransom. We will contact you on Tuesday with instructions.

Chloe dialed a number on her phone.

"Who are you calling?" Eric asked.

She held up a finger and shook her head. "Detective Gardner, we've received a ransom."

"You're calling the police?" Eric interrupted.

Chloe pointed to his phone. "They didn't say not to." She gripped the phone with shaking hands. "Yes, they asked for ten million dollars."

A few minutes later, she ended the call. "Detective Gardner is contacting the FBI. He's on his way here now. He says not to answer any calls until he arrives."

"What if they're watching us?" Eric said.

Her fingers wrapped tightly around the phone, and Eric noticed her hand shaking. She looked up at her husband. "This isn't a movie, Eric. They have Courtney, and we've got to get her back alive."

"But Tuesday? I can't get that much money by Tuesday." Eric raked his fingers through his dark hair.

"We'll figure something out," Chloe said. "The FBI will help us get Courtney back."

Jason Edwards paced in front of his living room window. Agent Dylan Pierson had called fifteen minutes ago—a kidnapping had been reported, and he was on his way over. Jason mulled over the brief conversation.

"What happened?" he'd asked Agent Pierson.

"I'll bring you up to speed when I get there, but it's a girl in her twenties who has been missing, and a ransom was just called in."

"I can come to the office," Jason offered.

"Your house is on the way to the crime scene, so I'll save some time and pick you up."

Since his move to Utah, Jason hadn't worked any high-profile cases. The Salt Lake City FBI office kept plenty busy, but the cases that had come his way were mostly involved in the drug trafficking occurring in the state.

His hand strayed to the gun in his holster, and he fingered the cool metal grip of the .40-caliber Glock. He'd spent a lot of time at the shooting range with his new weapon, and he was more accurate with it than he had been with his previous guns. He was still working on settling into his new area—all the changes had made him reevaluate his life.

He was starting to feel like his heart had mended after the Stewart case in San Diego. Enough time had gone by that he felt ready for a change, and that's what had brought him to Utah.

Jason knew it was nearing Aubree's second wedding anniversary. A card with a family photo had been forwarded to his office. A year after he attended Aubree and Wyatt's wedding, Jason had felt the need for a change of pace and some new scenery. The mountains of Utah had provided plenty of distractions, and his job kept him busy.

When Aubree had sent the family picture with an update, Jason felt happy for her, but he still experienced the familiar pangs of "What if?" that tried to set him back. Before he put in for a transfer from California, he had promised himself he wouldn't let another opportunity for happiness pass him by.

He frowned as he stared out the window. He was twenty-nine years old and still trying to figure things out. It wasn't so much that he was unhappy—more that he felt unfulfilled. Like there was something he needed to do, and staying in the same spot wasn't getting the job done. So he'd decided to embark on a different journey.

Pierson pulled in front of the house and flashed his lights. Jason locked his door and hurried out to the car. "What's going on?"

Pierson lifted his chin and motioned to the computer screen mounted on the dash between them. "The vic is a twenty-three-year-old college student, lives at home with her millionaire parents, Eric and Chloe Beckham. That name won't mean much to you, being new around here, but the Beckham name is synonymous with success and cash. He knows how to get the ball rolling, so he'll expect us to come in with all the answers and guns blazing."

"I get it—we need to act confident, then?"

"You're cocky enough. Just be yourself," Pierson bantered.

Jason laughed, then his eyes narrowed as he looked at the print-out Pierson handed him. A grainy black-and-white picture of a beautiful dark-haired girl with almond-shaped eyes stared back at him.

Pierson pulled out onto the main highway. "She's a looker—let's hope that isn't why she was picked up in the first place."

Jason grimaced. "When was the ransom called in?"

"About an hour ago."

"Suspects?"

Pierson shook his head. "Boyfriends, enemies of the Beckham Development company—not a lot to go on right now." He motioned to the computer. "Detective Gardner has already sent along some intel."

"We'll figure it out." Jason scrolled through the information coming in on the laptop.

Pierson squeezed the steering wheel. "Something tells me this is going to be more complicated than it looks."

Jason frowned as he read the reports about the family dog and a horse-ride gone wrong. He glanced back at Courtney's smile, inhaled slowly, and prepared his mind to be alert to every detail so he could help bring her home.

Two hours after receiving the ransom message, Eric watched as a black Crown Victoria pulled onto his circular driveway. "They're here."

A thickset man in his midforties stepped out of the car and smoothed a hand over his sandy brown hair. He was followed by a younger man with blond hair. The young man looked fit, and he walked purposefully toward the front door.

Eric moved to stand next to Chloe, who wrung her hands and

then clasped them together. Detective Gardner answered the door.

"Hey, Dylan. Good to see you." Gardner clapped the older agent on the back and turned to Eric and Chloe. "This is Agent Pierson and . . ." He held his hand out to the other man. "Our new addition to this area."

The second agent stepped forward. He stood a few inches taller than Eric's five-foot-ten frame. "Agent Jason Edwards. I transferred here six months ago." He shook hands with the detective, then extended his hand to Chloe. "We're going to get to the bottom of this."

"Thank you," Chloe murmured.

Eric gripped Agent Edward's hand. "I'm counting on it." He motioned past the entryway. "Come into the living room. Tell me what to do. We have to find her."

Jason pushed at an errant strand of white-blond hair near his ear and met Eric's gaze. "I won't let you down."

Eric took in the determination in Jason's vivid green eyes. "She's our only child."

Jason nodded. "Let's get to work. I'd like to see your phone first. We're going to hook it up to some of our equipment and hope they contact you again soon."

Eric handed over his phone and settled onto the couch next to Chloe. The agents had just finished hooking the phone up when it rang. Eric jumped.

"It says 'Sandra,'" Agent Pierson said.

"It's my secretary. I called her to see if she knew anything about Courtney's plans for this weekend, but I guess it doesn't matter now."

Jason handed him the phone. "It still matters."

Eric answered the call and watched the federal agents hang on his every word. It took him a few seconds to calm Sandra down once he told her Courtney had been kidnapped. "Listen, I need to know if you talked to Courtney or overheard what she had planned for Saturday."

"Um, I'm pretty sure Corbin set something up with her for Saturday afternoon," Sandra said. "I overheard him talking to Jake about it. I think he was planning to take her out on his boat."

Eric frowned. "I don't think she went with him, but I'll do some checking. If you think of anything else, will you call me?"

"Sure, and Eric—I'm so sorry," Sandra said.

"Thanks. I appreciate it." He ended the call and handed the phone back to Jason. "She had a date to go boating with one of my employees, Corbin Whittier, on Saturday afternoon." Eric shook his head. "I wonder why he hasn't called—Court's all over the news."

"He might not have seen it yet." Jason motioned to the cell phone. "Why don't you give him a call? Is he in your phone book?"

"He goes by Cobra. That's what it's under."

Jason selected the number and handed the phone back to Eric. When it went to the answering machine, Jason said, "Don't leave a message."

Eric ended the call, and Agent Pierson stepped forward. "Corbin lives at 931 Sage Drive, right?"

Eric raised his eyebrows. "I think so."

"We'll stop by and see if he saw Courtney at all on Saturday. Is there anyone else she might've had contact with?"

Chloe stood. "She has a boyfriend—Sean. But like I told Detective Gardner earlier, she canceled their date Friday night and hasn't answered his calls."

Jason rolled up the sleeves of his dress shirt, and Eric noticed a fiery tattoo encircling his right arm just below his bicep. After jotting down a few notes in a small notebook, Jason looked at Chloe. "She had a boyfriend but was planning to go out with Cobra?"

"Yes, but she told me on Friday that she and Sean had a fight and she wanted to break up with him."

"This Sean—would he be upset if Courtney dumped him?" Jason lifted his eyebrows and focused on Chloe's reaction.

Chloe twisted her wedding ring around her finger. "You don't think he had something to do with her kidnapping?"

"At this stage, everyone is a suspect, and we like to ask as many questions as possible to narrow the field," Agent Pierson said.

"But I don't think Sean would hurt Court," Chloe said.

Eric cleared his throat. "He's a football player. He goes running with Court a lot. She mentioned to me once that he was all hands, but nothing she couldn't handle."

Jason coughed and lowered his eyes. "So, did Courtney date a lot of different men?"

"Yes," Eric said.

"No," Chloe answered simultaneously.

They looked at each other, and Chloe lifted her palms. "She usually stuck with the same guy for a few weeks. Court's a good girl. I think she was frustrated that so many men she dated wanted to move too quickly into a physical relationship."

"Has she ever had any run-ins with these boyfriends after breaking up?" Jason asked.

Eric looked at his wife, and she pulled her bottom lip between her teeth. "There was one about two years ago. He took her for a ride up the canyon, and . . ." Chloe glanced at Eric.

"Mrs. Beckham, anything you can share at this point is helpful," Agent Pierson said.

Chloe tensed. "He scared Court because he wouldn't leave her alone. She said it started innocently, but then he didn't want to stop. Courtney got out of the car and ran. She called one of her friends to bring her home."

"What?" Eric said. "Are you saying someone sexually assaulted our daughter and you didn't tell me?"

Chloe turned to him with pleading eyes. "She didn't even tell *me* until a few months after it happened. She made me promise not to tell you. After that night, he kept calling and texting her for weeks. She told him that if he didn't stop, she'd tell you."

"Felix Haran?" Eric thought of the bright young man who had worked for him all through high school. He remembered that after Felix started college, he always seemed nervous and fidgety. Eric had figured it had something to do with his stress over his studies.

Chloe nodded, and her eyes filled with tears again.

"But why didn't you tell me? I would've fired him."

"That's why," Chloe said. "Court made me promise. He was working his way through college, and she didn't want to antagonize him and upset his plans to leave for graduate school. She said he'd get busy with school and forget about her, and he did."

"But still, you should've told me."

"I'm sorry to interrupt, but does Felix live around here?" Jason asked.

Eric rubbed his eyes and sighed. "Felix is in the masters program for engineering at Utah State University. He's been living in Logan for the past year. Before that, he worked for me." Eric glanced at Chloe. "Now I understand why he was always so nervous around me."

"We'll check on Felix and see what he was doing the past few days," Jason said.

"Yes, and we'll check up on Sean too," Pierson said. "Chloe, if you could write down the names of any of the guys she's dated in the last few months, that'd be helpful."

"But you don't think it's someone like that, do you?" Eric said. "I mean, these people kidnapped her. Did you see her face? A past boyfriend wouldn't do that." Eric sank back onto the couch and lowered his face to his hands. "They're asking for ten million dollars."

"You have a good point, Mr. Beckham, but people do things out of character all the time. It may or may not be someone she dated, but it's very likely the kidnapper planned this out and waited for an opportunity," Jason said. "Don't worry about the money right now. We'll do our best to stall on that part and see what we can find."

"But I have to pay the ransom. They'll kill her otherwise," Eric said.

"It all depends on how they want to handle the transfer," Jason said. "I want you to be aware of the possibility that the kidnapper may intend to harm your daughter, even if you pay him."

"No." Chloe covered her face with her hands. "I don't want to think of that possibility. I just want her to be safe."

Agent Pierson crouched beside her. "We're going to do everything in our power to bring her home." He glanced at Jason. "In order to do that, we've got to think like a man who's desperate enough to kidnap a woman for ten million dollars."

11

JASON WAS waiting in Cobra's office when he showed up at nine o'clock the next morning. Cobra hummed as he came through the door but stopped short when he saw Jason. "What the—"

"I'm Special Agent Edwards, FBI."

Cobra dropped his shoulder bag. "Is this about Courtney? I just heard she was missing. Have they found her?"

"Why don't you have a seat?" Jason motioned to the chair next to him, and Cobra sank into it.

Jason remained standing. "Could you tell me what you did this weekend?"

"Why?" Cobra grasped the arm of the chair, and Jason could see the snake tattoo winding along his forearm.

"We're just trying to put together a timeline of what Courtney did over the weekend. Did you have plans with her?"

"You don't think I had something to do with this, do you?"

"Like I said, we're trying to fill in the blanks," Jason answered.

"Sure, but I swear I never saw Courtney after Friday morning." Cobra's eyes flicked to the screen saver on the computer. Jason saw a picture of Cobra wakeboarding before it changed to another of him standing by a boat with a group of friends. Cobra frowned and continued, "I asked her to go boating on Saturday afternoon. I thought she ditched me, because I came by the house to pick her up and there wasn't anyone around."

"Were you angry about that?" Jason asked.

"Have you seen a picture of Courtney Beckham?"

Jason stared at Cobra, wondering what angle he would use to defend himself.

"Well, wouldn't you be mad if you missed a chance of seeing her in a swimsuit?"

Jason didn't smile.

"Look, dude. I like Courtney. Why would I hurt her? I work for her father." He leaned forward. "Are you gonna tell me what happened or not?"

"Courtney's been kidnapped." Jason watched Cobra's reaction.

He pressed his palms against his knees. "Is she okay? I mean, she's alive and everything, right?"

"Yes, but there's been a ransom demand," Jason said.

Cobra's neck muscles jutted out as he struggled to swallow. "Ransom? But who would—"

"So the last time you saw Courtney was on Friday here in your office," Jason confirmed. "What was she doing here?"

"She created an Excel spreadsheet for me. She's a whiz at that kind of stuff."

Jason noticed the slight flush creeping up Cobra's neck. "Were you romantically involved with Courtney?"

Cobra flexed his fingers. "Saturday would've been our first date."

"What time did you arrive at the Beckham residence?" Jason asked.

"It was about 1:45. I'd told her I would be there by two to get her."

Jason wrote down the time and watched Cobra out of the corner of his eye. The phone rang and Cobra moved to answer it, but then he sank back in his chair. "It can wait," he muttered.

Jason tapped his pen against the notebook. "So what did you do when you didn't find Courtney at home?"

"I walked around the house, knocked on the back door, and tried to call her cell."

"Did you notice anything out of the ordinary?"

Cobra tapped his fingers on the desk. "I thought I heard some ATVs. It's usually pretty quiet up there—private property, you know."

Jason gripped his notepad. Maybe Cobra would give him something useful after all. "How many do you think you heard?"

"There may have been two, but I don't know. I just remember hearing one rev its engines when I walked around the house."

"About how far away do you think they were?"

"They must have been a ways off because I didn't see anything," Cobra said. "The sound carried because it's so quiet up there. Probably somewhere up in the mountains."

Jason scribbled on his notepad. "Anything else?"

"No, I left after that. Like I said, I figured she was a no-show."

Jason sat on the edge of Cobra's desk. "I'm trying to understand why you didn't contact her father about this when you heard she went missing."

"I just found out when I came in this morning." Cobra motioned to the hallway. "Sandra told me about it and asked if Eric had been in touch with me. After I went boating Saturday, I headed down to Moab with some buddies, and we got back late last night."

Jason studied Cobra's face. The man's wide blue eyes hardened under Jason's gaze. "Would you mind giving me the names and phone numbers of a few of your buddies to corroborate your story?"

"So I'm a suspect?" Cobra leaned back in his chair, pushing his arms straight against his desk.

"We're just gathering information, and I'd rather not have to come back when my boss asks for details later."

"Sure, happy to help." Cobra gave Jason a fake smile. He jerked a sheet of paper from his printer and scrolled through his cell phone, writing down numbers. He handed the page to Jason. "I guess that's my alibi?"

"Yeah, something like that. If you think of anything else—anything—give me a call." Jason flipped out his contact card and handed it to Cobra.

Jason met up with Agent Pierson thirty minutes later. "Any news from the boyfriend?"

"Sean? No, he didn't have anything to add." Pierson scrolled through pages on the Internet as Jason drove. "I'm pretty sure he's not our guy."

"Solid alibi?"

"Yeah, and Felix Haran is in Europe, so he's not our man either." Pierson rolled his shoulders. "I think this is bigger than a boyfriend anyway."

Jason watched Pierson reach into the cooler behind the seat with his signature move and pull out a candy bar.

"Don't you ever eat anything besides Snickers bars?" Jason asked.

Pierson laughed. "Hey, these are a lot better than those granola bars you're always carrying around."

"Really? How do you figure?"

Pierson ripped open the candy bar. "They're both sugar in different forms. And you might have noticed, they both have peanuts."

"Yeah, except one has caramel coating those peanuts." Jason grabbed a water bottle and took a swig.

"Well, Nature Boy, what do you think about our list of suspects so far?"

Jason chuckled. Pierson's good-natured ribbing didn't hit far from the mark. He worked hard to be fit, but he had his vices—one of which was a juicy hamburger with onion rings. "I don't know."

"Sure you do," Pierson said. "Gimme your gut."

Jason punched him in the arm. His partner loved to tease him about his gut instinct, and Jason took it in stride because he knew Pierson was aware of how accurate it had been in the past.

"I don't feel like our man is on the list yet, but I'm hoping he'll make an appearance soon."

"And," Pierson nudged him.

"Someone is hiding something. I think it's someone close to Courtney." Jason glanced at Pierson.

"What makes you think that?"

"My gut." Jason looked straight ahead, trying to ignore the grin he knew was spreading across Pierson's face.

"So where is your gut taking us?"

"Out to the Beckhams', but my gut isn't taking us—information is." Jason put on a pair of chrome sunglasses. "Cobra said he heard ATVs driving by around two o'clock on Saturday. He mentioned he thought it was usually quiet up there because it's private property. Did you know after a quarter mile, the Beckhams are surrounded by the National Forest?"

"Yeah, it's pretty secluded."

Jason tapped the steering wheel. "I have a question."

"Shoot."

"You've got teenage girls, right?"

"Yeah." Pierson shook his head. "See all these gray hairs?"

Jason smiled. "A girl like her." He pointed to the picture of Courtney pulled up on Pierson's laptop. "How much time would she take to get ready for a date?"

Pierson chuckled. "You can never tell—too long, probably." He stared at the picture. "My girls take at least an hour in the bathroom. I don't know how much time it takes them to decide what to wear."

"So, if Courtney had a date with Cobra at two, it'd make sense for her to be home from her horse ride by one o'clock at the latest, but probably much earlier," Jason said. "With the heat this time of year, she probably would have left early."

"So you're thinking she went missing sometime Saturday morning?"

"I'm thinking she's been held captive for forty-eight hours now." Jason pushed the kidnapping statistics from his mind and focused on the information he'd gathered. Pierson had come up with a list of possible enemies of Beckham Development. The list was so long, it'd take a week to analyze and narrow down suspects.

"After this, we need to talk to Detective Gardner. He's probably getting all kinds of dirt on Eric," Pierson said.

"I saw the dollar amounts that business is pulling—he's ruthless," Jason said. "I wonder how many hours he works in a week?"

"Enough to make him feel guilty and plan a surprise getaway for his wife."

Jason tapped on the brakes as they rounded the curve in the paved drive to the Beckham residence. "I want to walk around the property again, get a feel for the area and see if there's anything we might have missed. Is that good with you?"

"Yeah, I wanted to ask their ranch hand a few more questions anyway." Pierson stepped out of the car and headed for the stables.

Jason walked the perimeter of the property slowly, listening to the quiet movement of the forest beyond the heat-stricken pastures. A few birds trilled, and he heard the screech of a hawk. He shielded his eyes against the sun to see the bird drifting on the currents of air high above.

Stepping carefully around the water trough, he noted again the crumbling footprints Richie had shown him yesterday by flashlight. About thirty yards into the field, Jason bent to examine hoofprints in a barren patch of ground. He ran his fingertips over the prints and watched as the dirt trickled away from his touch.

Completely dry, the horseshoe-shaped imprints would disappear in the first gusts of wind that blew out of the canyon. Jason stood and pulled his phone from his belt clip. He took a picture, and as he did, he caught movement in his peripheral vision. He turned to see Eric walking toward him. Jason marked his bearings against the tree line so he could remember the location of the hoofprints, then hooked his phone on his belt.

Eric smiled as he approached. "Agent Edwards, good to see you today. Is there something I can help you with?"

Jason brushed the dirt from his hands. "Just wanted to see the lay of the land. It's pretty up here. Do you get many trespassers?"

"No, we're lucky that way."

"I bet you have the occasional rogue ATV, though. It'd be hard to resist these open stretches."

"No, I think most people are smart enough. The Forest Service is serious about keeping these parts unscathed, and so am I."

Jason rubbed the sweat from his forehead. "You said Courtney liked to take that ride into the canyon a lot. What direction did she usually head from the stables?"

"She'd go straight down the drive and cross over the south pasture."

Jason pointed to the field. "So she wouldn't ride out there and come out somewhere else?"

Eric shook his head. "No, that's in the opposite direction and would add too much time to her rides. She usually didn't like to be gone for more than three hours."

Jason walked with Eric toward the house. "There's a source of water for the horses in the stable, correct?"

"Yes, we have fresh water for them there."

"Does Richie take care of that every day?"

"Twice a day, except weekends." Eric stopped at the edge of the field and looked at the stables. "We give him the evenings off on the weekend."

Jason stopped at the water trough and pointed at the disintegrating hoofprints. "I'm just wondering why Courtney would come all the way over to this trough for water when the stable has ample water resources."

"Well, Richie usually comes around five in the morning on Saturday, and the horses can drink quite a bit after they eat," Eric said. "When it's hot, they'll take a drink of fresh water whenever they can, and Court is pretty mindful of Tika."

"But Richie said she filled up the water trough here. If she was going to fill up a trough, why not the closer one in the stable?"

Eric looked at him and squinted in the sunlight. "Are you going somewhere with all these questions?"

Jason met his gaze. "Just trying to narrow down the timeline by figuring out exactly what she did Saturday morning."

"Shouldn't you be spending time searching the area where we know Courtney was kidnapped?"

"But that's the problem—we don't know for certain where she was abducted." His cell phone rang, and he answered. "Yeah?"

Pierson was the caller. "Come in the house. I found something in Courtney's room."

"Be right in." Jason replaced his phone on his belt clip and headed for the house. "Pierson is checking out Courtney's room again. I hope that's okay."

"Certainly," Eric said. "Let me know if there's anything else you need. I'm heading over to the office to see what I can do about the financial side of this problem."

Jason wished he could tell Eric not to worry about the money because it was his plan to solve the case, not pay criminals. Instead, he smiled. "Mr. Beckham, we're going to try our best to see that you won't even have to meet up with the perpetrator."

Eric nodded as he walked to the silver automobile with a poised jaguar as the hood ornament. "I want to be ready just in case."

Jason jogged up the stairs to Courtney's room, admiring the elaborate furnishings throughout the house. He wondered just how much money Eric would be able to pull together in the next twenty-four hours—probably a hefty sum.

"Courtney planned on going out with this Cobra guy," Pierson said when Jason entered the bedroom. He pointed to the black-and-green swimsuit draped over a chair. A bag with a towel and other swim gear hung on the arm of the chair.

"So she had to have been taken before noon," Jason said.

"I'm betting a couple of hours before that. Like you were saying, she'd want to get ready, and plus, it must've been close to ninety-five degrees by noon." Pierson nudged the bag with his toe.

"I think we're narrowing down the window pretty tight as to when she was abducted," Jason said. "If they did take her Saturday morning, why wait until Sunday night to put in a ransom note?"

Pierson clicked his ball-point pen back and forth. "That's a good question. I'm surprised they would risk holding onto the victim for that long, unless they were worried Eric wouldn't be able to get the money over the weekend."

"Or if she was seriously injured when they abducted her and they had to wait for her to be coherent enough to send the voice message." Jason paced around Courtney's room. He noticed her pink laptop. Detective Gardner and his unit had performed the first search of her room for any signs as to why she was missing, but now they were searching from a different angle. "I think we should take her laptop to the office and have the guys look at it."

"Yeah, I'm planning on it," Pierson said. "Her mom looked through the room initially to see if anything was missing. At first, the guys wondered if she'd run off somewhere, but nothing was missing."

"So now we're trying to find anything that would hint as to what she had planned for the weekend." Jason looked through a stack of papers on her desk. "I think whoever took her did so with an ATV not far from the house."

"The only problem with that theory is the horse was found five miles from here, closer to a major road." Pierson slid the laptop and a few more of her personal belongings into an evidence bag. "Why would they risk coming close to the house when they could just exit the canyon on the highway?"

Jason sat on the edge of the bed. "What about the ATVs Corbin Whittier said he heard? We need to figure out who they were and why they were on restricted property."

"I don't think we have the resources right now to follow up on that. You know kids are always out riding where they aren't supposed to, and he probably made that up to make his story sound realistic."

"But maybe someone saw something," Jason insisted.

Pierson shook his head. "We haven't heard anything so far."

"What's the search radius?"

"Search and Rescue was increasing it to five miles from the clearing where the dog was shot, but they called it off once the ransom note came in."

Jason clenched his jaw. He had a strong opinion about the decision to call off the search, but it wouldn't do him any good to voice it now. He glanced around Courtney's room again. Her closet overflowed with clothes, but the room was relatively tidy. The bookshelf was crammed with an assortment of fiction titles from fantasy to suspense and romance.

Outward appearances of Courtney Beckham painted her to be a shallow, spoiled little rich girl, but Jason could see there was more to this woman. A cushioned window seat was scattered with books and notebooks, not the fashion magazines Jason would have expected. The large bay window overlooked the mountain range and would catch the sun's first eastern rays. Jason imagined Courtney sitting in the sunlight reading a book.

The pillows on the window seat were arranged neatly, and Jason walked over and lifted the cushions one at a time. Under the third pillow, he noticed the spine of a hardback book. He pulled the dark green book out and discovered it was actually a leather-bound journal. Courtney's name was embossed in silver script across the front.

Jason lifted the journal up. "Do you think they already snooped through this?"

Pierson looked up and narrowed his eyes. "No, looks like it was pretty well hidden over there."

Relaxing back against the cushions, Jason opened the journal and flipped to the most recent entry. "I don't think this will give us any inside info. The last entry is from almost three months ago."

"Yeah, we usually have better luck reading people's emails." Pierson continued his methodical search of Courtney's dresser drawers.

Jason studied the last entry Courtney had penned during the first week of May:

I can't believe another year of school has come to a close. I'm so excited to be done with finals! My human physiology class was a killer. But it was also one of my favorite classes ever. I loved learning so much and really feeling like my brain was being stretched and pulled in so many directions to grasp the concepts. I hope I'll feel the same way about next year's classes. If I hadn't changed my major so many times, I'd probably have my business degree by now—sometimes I still wonder if I made the right choice. Oh well, I can always minor in a few more subjects.

My best friend, Jenica, is getting married in the fall. I'm okay with being single, but can I just say how sick I am of the whole dating scene?!

I know it's mostly my fault, but I seem to attract the wrong kind of guys. I'd like to meet someone who could carry on a conversation about something besides sports or how tight my rear end is. My study partner this term was so nice. Henry totally understood how my mind worked when we were trying to memorize the process of cell breakdown for human phys. And he helped me figure out a way to memorize it. I think he was into me, but I could never date someone like him. Mom and Dad wouldn't approve, and it was too hard for me to get past the geek factor anyway.

Rick thought he was right when he called me shallow, but I wish I could have told him the truth. It's been two years, but I still get nervous when I think about Felix. I probably would have never dated again if I didn't have to deal with the pressure I have from my friends and family to date just the right kind of guys. Sometimes I think I'll never find the guy for me.

That's why this summer I decided I'm just gonna have fun while I can, and then next fall I'll concentrate on finishing up with school. It'll be kind of a relief to get a job and go out on my own. Mom and Dad are never around, but when they are, you could cut the tension with a knife. I think they've stopped trying. If that's all I have to look forward to, then I guess I better get busy having fun!

"Anything good there, Edwards?"

Jason looked up and held the journal toward Pierson. "Actually kind of interesting. She wrote something about her parents not getting along anymore—like they've stopped trying."

Pierson took the journal and read where Jason indicated. "Hmm, I didn't catch that vibe from them. Did you?"

"No." Jason rubbed the stubble on his chin. "Of course, people act differently under stress, but I didn't sense any tension."

Pierson closed the journal. "They must be good at hiding it, but let's keep that tidbit on the radar. If one of them was fooling around, things could have gotten nasty."

"You mean like an ex-lover?"

"Exactly." Pierson put Courtney's journal into his evidence bag. "We'd better start a new line of questioning to see what we come up with."

"I bet the secretary at Beckham's office would know," Jason said. "The wife, though—it might be harder to uncover her secrets."

"We need to let Gardner know about this—make sure his men look at possible scenarios." Pierson pulled his cell phone from his belt but stopped when Chloe poked her head in the room.

"Is there anything I can help you with?"

Jason looked at Pierson. "Hey, I was looking at a few things outside when you called. I'm going to take a walk while you finish up in here." He patted his cell phone, and Pierson nodded.

"Mrs. Beckham said she'd help me look through Courtney's things to see if anything else was out of the ordinary." Pierson turned to Chloe. "It shouldn't take too much longer."

Jason walked outside. The weight of the summer heat hung heavy as he strode back to the water trough and the entrance to the east pasture. He called Gardner and relayed the information he'd read from Courtney's journal.

"We'll start questioning some of their friends," Gardner said.

"But be discreet," Jason said. "We don't want people to get wind of this."

"Sure, no problem." Gardner ended the call.

Jason let his mind wander to the contents of Courtney's room. He chuckled when he thought about what Courtney had written in her journal. Why was she dating a football player if she was tired of talking about sports? The journal entry had given him a good snap-shot into the real Courtney Beckham, and it had him concerned in more ways than one. She'd mentioned attracting the wrong guys and just wanting to have fun, and he couldn't think of a worse combination for trouble. Whatever had happened with Felix Haran seemed to still be affecting her.

A few wasps hung on to the edge of the trough, drinking the water. Jason's boots crunched against the leftover bits of dried June grass as he walked across the pasture. The ground was packed, and Jason shook his head. His search for hoofprints would be fruitless in this dry climate.

He shaded his eyes against the sun as he looked at the mountains and continued walking. A grove of aspen trees grew in a tight cluster at the edge of the woods. He figured the terrain should alter slightly with the shift from the dry pasture to the rocky ground dotted with scrub oak. He saw Richie by the stables and picked up his pace.

"Hey, Richie," Jason said as he entered the stables. "Would it be okay if I borrowed the ATV to drive across the field?"

"No problem. Feel free to use anything you need to help find Courtney." Richie stepped back and motioned to the ATV. "I just filled her up."

"Thanks. I'll park it back here when I'm finished." Jason straddled the machine and started the engine.

He drove slowly back to the water trough and looked for any signs that the horse had entered the pasture. Some of the dry grass was trampled a few yards from the water trough, and Jason felt he was heading in the right direction as he continued across the field.

Keeping a close lookout, he headed for the aspen grove and ignored the beads of sweat rolling down his back. The expanse of the field made the search nearly impossible, and Jason couldn't find anything definitive to indicate that a horse and rider had come this way, but he continued toward the edge of the woods. When he approached the perimeter of the open field, he cut the engine and walked toward the tree line, looking for any areas in the dry grasses that had been disturbed.

When Jason stepped into the shade of the trees, he inhaled, noting the difference in temperature. He wiped a hand across his brow and turned back to look at the pasture. The sprawling mansion was no longer in sight. He'd probably driven nearly two miles—further than he'd intended, but he decided to have a look around before heading back.

He leaned against a tree that was actually two separate trees winding around each other. He traced the curve of growth until the trees merged and continued to branch out, reaching toward the bright blue sky. The golden green leaves fluttered above his head, and he grabbed hold of a branch and felt the smooth bark scattered with knobby outgrowths.

His hand stilled on an abrasion in the bark. Green lines where something had chaffed against the bark revealed the vivid life within the trees. Jason's heartbeat quickened as he fingered the two separate marks winding around the limb. He stepped away from the tree and examined the ground.

The weeds were trampled down in some places. Taking in the full diameter of the tree, Jason stopped and crouched. He grabbed a stick and prodded the pile of horse manure sitting in front of him. Flies buzzed around it, and he caught a whiff of the droppings. A horse had been here in the last two days.

Jason stood and walked out a few paces from the tree, circling wider. He dialed Pierson's cell. He answered on the first ring. "Jason, where are you? Eric Beckham just received another text message. They're making their move."

"What? But how?"

"They want Eric to pick up instructions for the drop at Liberty Park in Salt Lake City tomorrow night at ten. I can't see you—how far did you walk?"

Jason stepped out from the tree line. "I actually borrowed the ATV. I'm clear across the pasture at the edge of the woods. I found some horse droppings out here, semi-fresh."

"I didn't know you were going that far. We need to get a move on."

"Something's not right." Jason scanned the area near the horse droppings again. "A horse has been here in the last two days."

Pierson grunted. "So she rode her horse over there. It doesn't matter now because I got a call, and we're about to get some intel on these guys."

"I'm a few miles away." Jason hesitated. "I want to come back and check this later, or maybe we could send someone out."

"And look at horse crap? C'mon, Edwards, we need to hurry."

"Be right there." Jason frowned. He turned back to look at the tree and the wooded area beyond. "Where are you, Courtney?"

12

B Y THE time Jason drove back to the stables, Pierson was pacing by the car. Jason jogged to the vehicle and climbed inside. "Sorry, I didn't mean to be gone so long."

Pierson waved his hand and slid into the driver's seat. "It's okay. The tech guys just called. They traced the text to an email account at Beckham Development. The sender was Corbin Whittier."

"Let's bring him in," Jason said. "I knew he was hiding something."

"We're getting a search warrant for Beckham's office so we can search the mainframe of the office computers."

"What did Beckham say?"

"Eric's not too happy about the impending search." Pierson raised his eyebrows. "It makes me wonder if his business has a shady side."

"Most of those developers have a few underhanded deals lining their pockets." Jason turned up the AC. His thoughts returned to the grove of trees he'd just visited. A nagging feeling itched at his insides, and he couldn't stop thinking about Courtney's journal entry. She seemed like a smart girl. It was unlikely she'd willingly follow someone like Cobra into a trap.

Pierson interrupted his thoughts. "Hopefully we can find enough info to get a lead on where he's stashed Courtney."

Jason gazed out the window for a few moments, following the sharp curves of the road as they headed back to the city. "You know, I would've pegged this case differently."

"How so?" Pierson glanced over at him.

"I wouldn't have thought the kidnapper would turn out to be someone Courtney knew personally. Cobra was supposed to pick her up for a date, remember?"

"Good cover story." Pierson drove with one hand on the steering wheel. "It's possible Corbin is the businessman and he has someone else doing his dirty work."

"Any idea on motive?"

"Besides money?" Pierson chuckled.

Jason worked a kink out of his neck with his knuckles. "You know what I mean. Why does someone suddenly need a huge amount of cash when they're already pulling in the kind of income he's showing?"

"Yeah, we're running analysis on everything, but there aren't any red flags waving yet."

The trees thinned as they approached the mouth of Big Cottonwood Canyon. Jason tried to ignore the images in his mind that kept circling around Courtney and the grove of aspen trees at the edge of the pasture.

At the next stop sign, Pierson reached behind his seat and pulled a candy bar from the cooler on the floor. "You want some lunch?"

"No, thanks." Jason shook his head.

Pierson unwrapped the Snickers bar and took a big bite. He chewed around a mouthful that constituted nearly half the candy bar, then glanced at Jason. "You've got a lot on your mind today."

Jason rubbed his stomach. "Something about this case is giving me indigestion."

Pierson laughed. "They all do that to me. The Tums are in the glove box, if you need 'em."

When they pulled into Beckham Development, Pierson licked the chocolate off the wrapper of his Snickers bar, wadded it up, and tossed it on the floor. "It'd be nice if this is our guy—have an open-and-shut case."

Jason smiled. "Yeah, too bad those only happen on TV."

"Not even there anymore. *Law & Order* has some pretty complex episodes these days."

Jason laughed and slapped him on the back. "Let's go see if the snake can give us an interview."

They nearly collided with Sandra when they entered the reception area.

"Oh! I'm so sorry," she said, and her face paled. "Are you here to do the search already?"

"No, but our guys should be here soon," Pierson said. "We're here to talk to Mr. Whittier."

"His office is just down the hall to your right." Sandra pointed, and Jason noticed her hands trembling.

"Thanks," Pierson said. They walked down the hall, and he looked at Jason with raised eyebrows. "She seemed pretty nervous."

Jason motioned to an office worker hurrying down the hall with a pile of papers. "Do you think they're cleaning out?"

"It won't be good for them if they are." Pierson stopped in front of Cobra's office door and knocked three times.

Cobra opened the door and frowned when he saw the agents.

"Corbin Whittier?" Pierson asked.

"Yes, that's me."

"I'm Agent Pierson, and you know Agent Edwards. We'd like you to come with us to answer a few questions."

"What! Why?" Cobra took a step back. "Why can't you just ask your questions here?"

"The case is sensitive, and it'd be easier if you'd just come with us."

"Okay, let me log off my computer." Cobra turned to his monitor. Just before his fingers could graze the mouse, Pierson cleared his throat.

"That won't be necessary, Mr. Whittier. We have a search warrant for the premises, and our tech guys will be here within the hour to analyze all of the computers."

Cobra spun around. "Can you at least tell me what this is about?"

Jason kept his face impassive but answered the question. "It concerns the kidnapping of Courtney Beckham."

"But I already gave you my alibi." Cobra's fists tightened. "I didn't do anything to Court."

"Mr. Whittier, you can either come with us, or we can place you under arrest." Jason stepped forward and patted the cuffs hanging from his belt.

Cobra looked from Pierson to Jason, then let out a sigh. "Okay, I'll come."

Jason cranked up the radio as they drove, not eager to hear any more of Cobra's excuses. Cobra kept quiet, with his head down, during the ride to the FBI office. They escorted him inside and settled him in a secure room.

Pierson sat at Cobra's left to begin the questioning. "Mr. Whittier—"

"Just call me Cobra—everyone else does."

Pierson nodded. "Cobra, as you're aware, Courtney Beckham was kidnapped this past weekend and a ransom note was sent Sunday night."

"Yeah, and I told you guys everything I know."

Jason held up his hand. "More has developed since we spoke." He leaned forward and waited until Cobra met his gaze. "Earlier this afternoon, Eric was contacted again by the kidnappers via text message."

"The text message didn't come from another cell phone." Pierson paused and looked directly at Cobra. "It came from an email account with your name on it."

"What?" Cobra's forehead creased with concern. "Are you saying that I sent a ransom note to Eric?"

"We're saying Eric received instructions from the kidnappers, and those instructions came from your email account."

"Then it must have been hacked," Cobra said. "It happens all the time nowadays."

"That's why we brought you in for questioning," Jason explained.

"I'm being set up." Cobra pounded the table with his fist. The movement appeared to make the snake tattoo slither up his arm. "There's no way I would ever hurt Court. Who would be stupid enough to send a ransom message from a traceable account?"

"For your sake, I hope we come to that conclusion, but in the meantime, we have to investigate everything," Jason said.

Pierson cleared his throat. "Where were you at 1:30 today?"

"I was out on a business lunch."

"Late lunch. Where'd you eat?" Pierson jotted down a timeline on his notepad.

"The Market Street Grill." Cobra exhaled. "I take clients out for lunch regularly. I can give you the number of the business partners I was with."

"That'd be great." Jason tossed Cobra a pen and notebook.

Cobra picked up the pen and gave them a smug grin. "So I couldn't have sent the email because I was at lunch."

"That might've worked, before the days of email scheduling," Jason said.

Cobra gave him a puzzled look.

Jason motioned to the laptop in front of him. "You can schedule emails months in advance to send out at precisely the time you want."

"But how do you guys prove that? Can't you see I'm being set up?"

"We'd like you to stay here until we can ascertain how the email was sent," Pierson said.

"Do I need a lawyer?" Cobra asked.

"You have a right to representation, but we're not charging you with anything yet," Jason said.

"Then I'm not staying here." Cobra moved to stand.

"It would be in your best interest to stay here and help us sort this out," Pierson said.

Cobra frowned and sank back into the chair. "Does Eric know about this? He could vouch for me."

"Mr. Beckham isn't aware of our investigation at this point," Pierson said. "But we'll be meeting with him shortly. Unfortunately, his word isn't enough to clear things up, and I don't think he's willing to give it anyway."

"Did he say that?" Cobra's face darkened in anger. "Eric Beckham will throw anyone under the bus if it means finding his daughter." Cobra raised his voice, and the tendons on his neck stood out.

"All we know right now is that Eric said you had full access to the business computers," Pierson said.

Cobra swore. "I can't believe you guys are trying to pin this on me."

"If you're innocent, you have nothing to worry about," Pierson said. "We'll get to the bottom of this. Just sit tight while we sort things out."

Cobra leaned back in his chair and covered his face with his hands.

"We'll keep you updated on our progress," Jason said as they exited the room.

Back in their office, the agents organized all of their notes and the information they had on the case.

Pierson pinched the bridge of his nose. "A little over twenty-four hours until the drop, and I don't think Whittier's our man."

"I know." Jason raked his fingers through his hair. "I just keep thinking that things aren't adding up right."

"That's for sure, but what part of the equation are you talking about?" Pierson said.

"You know—like, why shoot the dog?" Jason tapped his notebook. "If it was Corbin, then it sounds like he's been over to the Beckham place enough that the dog would know him. If someone wanted to throw us off their trail, it would be pretty easy to move that horse and plant the dog."

"But the evidence they collected says otherwise," Pierson said. "Forensics said the dog was shot there in the meadow."

"What about the blood on her shirt? Are we sure it was hers?"

Pierson stopped typing and looked at his notebook. "We don't know yet. Are you thinking it was from the dog?"

Jason grunted. "I don't know." He slumped into his office chair and spun it halfway around. "Just hoping she's not injured."

Pierson's phone rang, and Jason checked his email, half-listening to the conversation. He could tell it was the tech department and that the news wasn't good.

After a few minutes, Pierson hung up. "Someone hacked into the system and covered their trail."

"So we're back to square one?"

"We don't have enough evidence to arrest him," Pierson said.

"You don't think he's our man, do you?"

"No, but it would make things a lot easier if he were."

Jason shook his head. "I'll go give him the good news."

Cobra leaned against the table with his head resting on his hands, but he jerked up when Jason opened the door.

"You're free to go, but don't leave town." Jason watched the different emotions flicker over Cobra's face. He looked afraid, angry, and relieved.

"I told you I'm innocent."

"Let's hope nothing else comes up to the contrary." He stepped aside so Cobra could exit the room, then walked with him down the hallway. "And if you think of anything that might help, let us know."

"I will," Cobra said. "I hope you find her."

"Guess we'll head back over to Beckham Development and ask a few more questions," Pierson said.

"Good plan." Jason followed him out to the black car soaking up the sun. "With the search warrant, people should be spooked enough to spill anything that might implicate them."

"You think the secretary's been holding back?" Pierson lifted a brow.

Jason shrugged. "Not necessarily, but I bet she'll be more than helpful now."

The parking lot of Eric's building was nearly empty when they returned.

"He must have sent everyone home when they started the search." Pierson parked the car in front of the building.

"Let's hope the secretary is still here." Jason followed Pierson inside and smiled when he saw Sandra.

They approached the front desk, and he noted the tension in the atmosphere. Sandra dumped a pile of office supplies into a box and lifted her eyes in greeting. "I figured I'd reorganize my desk while we were at it."

Pierson nodded. "We'd like to ask you a few questions, if that's okay."

"Sure, anything to help Courtney," Sandra said. "I can't believe it—I hope she's all right."

Jason took a step closer to the desk. "We're moving as quickly as we can with the investigation."

"Do you know anyone who might want to do harm to the Beckham family?" Pierson asked.

Sandra looked taken aback. "You think this was someone we worked with?"

"At this point, we're trying to rule everything out," Jason said. "Narrow down the list of persons of interest so we can focus on a probable suspect."

Sandra glanced at her computer. "There were some clients who defaulted, and we had to take them to court, but I can't imagine them doing anything so violent."

"Would you mind taking a look through your database? If anything catches your eye, let us know."

She sat down and swiveled her chair back toward her computer. She clicked the mouse and opened up a few folders.

Pierson leaned over the desk. "Does Mr. Beckham work pretty long hours?"

"Yes, he's often still here when I close up and head home."

Jason watched her scrolling through pages on her screen. "Does he ever spend the night here?"

"I think he's slept on the couch a few times, but I don't know how often," Sandra said. "Sometimes he stays at the condo in Park City if he's working in that area anyway."

"Do he and Chloe get along pretty well?" Pierson pulled out his notebook.

Sandra looked like she was trying to figure out where the questions were headed. "Um, I really didn't socialize with them much. She's pretty busy with her organizations and the spa group. Sometimes I've helped make appointments for her, but that's about all."

Jason cleared his throat. "We're just trying to find weak spots, to try to see what our perpetrator might have observed before making his move."

"Chloe isn't the type to have enemies, and she keeps herself unaware of the difficult side of Eric's business."

Pierson scribbled a few notes and then asked, "Who usually deals with the nasty side of the business?"

"Eric was pretty efficient in dealing with those types his assistants couldn't take care of, but if he wasn't available, it was Cobra." Sandra motioned down the hall to his office.

"What about accounting? Who's the go-to person there?"

"Well, Courtney helps out a lot with that." Sandra rolled a pencil between her fingers. "She streamlined a lot of our accounts and made the bookkeeping so much simpler."

"Do you think anyone held her responsible for their unpaid accounts with the company?" Jason asked.

"Oh, I see," Sandra said. "There were some clients who had been able to slip through the cracks, so to speak, because our bookkeeping wasn't up to date. When we were in our heyday, we were running ragged. We just couldn't keep track of everything."

Sandra pushed a strand of light brown hair behind her ear. "After Court's first year of college, she came in and cleaned everything up. She found deficits of nearly 450,000 dollars by the time she was done analyzing everything."

Pierson let out a low whistle.

"She also found some other strange things that had Eric pretty worked up."

Jason straightened and clicked his pen. "When was that?"

"About a month ago." Sandra opened a new window on the computer screen and pointed to it. "She was trying out some new spreadsheets she'd developed in one of her college classes and picked up on some discrepancies."

"What kind of discrepancies?" Pierson asked.

Sandra shook her head. "I'm not really sure. I overheard her discussing it with Cobra and Eric. Maybe they can explain it."

"Can you think of anything else out of the ordinary?" Jason asked.

Sandra pressed her lips together and looked at the floor, then she sighed and met Jason's gaze. "I wish there was something that jumped out at me, but no, I can't think of anything right now."

"Thank you for your help." Pierson slid a card across the desk. "Here's our contact info in case you think of something else."

On the way back to the office, Jason scribbled notes as fast as he could, thinking about all of the information Sandra had just given them. "We should be able to get a new line of questioning going based on the accounts she referred to."

"I don't know if we're barking up the wrong tree, though," Pierson said. "It still doesn't seem like Cobra is our guy."

"But the motive is there," Jason said. "Let's check to see if he had any travel plans in the near future."

"Our biggest problem is that this avenue of questioning isn't going to lead us to who has Courtney right now." Pierson glanced at him. "All of these types would have someone else doing their dirty work, so of course they would alibi out."

"Yeah, you're right," Jason said.

After they returned to the FBI office, Jason pulled out a green folder and labeled it COURTNEY BECKHAM. He placed a sheet with her pertinent information in the front and added a few pages of notes he'd taken. Last, he slid the eight-by-ten-inch color photo provided by her parents into the folder. He ran his finger along the edge of the folder and pulled the photo back out.

There was no argument that Courtney was a beauty. Her long black hair reminded him of her father's coloring. A small dimple under her right eye fit the fun-loving personality everyone had painted of her, but when he focused on her dark hazel eyes, he wondered what story they were hiding. There was more to Courtney than the smiling diva in this photo. He hoped he'd have a chance to figure out what that was before it was too late.

He tapped a finger on the picture, noting her pale complexion. He wondered if her skin darkened up in the summer from the hours she spent outdoors. Dozens of questions flitted across his mind as he continued to study Courtney's photo. Jason did this with all of his investigations—overanalyzed them to try to figure out some hidden motivation to the case. Sometimes it worked—other times it didn't. But he always felt it helped him as an investigator to notice intricate details he might have missed. Something that might be out of place.

If he could find out enough about Courtney, maybe when they went back out to the Beckham residence tomorrow, something might show up as a red flag. Jason stared at the photo, scrutinizing each part of the fine curves of her face. He jotted down a handful of questions, then placed the green folder in his shoulder bag.

Next, he pulled out a red folder from a stack on his desk. He used this color to store information about potential suspects. It bothered him that they still didn't have a good lead on who might be responsible for the kidnapping. He clenched his jaw and wrote down the few notes they had collected.

13

RAMIRO WAS kicking back on the couch in the cabin's loft with his eyes closed when the phone rang. He jumped up and hurried into the office, grabbing it by the second ring. His boss was the only one who had this number. "Hey, Honcho." He knew his boss didn't like the nickname, but he'd never come out and told Ramiro to address him differently.

"How's Courtney?"

"She's fine. Feisty, but she'll be okay." Ramiro kept his voice low and looked toward her bedroom door.

"Keep an eye on her. Look, the feds are nosing around too much. We need to move," Honcho said.

"The guys are almost done harvesting the first crop, but we don't have enough men. They haven't started on the second. We're losing a lot of money as it is, taking it so early."

"We'll take a hit this time, but we've got to keep the operation safe," Honcho replied. "I don't have any more men to spare on these crops. Do what you can, and be sure to destroy all the evidence."

"How much time do you think we have?" Ramiro asked.

"I'll check around and call you as soon as I know," Honcho replied. "Probably only forty-eight hours. Be ready to move out."

A sound broke into Courtney's troubled thoughts. A telephone ringing—not a cell phone, but an actual landline. The ringing cut short, and Courtney tiptoed across the room and put her ear to the door. She could hear someone speaking just down the hall. Could there actually be a phone line to this cabin? If so, they must be closer to the cluster of cabins settled in this forest than she thought.

Courtney dropped to her knees, crawling slowly along the carpet. When she ducked her head under the bed and saw the phone jack in the wall, her breath caught. There *was* a landline. Her hands shook with nervous anxiety as she absorbed what this might mean.

There was definitely someone bigger than Ramiro running the drug operation, and they were in contact. If Courtney could get to that phone and dial 9-1-1, the police could come and find her. She sat on the floor and leaned against the bed, looking down at her watch. Both hands pointed to the four. The second hand ticked nervously around the face, as if counting the seconds until Ramiro would return. She felt every nerve in her body following those silent ticks as she tried to decide what to do.

When the hands pointed to five o'clock, Courtney moved across her bedroom toward the door. She opened it a crack and listened. Ramiro was downstairs. She'd heard him clomp by minutes after the phone rang. She couldn't hear anyone else in the house. Courtney listened to find out if Ramiro would come back upstairs. The stillness of the cabin emphasized the beating of her heart, and she swallowed hard, thinking about her next move.

Inch by inch, she opened the door wider, praying that the hinges wouldn't squeak. She looked down the hallway and saw two more doors. The first was open, so that made her decision easier. She wouldn't have much time.

Courtney edged out of her room, keeping her body flush against the wall. Her ears strained for any sound. The adrenaline pumping through her veins brought beads of sweat to her hairline.

Remembering Ramiro's warning not to leave the room, Courtney closed the door and took two steps across the hall. One floorboard creaked, and she held her breath as she slid her foot forward. With each step, her heartbeat grew louder in her ears until she was certain she wouldn't be able to hear Ramiro approach if he came looking for her. She tiptoed the last few steps into the other bedroom.

It was carpeted, and she exhaled when she noticed the makeshift office set up in the corner of the room. A black cordless phone sat on the charger a few feet away. Her heart soared as she crept across the floor. Visions of someone coming to her rescue ran through her mind as she reached for the phone.

Her fingers had just grazed the black plastic when it rang again. Courtney pulled her hand back abruptly. She turned, wondering if she should sprint back to her room or try to hide. Her eyes darted across the room, but there wasn't a big enough space to crawl into— she was trapped with nowhere to hide.

Crouching down, she saw boxes underneath the bed and wondered if she could wriggle between them. She hesitated, listening for the sound of Ramiro's boots as the phone continued to ring. Then Courtney glanced at the name on the caller ID. The words sent ice through her veins.

She squinted and watched the name Tropical Resources move across the screen followed by a phone number. Courtney swallowed and took a step back. The ringing stopped, and every muscle in her body tensed. Ramiro must've grabbed a different handset downstairs. Her insides buzzed as she thought about the last time she'd seen the name Tropical Resources. It didn't make sense, and she had to find out what was going on.

Courtney sucked in a breath as she thought of the consequences of staying in the room longer. Ignoring the panicked voice telling her to run, she picked up the phone and pushed the talk button. She didn't hear a noticeable beep, and she relaxed her stance, holding the phone by her ear.

"Make sure she doesn't know where you're taking her. If we don't get that crop out tonight, it'll be too late. One of the agents was asking a bunch of questions—he's suspicious."

The phone felt like a searing red torch in her hand, and Courtney's fingers trembled. Tropical Resources. Her heart raced as the sound of the voice clicked with thousands of memories in her brain.

The voice she knew so well sent shock waves rolling through her body. Frozen to the spot, Courtney tilted the phone away from her mouth to let a trembling breath escape.

She heard Ramiro speak. "Courtney will tell them what she saw."

"It'll be too late. Everything will be cleaned up, and there won't be any evidence. We'll have the other patch harvested by then. Next year, we'll move farther into the mountains. It was a risky move, placing it so close to the property."

Courtney bit her lip to keep from screaming. Her stomach twisted, and she leaned against the desk, overcome with what she heard. The voice continued on in a clipped, steady rhythm, and she relaxed her jaw when she tasted blood on her lip.

"When we do the information drop, you'll take the money and then demand more." He lowered his voice to a whisper. "Hold onto her for two more days, but whatever you do, keep your hands off Courtney or I'll kill you. But get her moved tonight. I'll check on—"

Courtney forced herself into action. Pulling the phone away from her ear, she hesitated before pushing the talk button to disconnect from the conversation. If she did, it would beep, and Ramiro might know she was listening in. She eyed the charger and decided that would be a better way. With trembling hands, she replaced the phone in the cradle. It beeped, and the hairs on the back of her neck stood on end. She ran on tiptoe down the hall and back into her room.

Diving for the bed, she burrowed under the covers and gasped for air, trying to even out her breathing. She concentrated on quieting the pounding rhythm of pulsing blood through her body.

Ramiro would be coming. He had orders to move her somewhere. She wished she could've listened to more details of the conversation, but it was too risky.

The scream she'd held inside felt tight against her throat. She pushed her face into the pillow to try to stop the tears. The betrayal of her trust burned against the backs of her eyes. She had recognized his voice immediately. Her father was behind this. Eric Beckham had kidnapped his own daughter.

For a few moments, she struggled to combat the hysteria she felt attached to this bizarre turn of events. Her own father. A few hot tears escaped her tightly closed eyes and dropped onto the pillow. Her insides burned with angry sobs, but then a thought stopped the overwhelming sense of loss from engulfing her.

Courtney's toes tingled with the realization of the situation before her. She was not going to die, and they couldn't hurt her even if she tried to escape.

Her father was some kind of drug lord, growing marijuana a few miles from his own backyard. And it looked like he was willing to do anything to keep his secrets. But he'd instructed Ramiro to keep his hands off.

After a few minutes, she roused herself from the bed and massaged her temples, trying to clear her head. She couldn't let Ramiro take her somewhere else. She had to get free before her dad could hide the evidence.

Courtney chewed on her thumbnail. She visualized their beautiful home in the foothills and the parties her mother had planned. Her mother's lifestyle and her own. If she kept quiet, nothing would have to change. Chloe Beckham would be crushed when Eric's illegal activities were exposed.

Courtney knew she had a choice. She held her family's fate in her hands. She shook her head vehemently—there was no choice. Images of hopeless individuals addicted to drugs flashed through her mind. She wouldn't stand by while her father destroyed other people's lives through drug dealing.

She jumped off the bed and searched the room again for anything that might help her escape. Courtney went through every drawer in the bathroom with renewed fervor, but a tube of toothpaste and a rattail comb weren't going to be much help.

Her father was a criminal. Not the kind who cheated on his taxes and took money under the table—he was a drug dealer. Courtney wiped at her eyes in frustration. Her own father was behind her kidnapping. But she couldn't make her heart understand the betrayal of the man she called Daddy.

She splashed her face with water and looked in the mirror. Water droplets rolled down her cheeks, merging with her tears and splashing onto the countertop. Her eyes always looked black when she cried, as if the iris absorbed the torment of the moment and imbued the darkness she felt. Courtney pulled the band from her hair and shook out her dark ponytail. She massaged her scalp and took deep, cleansing breaths to rid her body of tension.

She straightened and pulled her hair back into the elastic. Escape was the only way out. If she stayed and something went wrong, her father might decide not to let her come home. He had said the FBI was involved and nosing around. Wouldn't they have found the marijuana crop by now?

Courtney covered her mouth. What if they had done something to Tika? She had to get out of this cabin. She closed her eyes and pulled up the memory of when Ramiro had brought her to the cabin. There had to be a back door, but she hadn't seen it from the kitchen. The fastest way out would be down the stairs and out the front entrance. But then she'd have to deal with Ramiro. If the other men were around, it'd be impossible to move without their notice. Courtney wiped her eyes. So far she had been a good prisoner, not attempting to escape. It was time to play dirty.

As night fell, Courtney grew more anxious. She was unfamiliar with this wooded area. Her plan was to make a run for it, but that would be life-threatening in the dark. Even though she tried to keep from checking her watch, she found herself noting the time every few minutes as the hour grew later.

It was almost ten o'clock when Ramiro entered the bedroom. Courtney noticed the rope coiled in his hand before he spoke. "We're going to move you tonight. I need to tie you up."

Her stomach growled, and she glared at Ramiro. "I haven't had anything to eat since breakfast."

He flinched. She guessed that he'd been preoccupied with the change of plans. "I'll get you something later."

Courtney's stomach grumbled again. Ramiro frowned. "Put your hands behind your back."

She tried to hide her fear as he pulled the rope tight around her hands. Courtney hunched her shoulders forward as he knotted the rope, pulling her hands apart slightly.

"Hold still," Ramiro commanded.

A thousand ideas ran through Courtney's head—different scenarios where she could convince Ramiro of what her father would do with him once his crop was harvested. But she couldn't let on that she knew who was behind her kidnapping. There was no telling what Eric Beckham was capable of doing to save his drug operation.

Ramiro tugged on the rope, and Courtney gasped as her shoulders pulled back taut. She struggled to hold still. "You're quiet tonight." He moved around to face her.

"I'm hungry. Can't you at least bring me some crackers?" She met his gaze and didn't look away when he leered at her. But when he reached out, she turned her head, and his fingers grazed the side of her cheek.

"I'll be right back. You try anything with those ropes, and I'll tie your feet and gag you." Ramiro closed the door, and Courtney leaned against the bed. Now was the time for action.

She couldn't outrun Ramiro with her hands tied behind her back. She needed to change position. She rolled her shoulders and bent her elbows until there was space enough to sit. With a deep exhale, Courtney remembered the yoga positions her mother's expensive trainer had taught her. He had said that flexibility would aid her running and help prevent injuries. And the exercises had helped her to become more sure-footed. She loved the release of tension every time she moved through the yogic postures.

Courtney pulled her hands apart until the rope bit into her skin. She forced herself to breathe through the explosions of pain and arched her back until she had pulled her rear end past the rope. She hurriedly pulled first one foot and then the other through the tight circle of her arms. Her foot caught on her hands, and her shoulders burned with agony as the muscles stretched farther, almost reaching the bursting point.

With another inhale, Courtney forced her foot through the opening and pulled her arms in front of her. Beads of sweat clung to her hairline, and she pushed her head back against the bed, willing the staccato race of her heart to slow down.

The first part of her plan had worked. Her mind launched forward, and she tried to think of her next best move.

She rolled her shoulders gently, the pain still throbbing as if she could feel the tiny ruptures she'd just created in the muscle fiber. Courtney didn't have a plan, other than to run, so she pushed her feet into her tennis shoes and laced them up, cursing at her lack of dexterity as the ropes impeded her movement.

As she rested on the floor, she glanced at the ornate glass bowl filled with potpourri on the nightstand. She heard Ramiro's boots clunk on the stairs, and she moved in rapid-fire succession with each footfall.

She jumped up, grabbed the bowl, and slid back down to the floor. As Ramiro opened the door, Courtney fumbled with the heavy dish to get a good grip.

She heard his steps falter before he saw the top of her head barely poking above the comforter. "What are you doing?" he muttered as he walked near the bed. "I brought you a sandwich."

"I'm too hungry. I feel like I'm going to pass out." She had her head tilted slightly to the left, so she could see when Ramiro rounded the side of the bed. He bent down, and in the same instant, Courtney rose from her squatting position and swung the bowl at his head.

The sound it made on impact ripped a ragged gasp from Courtney's chest. Ramiro fell in unison with the broken halves of the bowl, both making a loud thud on the rug.

Courtney jumped on his back and put her bound hands around his neck. She pulled back hard. The rope tugged against his skin and chafed the red welts on her wrists, but she kept pulling.

He choked and struggled, but Courtney thought about Pepper, Tika, her father, and the way Ramiro had touched her, and she ground her teeth together. She had to escape, and it wouldn't do her any good if Ramiro followed her. His body slumped against her hands, and Courtney swallowed a cry. She unhooked her hands from around his neck and dragged her eyes away from the raw flesh.

The sharp glass sparkled in the light. Courtney knelt beside it and pushed the rope against the jagged curve of the broken bowl. With careful movements, she rotated her hand to provide enough pressure to cut the rope.

She tried to remain calm and listen, but her heart pounded in her ears as she struggled to get free. She couldn't hear anything but the rhythmic sawing of the rope and the popping of each fiber as she worked to loosen the bonds.

When she had cut through enough strands of one of the ropes, she wriggled her hand free and glanced at Ramiro. He lay still, and she couldn't tell if he was breathing. If she thought too hard about what she had just done, she would fall apart. She touched her bruised cheek and reminded herself that Ramiro meant to do her more harm. Courtney listened again before moving, but she didn't hear anyone coming up the stairs.

She swallowed and hurried for the door. In three soft steps, she made it to the head of the stairs. Courtney pressed her body close to the wall and continued down, the hair on the back of her neck tingling with fear. She was four steps from the bottom when she heard Spanish. The accented voices were coming from the kitchen area, but they were subdued.

Courtney gauged the distance to the front door and took a shaky breath. *It's now or never*, she thought. The fear coursing through her veins caused her limbs to shake.

Tears pricked the corners of her eyes, but she pushed back the panic and continued down the stairs. She darted for the door, flung it open, and headed outside, pulling the door half-shut behind her.

As her foot hit the hard ground at the bottom of the front steps, she heard the men yelling. They had seen her.

She was ready to sprint into the darkness, but as she rounded the corner, she noticed the four-wheelers. Two of them were parked in front of the cabin. With the high-beam headlights, the men would find her easily. Courtney heard the front door bang against the cabin wall and footsteps coming after her. She redirected her steps, and as her eyes adjusted to the darkness around her, she fumbled for the key hanging in the ignition. She pulled it out and scrambled for the other four-wheeler's key.

A man yelled, and Courtney jumped, her fingers grazing the second key. She turned it and hopped on at the same time. She gunned the engine and was pushing into second gear as Adán grabbed for her. Courtney felt his fingers clutch the fabric of her tank top and heard the material ripping as she fed the four-wheeler more gas. Adán lost his grip, and she heard shouting behind her as she moved into third gear and sped down the trail.

Her lungs protested against the adrenaline rush and the short, gasping breaths she took as she drove down the rocky path. The headlights illuminated the path before her, but she still had no idea where she was.

Just in time, she remembered the steep incline Ramiro had climbed to get to the cabin, and she geared down. With the rumbling of the engine, she couldn't hear her pursuers, but unless they had another key handy, they wouldn't catch her.

Courtney drove for about ten minutes and then stopped. She was heading back to the marijuana grove. If Adán and Jesse were at the cabin, more workers had to be harvesting the grove by cover of night.

It wouldn't do her any good to jump from the frying pan to the fire. Courtney didn't know how close she was to the marijuana patch, and she didn't know the woods well enough to gauge the distance to her house. She drove farther, scanning her surroundings through the headlights of the four-wheeler.

She edged her way off the trail in what she thought was the direction of the creek. A few minutes later, Courtney admitted to herself that she had no idea where she was headed. It would be stupid to drive right into her enemies. She cut the engine and pocketed the key. She listened to the night sounds of the woods and followed the rushing call of the water.

The gurgling overlapped the trilling of the crickets and the rustling pine boughs. With her hand outstretched, she maneuvered through a close grouping of Scotch pine trees. When she reached a thicket of bushes, she stopped and squinted into the darkness. The water rushed by only a few feet from where she stood.

The creek would lead her closer to home. With that thought, Courtney felt the truth settle in her stomach like the rocks tumbling along the bottom of the creek bed. She couldn't go home. Her father had held her hostage so he could harvest his crop. She had heard him tell Ramiro that he needed to get the marijuana harvested within forty-eight hours. If Courtney returned home now with her story of abduction and marijuana plants, what would Eric do to protect his investments?

Courtney sank to her knees beside the stream of water and thrust her hands into the icy-cold channel. She had to get help. Her mother would be home, and the cops would probably be nearby. Did her mom know about her father's illegal activity? If she did, what would she do to protect their money?

Courtney lowered her head closer to the running water and swallowed several handfuls. It was too risky to go home now. She felt like crying as she realized she would have to backtrack from where she had just come. The cabin where she had been held hostage couldn't be too far from other cabins in these mountains.

A thought tickled the back of her brain. Did her father own the cabin? If he did, it must be a hidden asset or the police would've surely checked it out when she went missing. Courtney thought about all the resources her dad had at his fingertips and shuddered. Eric Beckham was an intelligent man. He wasn't someone who would leave any loose ends leading back to him. Tropical Resources—that must be the name of a company set up as a front for his marijuana business.

Even if Courtney returned and told the police her suspicions, her father was too smart to be taken down that easily. She needed some kind of evidence. Her dad had mentioned the feds, so the FBI must be involved in her kidnapping case. But if he needed to get the crops harvested, why did Ramiro send in a ransom note? Why not just hold her captive until the evidence was removed?

Something must have gone wrong. Courtney thought about her father—he was a successful businessman because he paid attention to every detail. She tried to think like him and analyze what would motivate him to make her case look like a kidnapping instead of a missing person. Her shoulders slumped in defeat as she realized the answer.

People had been looking for her, and they would have found the crop, so her father had to stop the search. The ransom note did that effectively. The search would have halted because the effort would be expended on getting her back from the kidnappers.

She wondered how close they had come to discovering the marijuana. Courtney walked back to the ATV. She needed to drive back the way she'd come. It would take too long to walk on foot. After listening carefully for any sign of her pursuers, she started up the engine. She drove slowly, staying off the trail and as close to the creek bed as she dared. It was the only way she could keep from getting lost.

Within a few minutes, the fear of being discovered was too great, so she drove closer to the creek bed and parked in a thick stand of trees. She kept the key—pocketing it alongside the other. It was only a matter of time until the men would contact the other workers to start looking for her. She would have to skirt the cabin and keep heading south.

Anxiety boiled in her empty stomach, and for a moment, Courtney thought she might be sick. But she forced herself to keep moving, picking her way through the low-hanging scrub oaks that populated this part of the woods.

Courtney glanced at her wrist and frowned. There was no way to track the time—the clasp on her designer watch must have broke in her scuffle with Ramiro, and the timepiece was gone. She felt like she'd been walking for miles, when in reality it was probably considerably less. Her head ached from the constant awareness of every sound, her hearing amplified by the fear of being caught.

She came to a clearing in the trees and saw a sliver of the moon hanging in the sky. The stars twinkled above her as they had on so many nights past, and she wished she had paid better attention to the constellations and the guidance they represented. With her face upturned to the heavens, she concentrated on locating the Big Dipper. She remembered something about being able to find the North Star from the constellation.

The handle of the Big Dipper hung low in the sky this time of year, and it was easy to identify. As her eyes traced the outline of the pot, Courtney's ears picked up a sound foreign to the woods, and her heart rate increased.

The familiar rumble of an engine in the distance echoed through the night. Courtney kept still, waiting for the right time to move. They were searching for her. Up ahead, she could see a bright light sweeping through the trees. Her eyes filled with tears when she realized they were searching with a spotlight. They must have had strong lights set up near the marijuana to aid in the harvest, and now they had stopped their work and were looking for her.

When she saw a second light, Courtney gasped and took off running.

14

COURTNEY'S EYES had adjusted to the darkness, but all she could see were shadows of trees and rocks as she ran through the woods. Branches scraped at her bare arms as she stumbled through the undergrowth. She forced herself into running mode and kept inhaling at a steady pace as if she were jogging through the canyon with Sean. *Stay calm, Court*, she told herself as she focused on keeping her feet light and avoiding the large roots crisscrossing the forest floor.

She could hear herself crashing through the woods, the trees grasping at her hair and swiping her cheeks. Somehow she'd left the path of the water cascading through the mountains. Even though the creek wasn't running strong this time of the summer, it would still provide enough noise to camouflage the ruckus she was making. She listened for the rush of water and headed toward it.

A light flashed nearby, and Courtney's heart felt as if it would jump out of her chest. The sound of the bubbling creek signaled her return to the water's edge. Leaping over a narrow part of the creek bed, she splashed in the water and groped in the darkness to get her bearings. She glanced behind her and could still see lights moving through the trees.

She couldn't stop running as long as the lights of her pursuers still followed. It was harder going on this side of the creek, though. Courtney noticed that she was running on a slight incline now. The smell of pine indicated that she had retreated deeper into the forest and was making a steady, yet gradual, climb up the mountain.

A pine bough scraped across her middle, and Courtney raised her arm to shield her face from other branches, straining her eyes to make out the shadowy trunks of trees in the darkness.

She thought she heard someone yelling not far behind and panicked, putting on a burst of speed. The small of her back was wet with perspiration, and she could feel the sweat clinging to the hair escaping from her ponytail. The terrain changed, and she struggled up a steep rise and then down a rocky slope.

The fear of being caught outweighed the nagging thought that she had no idea where she was headed. She crashed through the forest in a panic, away from the water. She ran like that for a few minutes before reminding herself that the creek was the only reliable guide she had. The path leveled out again, and Courtney picked up the pace once more, turning in the direction she thought the creek might be. The sound of water indicated she was nearing the winding creek bed again. She slowed her steps a bit, trying to gauge where the drop-off to the water would begin.

Her foot caught on a root, and before she could react, her face was in the dirt. Her ankle made a loud pop as it twisted in the wrong direction, and Courtney cried out in pain.

An arc of throbbing energy rose up her leg, and it seemed as though her foot were on fire. The pain stole her breath, and her lungs convulsed. It took a few seconds of gasping before she could inhale quietly again.

The urgency to keep moving hovered over her, but when she tried to stand, she fell in a painful heap. Her ankle was definitely sprained. Courtney sat up, leaned against a tree, and tried to examine her foot in the dark. She hoped it wasn't broken. The pain radiating from her right foot, added to the knowledge that she was being pursued by people her father had hired, was too much. She bit back a cry, but it still gurgled up from her chest. She rested her head on her knees and let the tears fall.

She allowed herself only a moment, and then the awareness of engines running and lights flashing in the distance overcame her frightened tears. From her sitting position, she took in her surroundings, trying to make out the shadowy forms of trees, rocks, and bushes. Courtney wiggled her foot and winced. There was no way she could walk or run right now, but she couldn't sit there and wait for the bright lights to sweep across her path.

The pressure from her ankle indicated it was already swollen, and Courtney's shoe was acting as a sort of tourniquet for the rest of her foot. She unlaced the shoe and pulled it off, sucking in a breath against the pain the movement caused. The creek was only a few yards in front of her. If she could make it down to the water, the freezing temperature would probably help with the swelling.

Moving to her knees, Courtney crawled near the water. The ground was covered with small rocks and hard roots that bit into her skin as she struggled forward. She put her right hand inside her shoe, ignoring the damp feeling of sweat, and used it as a glove to protect the skin of her palm. The sound of the water bubbling over rocks overtook the noise of engines as Courtney edged closer to the creek.

She crawled down a small embankment and sat at the water's edge. Setting her shoe in a safe spot, she pulled off her sock and thrust her foot into the water. She gasped as the frigid stream enveloped her foot. Her leg automatically jerked back. With determination, Courtney plunged her foot into the water again, holding it there until the needles of pain subsided to a numb coldness.

Careful not to get her other shoe wet, she bent down and drank the cool water. She couldn't be sure if this part of the creek was clean enough for drinking, but she figured it was worth the risk to keep from becoming dehydrated. Her stomach grumbled as she gulped the water. It was so tight with hunger that Courtney felt as if it was turning inside out. In the last forty-eight hours, she'd had the equivalent of one meal and a snack. She rinsed her face with the cold water, banishing thoughts of her extreme hunger and concentrating on her next move.

The freezing water reduced the pain in her ankle, but she knew she wouldn't be able to walk anywhere tonight. "What am I going to do?" Courtney whispered to herself.

She had no idea where she was and only hoped the morning light would provide enough of a sense of direction to help her escape the woods. There were plenty of people looking for her—but they were the wrong kind of people.

How long would they search before they returned to the other urgent task at hand? Courtney wondered how close they were to harvesting the marijuana and hiding any evidence that the grove had thrived mere miles from her home. She rubbed her forehead and attempted to focus. Right now she needed to hide.

When she could no longer feel her right foot and the water had soaked the bottom of her capris, Courtney lifted her leg from the creek. She waited for the cool night air to caress her foot, bringing sensation back to her swollen ankle. A dull ache radiated up her leg when she tried to move her toes. She shouldn't have been running through the woods in the dark, but the desperation of being chased overtook the logic of navigating the woods at a fast walk.

Her best bet would be to cross to the far side of the creek, putting a barrier between her and her hunters, and find somewhere to hide until morning. It took her a few minutes to remove her other shoe and sock and roll up her capris. She tied the laces of her shoes together and hung them from her neck. Courtney knew from hiking in these woods that the creek wasn't more than six feet wide in most places and usually less than two feet deep. She hoped that would be the case in this part of the woods.

She squinted in the darkness and could make out a gloomy shadow a few feet across the water in front of her. It was probably a large rock or a decaying log. She gazed further into the darkness and could see clumps of bushes growing on the other side of the creek. It would be painful, but Courtney knew she needed to cross this border of water and put more distance between herself and those searching for her. She scooted closer to the water's edge and slid both feet in, biting off a scream as the frigid stream rushed past her legs. She continued scooting until her knees were in the water and she could feel the cold seeping into the fabric of her capris.

She pushed herself up—ready to attempt standing on one foot. With balance learned from another yoga posture, tree pose, she stood on her left leg and reached toward the other side of the creek. Her toes gripped the bottom of the creek bed, and she rose up on tiptoe and hopped forward, wincing as sharp rocks connected with the ball of her foot. She fell forward and grabbed hold of the log half-submerged in the creek. Pulling a final burst of energy from her spent body, she lifted herself onto the rocky shoreline and crawled out of the water.

Her teeth chattered as she struggled up the side of the embankment, grabbing hold of roots to give herself some leverage. She unrolled her capris to protect her skin from the uneven terrain. The soggy material squelched when she moved, and she grimaced. She hadn't wanted to get so wet, but at least she'd made it across.

She wiped her hands on her thighs and untied her shoes from each other. Her feet were wet and covered with pine needles, leaves, and small pebbles. She dipped them back into the water and waited a few minutes for them to drip-dry. Then she pulled on her socks and her left shoe. Her right ankle was still too swollen for any type of footwear.

The hair on the back of her neck stood on end as Courtney rotated her head, gazing into the night for any signs of danger. Her heartbeat picked up the pace again as she thought about how close she might be to those hunting her. But all she could hear was the murmur of the creek and the sway of leaves in the light summer breeze moving through the trees.

She crawled forward again until she found a copse of bushes growing next to a cluster of scrub oak. Courtney prayed that it would provide cover in the daylight until she could figure out what to do next. She wriggled between the bushes and stretched out on the ground. It took her a few minutes to find a position where the rocky ground wasn't stabbing her in the back.

She hadn't seen any searchlights for a while and hoped that meant they were concentrating on the marijuana instead of her escape. She knew someone was definitely still looking for her, but they probably couldn't afford to waste precious time and manpower searching for a needle in a haystack.

After several minutes of shivering in the darkness and listening for the ATVs, Courtney felt the weight of her eyelids pressing down. She kept listening but only heard the forest sounds around her. When the rushing of the creek and the chirp of crickets continued to be the only music serenading her, she succumbed to exhaustion and closed her eyes in sleep.

15

THE VIBRATION in the pocket of Eric's suit coat stopped his senseless pacing in front of the office window. He stepped into the living room and glanced at his wife. She sat on the leather sofa, staring straight ahead. Her fists clenched and relaxed, and Eric avoided the hollow look in her eyes. Neither of them had slept much the night before. Chloe had tossed and turned, and Eric finally went down to his office and dozed in his ergonomic chair for a bit.

He made a show of getting an apple and a bagel from the kitchen pantry and then walked out the French doors. The patio extended several yards and widened to include a hot tub and several deck chairs. Eric walked the distance and sat in one of the chairs where he could view the comings and goings of his home. It was only seven o'clock in the morning, and the temperature was already on the rise. One more week, and his crops would have been at their peak in the summertime heat. He cursed as he grasped the sleek black cell phone and returned Ramiro's call.

The phone rang only once before Ramiro answered. "Honcho, we have a problem."

Eric ground his teeth together. "What happened now?"

"Your daughter tried to kill me, and she escaped."

Eric felt like someone had punched him in the gut. "Where is she?"

"I don't know, but she nearly strangled me to death and took off on one of our four-wheelers."

109

"I thought you had her tied up!" It took all of Eric's control to keep his voice down.

"She *was* tied up—with her hands behind her back. I don't know how she got loose."

Pinching the bridge of his nose, Eric's breath rumbled out slowly as he listened to Ramiro's frantic explanation of their fruitless search through the night. "We're hours away from getting this taken care of, and you let her escape." He paused, and Ramiro was silent for a full five seconds.

"We'll find her," he said.

"We need to fix this. As soon as I hang up, call Natalie and tell her to send another message with a change of plans. Tell her to say something about too many cops, then change the location and the time."

"And what if Courtney finds her way back home before—"

"If that happens, I'll finish what my daughter started," Eric cut him off. "Find her."

"Okay."

"And Ramiro, clear out. We're out of time. Salvage as much as you can and cover your tracks."

"I'll call you when we find her." Ramiro hesitated and then added, "If we don't find her by tonight, we might have to go to plan B."

"That's not going to happen," Eric growled and ended the call. He slipped the phone back into his pocket and took a bite of his apple. He made himself sit quietly and finish his breakfast before reentering the house.

Twenty minutes later, the cell phone on the dining room table jangled with an incoming text message. Chloe and Eric practically ran for the phone, and Detective Gardner was right behind them. Gardner felt his gut clench with worry as Eric picked up the phone and held it so they could all read the message.

Change of plans. Get rid of the cops or Courtney isn't coming home. Be ready tomorrow at 4 p.m. Meet at the scheduled time tonight at 10 p.m. for the info. An account number will be sent. Deposit the money, and we'll give you the address where you can pick up Courtney.

"No!" Chloe cried and slumped into a kitchen chair.

"This is impossible," Eric said.

"We're gonna nail these guys," Detective Gardner said as he reread the message. He dialed a number on his cell phone and parked himself in front of his laptop, scrolling through the information they'd gathered. Gardner hoped they could find enough data on the text.

"You have to leave," Eric said. "All of you. They must be watching the house."

Gardner looked up. "We can leave, but you should follow shortly after and have one of us ride back here with you."

"No, Eric's right," Chloe said. "It's too risky. I don't want them to hurt Courtney."

"That would be foolish." Gardner stood slowly. "Don't you understand? If you cooperate with these guys and give them the money, they'll kill your daughter. They're not planning on a transfer anymore."

Chloe covered her face with her hands and cried out. "Don't let them do this. Please, we have to find her."

"One man, that's all I want here." Eric stood and motioned to the vehicles outside. "Have everyone else leave. We can keep the monitoring equipment, and that should be enough."

"Something must have happened." Gardner stood and rubbed a hand over his forehead. "The FBI has extensive experience in kidnapping cases—they need to be here."

"I know, but this is my daughter," Eric snapped.

Gardner packed up his laptop. "I'll get my guys, and we'll be on our way, but I wouldn't dismiss the FBI agents."

"Please understand," Chloe whispered. "We're just trying to keep Court safe."

Gardner shook his head and walked out the door. As soon as he got in his car, he called Pierson and relayed the information.

"Why is he being so uncooperative all of a sudden?" Pierson said.

"He and his wife are scared," Gardner answered. "The change of plans really put them into a tailspin."

"We'll still keep an eye on them, but we'll be more discreet. Our tech guys said they found something at his office," Pierson said. "I'm on my way to go check it out, and then I guess we'll stop by the Beckhams' and talk to them."

"Something's gone wrong, Pierson." Gardner swallowed hard. "What if she's dead?"

"We'll keep working on the assumption that she's alive."

Gardner could hear the pain in his voice. "Keep me posted." He ended the call and glanced in his rearview mirror at the cops following him out of the canyon. He'd left one man behind in an unmarked vehicle and hoped it would be enough until they could persuade the Beckhams to allow more surveillance.

Arguing with Eric right now would waste precious time, and that was something they couldn't spare. The clock was ticking ominously toward a point of no return for Courtney—they needed to figure out what the kidnappers were up to.

16

SHORTLY AFTER digesting the news that Eric had ordered the uniforms off his property, Jason's work was interrupted again. Pierson entered the office with a triumphant smile.

"We found some interesting things over at Beckham Development today."

Jason sat up straight and pushed away from his desk. "You found some shade?"

Pierson nodded. "In a lot of areas. It seems like half his business is in the shade."

Jason pursed his lips. "I didn't like him from the start."

"We've been running the accounts, and it turns out Eric has received payments on several finished properties that aren't even in existence." Pierson handed Jason a file.

"How's that possible?" Jason asked.

"You seen some of the ghost towns around here?"

"Yeah, sure."

"Well, most of them are full of unfinished homes and developments, yet Eric has recorded payments for the jobs he started and never finished." Pierson flipped through a stack of papers. "Like this development out in Utah County. There was supposed to be this huge subdivision going in with over a hundred homes, a park, landscaped median—you get the idea. When we did some checking, we found that the area has only about thirty homes right now, with all kinds of unfinished projects. They were told the developer had to halt construction because he wasn't getting paid."

"So where's the money coming from?" Jason asked. "And is it really there, or just in the book work?"

"Your guess is as good as mine at this point, but the money was there." Pierson pointed to the file. "We're following the trail. It looks like we have some good motives, and Eric's going to have to answer a lot of questions."

Jason narrowed his eyes and tapped the desk. "See if he'll come down and talk to us. It'll save us a trip out there and get his cell phone closer to our office in case they contact him again."

"Good idea," Pierson said. "I'll give him a call."

Jason leaned back in his chair and focused on reading through the file again.

✳ ✳ ✳

It was after lunch before Eric made his appearance, and he wasn't too happy about having to leave Chloe at the house.

Pierson slid some papers across the table for Eric to look at.

"I've never seen this ledger before," Eric said. "You say you pulled this off my computer systems?"

"Yes." Pierson scowled at Eric. "Specifically, it was found under your account access."

Eric studied the printouts. "It doesn't make any sense."

"Actually, it does. We checked the main account for Beckham Development and found a number of smaller accounts tied to it. The money has been divided between these accounts." Jason slid another stack of papers across the table. "We've highlighted the deposits made within the last six months that are tied to the ledger of questionable accounts."

"Questionable?" Eric sputtered. "More like imaginary. No, something must have gone wrong with our computer systems. We do have an automatic account accrual system. Perhaps it went haywire and it just looks like we've collected on these accounts."

"Then how do you explain the extra money?" Pierson said.

"Wait a minute." Eric pointed at one of the highlighted rows of the ledger. "I just noticed something."

Jason leaned forward to see the lines he indicated.

"I didn't enter these numbers, but I'm pretty sure I know who did." Eric's eyes glinted as he smiled.

"Who?"

"Corbin Whittier."

"But only you had access to these ledgers," Jason said.

"Cobra also had access." Eric jabbed his finger at the page. "And he brought every single one of these accounts to the business."

Jason looked at Pierson. "Guess we'll have to bring him back in."

Eric stood, but Pierson held up his hand before he could move. "We'll need you to stay right here."

"But I need to be out there, available in case someone contacts me again about Courtney."

"Right here is probably the best place for you to be." Pierson pointed at the chair. "Nothing is going to happen before the info drop tonight."

"But what if they call?"

"You'll answer, and we'll be here to analyze the details with you." Jason smiled, but he knew the smile didn't reach his eyes as he watched Eric slide back into the chair.

* * *

Eric sat in the interrogation room and felt the perspiration gather under his armpits and drip down his sides. He felt like his insides were compressed in a vice, the stress radiating through his body as his thoughts raced through different scenarios. How would he get himself out of this mess?

Natalie had sent the text message delaying the meet for the transfer, and now the FBI waited for the kidnapper's next move, but he couldn't contact Ramiro until he was in a safe place. It had been difficult with the police activity in and around his house lately, but Eric was careful to hide any evidence before he came to the FBI office.

The clock moved toward two, each tick sounding like a threat to the empire Eric had built. His Adam's apple bobbed with a series of gulps as he tried to swallow the fear rushing up his esophagus. Natalie had directions to follow if he got into trouble.

In three hours, if they hadn't found Courtney, she would begin their "fail-safe" plan. From that point, there was no going back.

Eric's hands trembled, and he gripped the armrests of the chair. He had instructed Ramiro not to harm Courtney no matter what Natalie said, but which boss would Ramiro choose to heed?

17

JASON COULDN'T shake the feeling that they were missing something. The focus of the investigation had shifted to the kidnappers, and he kept wondering if that was exactly what was supposed to happen. He kept trying to glimpse the bigger picture—what weren't they seeing?

He thought about the Stewart case from two years ago. He had followed his gut and done a few unorthodox things that ended up helping to solve the case. But you couldn't just "follow your gut" in this line of work. You had to have something to back it up or risk going rogue.

His green file folder sat in the center of his desk. Jason flipped to the back and looked at Courtney's picture. An image of Aubree Stewart, with her strawberry-blonde hair and blue eyes, flashed through his mind. He remembered what had happened to Aubree when the FBI failed to protect her. Jason didn't want that to happen again.

With a sigh, he closed the green folder. He shook his head—now wasn't the time to think about his past or his future. He had to concentrate on the present and solving this case. Even though he'd tried, he couldn't shake the idea formulating in his mind.

"All we have to do now is wait until the drop." Pierson interrupted Jason's thoughts. "We've exhausted every lead and have the area under complete surveillance. Why don't you take a break, Edwards? You've been going strong for more than twenty-four hours."

Jason was about to shrug off the overtime he'd put in for this case, but a flicker of an idea stopped him. "You know, I think I will take a few hours."

"Yeah, get some shut-eye. We'll need to be on high alert later. You sleeping here?"

"No, I think I'll run home and get a change of clothes," Jason said. "What are we going to do about Beckham?"

"I just got off the phone with his lawyer." Pierson popped his knuckles. "I'll go tell him that he can be on his way."

"At least we made him sweat," Jason said. "We'll have to keep an eye on him. Are you bringing Cobra in again?"

"No, you and I both know that would be a waste of time." Pierson slapped him on the back. "I'll let you know if anything changes."

Jason closed down his workstation and headed for his vehicle. There was plenty of time to kill before the info drop was supposed to take place, but if he hurried, he'd only be gone for two or three hours. He drove home and changed into jeans and hiking boots and then put a clean white dress shirt and slacks in his car.

He stashed a few water bottles, some fruit and granola bars, and a first aid kit in a backpack. Jason tossed it in the backseat of his car and headed up the canyon.

When he got to the Beckham residence, he didn't park in front of their house. With a wave to the undercover cop, he drove past the sprawling home to the stables and pulled his car even with the building—out of sight. Jason remembered the Beckhams' orders of no cops, and he didn't want them worrying over what he was about to do. He adjusted his gun snug in his holster, slung on his backpack, and locked his vehicle.

Jason entered the stables and rubbed Tika's nose. "I wish you could tell me what's off about this investigation," he murmured. The horse snuffled his hand, looking for treats, and Jason scratched between her ears before heading to the back of the stable.

The dark blue ATV was parked in the corner where he had found it the first time. Richie had told him they were welcome to use it or anything else they needed. Jason turned the key in the ignition and drove slowly outside.

He imagined Courtney leading Tika to the watering trough near the open expanse of field that skirted the mountains. He wondered what she had been planning that morning. Richie reported that the horse had been ridden hard, something that stood out because he said although Courtney didn't spend much time grooming her horse, she was always aware of the animal's limits. In the extremely dry heat, she would have been careful not to overwork Tika.

Jason thought about what Richie had said. "I was surprised to find Tika that far away, all lathered up like she had obviously been on a hard ride."

"Why's that?" Jason had asked.

"Because that's at least a ten-mile ride round trip. If Courtney was planning to run Tika very hard, she did that right close to home." He motioned to the field next to the stables. "She'd usually ride her out there for a workout."

"And the meadow where Tika was found?"

"Courtney liked to go that route when she had plenty of time and someone to ride with."

Jason revved the engine and headed out across the field. Scanning the area as he drove, he willed his eyes to spot something out of the ordinary, but the two miles passed without event.

He pulled next to the aspen trees and continued his investigation from the day before. So much had happened in twenty-four hours that it was hard to believe only a day had passed. It took him a few minutes, but he found the branch with the markings. His fingers traveled around the branch, feeling the width of the grooves in the bark. It looked as if something had been tied around the branch— something like Tika's reins.

He walked around the trees and saw something he hadn't had time to notice yesterday. The grass was completely trampled and eaten down where a horse might have been tied to the tree. The horse droppings and hoofprints coincided with that theory.

Jason pulled out his camera and took several shots of the evidence. With the investigation into the email sent from Cobra's account, there hadn't been time yesterday to follow up. He thought about calling Gardner right then and asking him to send someone out to look things over with him, but he decided to see what else he might find first.

He stood still and listened. The woods were quiet, with only a trilling chickadee to break the silence. Jason turned in a slow circle, staring out in each direction for a sign of what might have enticed a rider to tie his or her horse there. He walked to the edge of the field and stepped on a rocky trail surrounded by scrub oak. He'd done enough hiking when he was younger to recognize the signs of recent activity—human activity—in the forest.

Jason remembered playing games of hide-and-seek with his brother on their family camping trips. His brother would leave clues as he traipsed through the forest to see if Jason could follow and find them. He learned to watch for the broken branch on a bush, the rock scuffed out of place on the trail, the trampled grass off the path. But those things were done purposely; tracking someone in a vast wilderness was an altogether different task.

Even so, it took him only about thirty yards to see the first definite sign that someone had recently walked this direction. He lifted his foot to step over the large root snaking across his path and stopped.

Someone had fallen here. He crouched near the ground and examined the bushes lining the walkway. The crumpled leaves on the otherwise vibrant green bush indicated that something heavy had made contact.

The root blended in nicely with the terrain—if someone had been walking along the trail and had tripped, it wasn't likely they would fall. But if that someone had been running, a fall would be inevitable.

Jason recalled the snapshot they had of Courtney Beckham. Her mother said she enjoyed running long distances and did so often with Sean. Would she have ridden out here and gone for a run through the woods? And what about the dog? He tried to think of a situation that would explain the canine's untimely demise, but nothing fit with the clues he had found.

Letting his fingers trail through the dirt, Jason surveyed the area around him. He studied the tree line and noticed the different species growing throughout the woods. As he walked, he surmised that there must be a creek nearby because he could see more undergrowth lining the path with a few wildflowers. He continued walking, keeping an eye out for other signs that Courtney had been in these woods.

It took him roughly twenty minutes of studious walking to discover the creek and the path Courtney might have taken to get to it. The shallow body of water ran lazily along the rocky creek bed. The late summer heat sucked the moisture from the foliage in the trees that surrounded him, and the roots reached for the water source greedily.

Jason crouched next to the water and felt the cool liquid rush against his fingertips. He bent lower and cupped a handful, tasting the icy-cold goodness of a pure mountain stream. The imprints in the mud near the creek caught his attention immediately, and he swallowed and moved closer for a better look. He focused his camera on a partial footprint, zooming in on the treads that looked like a cross-trainer—the type Courtney would probably wear.

The imprint wasn't deep, so the detail wasn't as fine as he'd like, but it was enough proof for him. He pulled out his cell phone to call Pierson. The number blinked on the screen, but the call wouldn't go through. The service must not be strong enough in this area of the forest.

Jason felt sure Courtney had come this way, but every clue had pointed away from this forest. Had she been kidnapped this close to home, or farther away where Tika had been found?

He looked at his watch. It was four thirty, and he needed to head back soon. He glanced at his camera and the trail he'd been following. There was evidence in this forest that might help their investigation into Courtney's abduction.

He didn't want to compromise any of the evidence, but if he could just get a few more solid indicators to support his hunch, Pierson would send the posse out here to investigate. If Jason could get some decent reception on his cell phone, he could have someone meet him, but for now he'd have to settle for showing Pierson the pictures.

He scoured the area around the creek, looking for signs of what direction Courtney might have headed, but he couldn't find anything definitive. He crossed and recrossed the stream a few times, but the undergrowth didn't give up any clues. About twenty-five yards ahead, Jason could see the terrain change, with more pine trees growing in clusters and less of the gnarled scrub oak he'd been skirting for the past half hour.

A large rock in the center of the creek provided a nice stepping stone for Jason as he crossed to the other side once more. The quiet of the forest emphasized his increased heart rate reverberating in his ears. The edges of his mouth curved into a smile when he pictured the look on Pierson's face after he reported the evidence he'd found today. This would open up a new facet of the investigation and maybe give them a better idea as to what the kidnappers were up to.

18

THE WARMTH of the sun shining through the bushes felt good on Courtney's cheek. As she rose through the levels of consciousness from a deep sleep, she struggled to understand why she'd been sleeping in the dirt.

The blessed, unconscious realm of sleep had erased the trauma of the last two days. But as soon as she moved and felt the stiffness in her joints, the sting of the scrapes and bruises that covered her body, and the mild throbbing of her ankle, Courtney remembered all too well.

Streams of sunlight filtered through the canopy of scrub oak leaves shading her from the morning's rising temperatures. She opened her eyes wider and concentrated on the erratic thumping of acorns falling from the branches. She remembered collecting handfuls of acorns from the scrub oak trees near her home as a little girl. Back then, she'd been wide-eyed and innocent, and today she wanted to return to that time.

How deep did her father's illegal activities run, and how far would he go to keep her from revealing the truth about Beckham Development? Courtney shuddered but took comfort in the fact that her dad didn't know she had overheard the conversation with Ramiro. Would she have to take the stand and testify against her own father?

Courtney rolled over and leaned against a slender tree trunk. She reviewed the past few days' events in her mind again, asking herself what she could have done differently to avoid being in this predicament.

If she had heeded her father's warning about riding in the mountains behind their home . . . but then she shook her head, interrupting that thought. It pained her to think of her father as a criminal, but she would rather know the truth. She wondered how long her dad had been involved with growing and distributing marijuana. Then an ache filled her gut—what if he did more than that?

It was all so overwhelming—like looking in the mirror one day and finding you didn't recognize the person in the reflection. Nothing made sense, but she was still glad to be made aware of her changed reality.

She shrugged off the ache in her bones and tried to concentrate on something else. Her mouth felt like it was lined with cotton. She needed a drink of water, but first she had to make sure no one was nearby. Pushing herself up to a sitting position, Courtney waited for the wave of dizziness to pass—her stomach had long since stopped protesting the lack of food. She felt so weak from last night's harrowing experience, she wondered how she would ever make it out of these woods.

After the buzzing in her ears subsided, Courtney focused on her surroundings. A gentle swaying of the trees around her punctuated the stillness with creaks and the sound of scattering pine needles. An occasional pine cone dropped from the evergreen branches and skittered along the ground. The heat felt intense, and Courtney looked at the sky, wondering how early or late she had slept. She figured it must be early afternoon, but without her watch, she had no idea of the time.

All she knew was that she felt extremely hot and thirsty, and her stomach had shrunk almost to nonexistence. The heat baking out every ounce of moisture from the grasses and bushes indicated that there would be no reprieve from high temperatures that day. Courtney was surprised she had slept that long. She also felt encouraged because it meant whoever was looking for her hadn't come near enough for the noise of an ATV to awaken her.

After gazing at the scorching sun with no revelations as to its course through the sky, Courtney decided to concentrate on getting some water. She pulled herself up slowly, listening to every chirp of the sparrows and crunch of pine needles under her feet. The creek wasn't far—she could hear the steady rushing of the water bubbling over the rocks, but it was far enough that she could still make out the isolated sounds of the forest.

Several moments later, she made it to a standing position, leaning heavily against the rough pine tree that had sheltered her during the night. An annoying sensation of pain slithered up her leg, and she glanced at her ankle and cried out.

A baseball-sized lump of purplish flesh where her ankle should have been indicated the severity of the sprain. Her chest tightened with anxiety as the reality of her predicament hit her hard. There would be no running today.

The wooded area around her didn't give off any hint that she was being hunted, and as she strained her eyes into the distance, all she could see was the undisturbed forest. Courtney had no idea where she was in relation to the cabin, the marijuana, or the stand of aspen trees where she had tied Tika a few days ago. If she had been able to hike, she could've climbed to higher ground to try to gain some knowledge of her whereabouts. She needed to get out of the mountains, but even more pressing, she needed to find something to eat.

Courtney hobbled painfully to the creek, carrying her right shoe. By the time she reached the water, the pain was so intense she felt like passing out. She scooted down the bank, removed her dirty sock, and plunged her foot into the stream once again. Tiny black dots appeared in her vision—she had been holding her breath. She exhaled slowly. As she did, she noticed the grime on her hands and wrinkled her nose. She scrubbed them together in the creek, then gulped the water hungrily. Her body reacted to the clear, cold water with a jolt. She could feel the water travel down her esophagus and hit her empty stomach.

The urgency to keep moving pressed on her, and her heart beat faster with the fear of being discovered. Courtney struggled to think of a plan of action in her weakened state. With her injury, she wouldn't be able to outrun her kidnappers if they found her. For today, at least, she would have to move slowly, keep hidden, and hope the swelling and pain would subside soon.

Courtney had never been big on wilderness survival, and her idea of camping was in her family's fully equipped cabin in Park City. But as she swirled her foot in the water, she realized the stream was a sort of map. With its downward current, the creek could guide her out of the mountains, but it would also bring her dangerously close to the marijuana grove that had started all her problems.

She wondered how many miles lay between her and the beautiful home her father had built for his family—the family he had so willingly betrayed for money. Courtney swallowed the lump in her throat and wiped her eyes.

At first, she figured she couldn't go home because of her father, but then she remembered what she had overheard on the phone. Eric had said that the feds were nosing around too much. That meant that the FBI was involved in her kidnapping case, so they would certainly be at her home or staked out nearby. If she could get to an FBI agent first, she could alert them that her father was behind her kidnapping.

Then an unsettling thought crashed down on her. If the marijuana was indeed harvested already and the evidence removed, what proof was there that Eric was involved?

Eric had mentioned another crop almost ready to harvest, but even if the police could find the marijuana, how would they link it back to her father? Her escape had certainly messed up her dad's plans. But part of her wondered if Ramiro even knew the identity of his boss.

The cold water had eased the swelling enough that Courtney could put her shoe on without tying the laces. For what seemed like hours, but was probably considerably less, she limped along the bank of the creek. With watchful eyes, she moved in and out of the large bushes that flanked the western side of the stream. She didn't hear or see any sign of the workers who were supposed to be harvesting marijuana and finding their escaped hostage.

When her foot throbbed in time to the beat of her heart, Courtney soaked it in the cold water again and then retreated to a thatch of bushes. The heat was too much, and she was so exhausted that she curled up on a smooth area of dirt to rest. She told herself she could just doze for a few minutes. As she tried to get comfortable, she listened intently for any sign of her hunters. Eventually, the fatigue overtook her, and she fell asleep in the shade.

19

JAGGED ROCKS surrounded the bank of the creek, so Jason hiked up about ten yards where it was easier to traverse and continued combing the area for any sign of human presence. He frowned when he glanced at his watch again—it was already after five, but if he hurried, maybe they could get some people out there before nightfall to continue the search. He shoved the camera into his backpack, wishing he could've found something else to bring the investigation out here with some urgency.

His boots were covered with the dark black soil that the plants thrived on in these mountains. He bent down to examine a pink-flowered fireweed. The stalk looked like it had been stepped on, and a few of the bright pink petals were crushed into the dirt. Jason lifted one of the dark green leaves and froze when he thought he saw a flash of movement. He jerked his head to the right and choked on his breath when he made eye contact with a young woman sitting next to a pine tree.

She was huddled against a large bush, trembling. The thin material of her tank top was so dirty the color was unrecognizable. Her skin was covered in abrasions and streaked with dirt. She cried out and scrambled against the rocks, trying to pull herself up.

Jason gaped in disbelief and took two steps forward. "Courtney?"

Her eyes were wild with fright, and she looked around as if trying to figure out how she could escape.

"Courtney, it's okay. I'm here to help." He held his hands out.

She studied him, her dark eyes flashing with worry.

Jason maintained eye contact and smiled. "I won't hurt you." He pulled out his badge. "I'm FBI agent Jason Edwards. You can call me Jason."

Courtney covered her mouth with a dirty hand and moaned. Jason was reminded of her mother reacting in the same way to the details of Courtney's case. He took a step forward. "How'd you escape your kidnappers?"

Her lips trembled, and her eyes glistened with tears. "Help me."

* * *

Courtney watched him approach and was overcome by a slew of emotions—fear, guarded relief, and a bit of hysteria that overshadowed rational thought.

Tears streamed down her cheeks, and when she wiped them away, she could feel the dirt and grime smear across her face. She was absolutely filthy.

Jason took off his shirt and crouched beside her. "Here, put this on. You're shaking." He held his shirt out.

"No, I couldn't," she said.

"I insist."

Courtney looked down at her tank top. Once a light blue, it was now dark brown, with a large rip in the fabric near the side seam where Adán had grabbed her last night during her escape.

She looked back at Jason and nodded. She held out her arms and allowed him to help her into the shirt. She tried not to stare at the toned muscles of his abdomen as he moved. Her hands were shaking so badly, her movements were jerky and uncontrolled.

"Take a deep breath." Jason spoke in a low voice. "I think you may be going into shock, and I need you to stay with me."

"I'm sorry about your shirt," she said between trembling breaths. She fingered the gray cotton T-shirt that dwarfed her small frame. The fabric was still warm, and the brisk citrus scent of his cologne tickled her nose.

"It's okay. I have a tank top here in my backpack." He nudged the pack with his toe, and hope flared in Courtney's chest.

"Do you have food?" she blurted and then dropped her chin as she felt warmth spread through her cheeks.

Jason touched her arm. "Hey, it's all right. You're going to be okay now. I have some granola bars and fruit. Want some?"

Courtney nodded, and her stomach roared to life at the thought of food. She watched him crouch beside the backpack to unzip it. "Where's your partner?" she glanced around her. "Why are you alone if you're with the FBI?"

Jason ducked his head. "I was following my gut." He thrust his hand into the pack and pulled out an apple and a peanut butter granola bar. "Here you go."

Courtney's mouth watered as she fumbled with the wrapper on the granola bar. When she took the first bite, she felt like crying, it tasted so good.

"Did they feed you at all?" Jason asked.

Courtney shrugged. "They gave me some crackers and a few other snacks. I haven't had an actual meal since Friday night."

"It's Tuesday afternoon. When did you escape?"

"Yesterday." She bit into the apple, and the sweet juice dribbled down her chin. Jason watched her eat. She knew she probably resembled a wild animal but didn't care. She couldn't recall a time in her life when she had gone this long without food.

"You'll want to chew slowly," Jason said. "Sometimes the stomach reacts violently after a long fast."

Courtney leaned her head back against the tree. "I've never been this hungry before. I feel so weak."

Jason handed her a water bottle. "Have you been drinking the creek water?"

"Yes, it's the only thing that's kept me going."

"Hopefully you won't get anything nasty from drinking it." He glanced back at the creek. "It tasted pretty clean when I tried it."

"I drank it in the past and never had a problem." Courtney took another big bite of apple. "Thank you, Agent . . ." she fumbled, trying to remember his last name.

"It's Jason—call me Jason."

She downed half of the water bottle and scrutinized him. "Okay, Jason. You didn't tell me where your partner is."

"He's back at the office. I'm supposed to be getting some sleep right now." Jason pulled a dark blue tank top from his pack.

Courtney noticed the contours of his muscles as he pulled the shirt over his head, and she struggled to pull her eyes from his toned chest. He zipped up his backpack and slung it on his shoulders again. As he did, she noticed the tattoo of a flame winding its way around the bicep of his right arm.

"When you went missing and everyone was searching, I checked out a different area and found fresh horse droppings. I wanted to investigate further, but then the kidnappers set up a meet, and we had to focus on that."

"Tika. Did you find Tika?"

"Yes, we found her tied up. She's fine." Jason kept talking. "But it kept bothering me—what I had found—so after the kidnappers delayed the transfer, I came out here today on my own time. Now I understand why they delayed things. What time did you escape?"

"Last night after dark. I stole one of their ATVs, but I didn't know where to go, so I left it and ran. They were searching for me with spotlights, and I shouldn't have been running in the dark, but I couldn't let them catch me." Courtney motioned to her swollen foot. "I tripped and sprained my ankle."

Jason crouched to examine her foot. "That doesn't look good. We'll need some help to get you out of here." He glanced at his watch. "I'm due back at the office soon. It took me longer than I thought, but I wasn't expecting to find you."

He pulled out his cell phone. "Your parents are going to be so relieved—the whole city will be."

"No, wait." Courtney grabbed for his cell phone. "You can't tell my parents—my dad—you can't let them know yet."

"You want to surprise them since we're so close?" Jason glanced at her. "I don't think we should make them wait." He frowned at his phone. "My phone isn't working. I'm not getting service out here today."

Courtney put a hand on Jason's arm. "Please, you can't tell anyone yet. It's not safe."

"Are you okay?" Jason looked into her eyes. "I'm worried you might be suffering from shock."

"No, you don't understand. It's my dad."

"Yes, he's been looking for you."

Courtney leaned forward, her bottom lip trembling. "No, he's the kidnapper."

Jason raised one eyebrow and then shrugged off his backpack. "I think you're dehydrated." He rummaged in his bag and handed her another water bottle.

Courtney shook her head. "I can't go with you. I need to show you the marijuana first."

"Marijuana?" Jason turned slowly and studied her face.

The story came spilling out in jumbled pieces. She recounted how she'd discovered the irrigation system feeding the illegal crop and was taken captive. She shuddered when she told him about how she'd choked Ramiro with the rope to escape. "I killed him. I've never even hit a person in my life, and now I've killed a man."

Jason frowned. "I'm sure you didn't kill him. How big did you say he was?"

"About your size. Maybe a little shorter," Courtney said.

"He probably just passed out."

"You mean you think he's still alive?"

"Unfortunately, there's a good chance of that. It all depends on how long you constricted his airway—kept his brain from receiving oxygen," Jason said. "If it was less than two minutes, he's probably still alive."

Courtney wiped fresh tears from her face as she told Jason about the phone call she'd overheard from Tropical Resources. "That's why I decided to escape, because he was going to take me someplace else. I decided I had to stop my father."

"I can't believe your dad did this," Jason said. "He's been with us the entire time, searching for you."

"And he's been delaying things so he could get the crop in and hide the evidence." Courtney squeezed the wrapper of the granola bar in a tight fist.

Jason's nostrils flared, and he shook his head. "I can't believe a man would do this to his own daughter."

Courtney noticed the tenseness in his jaw, the anger radiating from him as he contemplated the information she'd shared. A shiver ran through her shoulders. "And they're out here somewhere, looking for me and harvesting the marijuana."

Jason stood and turned in a slow circle surveying the area. "I didn't see any sign of another person on my way in. I figure I've come about a mile from the aspen trees where I found Tika's droppings."

"Do you mean that cluster of trees across the field by my house where I left Tika tied up?"

"That's not where we found your horse, but yes, I drove your ATV across that field and hiked in."

"We're that close?" Courtney sat up. "Wait—what do you mean that's not where you found Tika? I left her tied to a tree there Saturday morning so I could come looking for our dog, Pepper."

"I knew it. Someone moved your horse about five miles from your house in a clearing near the mouth of the canyon."

"But why would they do that?"

"To throw us off the trail." Jason grinned. "I knew things weren't adding up right. Search and Rescue was looking for you all day Sunday, and they'd canvassed a big area. They were going to increase the radius of the search, but then the ransom note came in." He put his hand to his forehead. "That's why they called the ransom in, because the police were getting too close."

"What about Pepper? Did he get home okay?"

Jason's shoulders slumped. His eyes flicked to hers and then to the ground. A pained expression tightened the corners of his mouth. He hesitated before murmuring, "I'm really sorry. He didn't make it."

Courtney looked down and allowed the horrible sensation of loss to wash over her. She didn't want to believe that what Jason told her was true. Every part of the past couple of days had been a living nightmare. Her throat tightened and her chin wobbled. "So they did kill him. Ramiro said he would, but I hoped he was just threatening me." She looked at Jason as her eyes filled with moisture. "How did he die?"

"I'm sorry," he repeated. "They shot him."

She wiped at the tears on her cheeks. "My dad has been behind everything, and he doesn't want me to get back home because he knows I'll lead you guys right to the marijuana crop." She pulled herself up to a standing position.

"What are you doing?" Jason asked.

"I was lost. I had no idea where I was last night. But if you walked a mile upstream from the aspen grove, then we need to get out of here." She pointed east of the creek. "The marijuana can't be far from here." She limped forward and winced when she put pressure on her foot.

"You won't get far on that ankle," Jason said. "Let me help you." He put his arm around her waist. "Is that okay?"

Their eyes met, and she nodded. Her heart skipped a beat, and she slid her arm around his waist. "Thanks."

"Just let me shoulder your weight so you don't put too much pressure on your foot."

Jason was a full head taller than her slight five-foot-six frame. They took a few steps together, then he paused. "Are you going to be all right?" His green eyes held her gaze for a moment, and she saw a flicker of something there.

"Yeah, I'm good." She looked away, wondering if it was nerves or if the fear she felt building in her chest colored everything she saw.

"You've been through a lot the past few days. I don't want you to push yourself too hard," Jason spoke softly as they continued down the uneven terrain.

Courtney bit her bottom lip to keep from wincing with each step. She just wanted to get out of these woods and to someplace safe.

20

PIERSON TRIED Jason's cell phone for the fifth time in twenty minutes. In the six months since he'd met Jason, the guy had never been more than five minutes late to anything. He waited another fifteen minutes and picked up the phone once again but dialed a different number. "Mercer, you out patrolling today?"

Thomas Mercer had been buddies with Pierson for over ten years. Even though he loved to harass Pierson about leaving the police ranks for the FBI so he could boss more people around, they were always available to help each other out in a bind.

"Yeah, what do you need?" Mercer answered.

"I can't reach my partner, and I'm wondering if you could stop by his apartment—see if he's sleeping."

"Sure, but you don't think he's sleeping, do you?" Mercer asked with a chuckle.

"No, but I can't think what else would make him this late. We've been working overtime here."

"You working the Beckham abduction?"

"That's the one. We need to be in place in less than two hours. We're supposed to be getting instructions for the transfer."

Pierson relayed Jason's address.

"I'll be there in fifteen minutes and give you a call," Mercer said.

Courtney struggled to put as little weight as possible on her sprained ankle as they walked. They were quiet for a few moments, navigating some rough terrain. She tried to think how to voice her fears to Jason. He wasn't how she'd pictured an FBI agent, and his ease and charm made her feel safe enough to speak. She licked her lips and glanced at him. "I don't want my dad to know you've found me."

"That's probably a good idea, if we want to figure out how involved he is in this drug operation."

"I'm telling you, he's it. Ramiro called him Honcho." Courtney stopped walking and turned to face Jason. "Dad was giving all the orders—about me, about the marijuana crop, everything."

"I'm sorry." He frowned, and she could see the worry lines around his eyes. "It's hard to wrap my head around. I could picture him doing some fraudulent business, but not drugs and kidnapping. Guess you never can tell."

"What do you mean by 'fraudulent business?' Did you already suspect my dad of something?"

He ran a hand across the top of his close-cropped hair. "Uh, yeah. That's now part of a federal investigation. Let's just say things aren't looking too good for your dad's business."

"I need to rest a minute." Courtney looked for a good place to sit down.

"Actually, do you mind if I just carry you? We could cover a lot more ground that way. My partner is probably going nuts right now because I should've been back at the office already."

She felt the warmth return to her cheeks. "Okay."

Jason hesitated half a second before scooping her into his arms. Her right arm rested across the back of his neck, and she inhaled the fresh scent of his aftershave.

"I must smell like a horse and look like a cave woman. Sorry," Courtney murmured.

Jason chuckled. "No problem. If it gets too bad, I can always toss you in the creek."

He glanced at Courtney as if to gauge her reaction to his teasing. She smiled. "That might not be a bad idea."

"It's nice to see you smile. I hope that means you're feeling better."

"The food helped."

Courtney felt his heart beating under the light material of his shirt. She was ultra-aware of the strength of his arms and tried not to think about how close she was to this FBI agent who was really still a stranger. He hefted her legs up as he stepped over a log, and the dark orange band of fire around his arm caught her attention again.

"Fire, huh?" She motioned to his tattoo.

"It symbolizes a bunch of things," Jason said. "Like it?"

"That depends on if you're going to tell me what it symbolizes."

He grinned. "Well, when I turned nineteen, I signed on for the volunteer fire department in Ventura County. I've always been fascinated with fire, and, of course, I knew women were fascinated with firemen, so I figured it was a win-win situation."

Courtney laughed. "Did it work? Did you get the girl?"

"I got some dates, but no, I still haven't got the girl—the right one is a pretty elusive thing."

"You're not telling me anything I don't already know." Courtney rolled her eyes. "Mr. Right is definitely not in my forecast."

"I can see why you think that, with the morons you've dated."

"What?" Courtney shifted in his arms. "How do you know anything about who I've dated?"

"I know everything about you." Jason's face flushed, and it made his blond hair look white in contrast. "We had to research everyone you've dated in the past six months and a few beyond that. Everyone was a suspect."

Closing her eyes, Courtney sighed. "So you met Sean and Ethan, I guess."

Jason raised his eyebrows. "Yes, and Travis, Pete, Drew. Oh, and can't forget Corbin the Cobra."

"I didn't actually get to date Cobra. I was kidnapped before we could go boating."

"I know," Jason said. "He's taken quite a bit of heat for your disappearance. I'm sure he'll be relieved to see you. Maybe you can go boating to celebrate."

Courtney shook her head. "No." She looked down. "I'm through with those kinds of guys. I don't feel like playing that part anymore."

Jason cleared his throat but didn't say anything.

After an awkward silence, she decided to change the subject. "And what else does that flame signify?"

He kept still for a moment, locking eyes with her. "That's a story for another time." He ducked under a low-hanging tree branch. "You said you found an irrigation line that led to where they were growing the marijuana. About how far was the patch from the creek?"

"I wasn't paying much attention to distance because I was looking for Pepper." Courtney chewed on her thumbnail. "I think it might have been about twenty yards or so."

"That's relatively close. I'm guessing they've finished the job because I didn't hear or see anything out of the ordinary where I hiked, and I was watching the ground pretty close for any signs of where you might have gone."

"From what my father was saying, I think there might be more marijuana growing in these mountains," Courtney said.

"I wouldn't doubt it. As soon as we get this reported, the drug task force is going to be crawling all over these hills."

Courtney heard the crunching of pine needles behind them and lifted her head to look over Jason's shoulder. He must have heard it too because he turned to glance behind. He shrugged and took a step forward. As he did, Courtney saw something from the corner of her eye.

She screamed, but it was too late. The thick branch connected with Jason's skull. With a grunt, he lunged forward, sending Courtney sprawling into the dirt. She cried out as fiery pain surged from her ankle and her elbows scraped against the ground in her attempt to catch herself.

A short Latino tackled Jason as he reached for his gun. The momentum knocked them both to the ground. Courtney watched as Jason lost his grip on the gun and the weapon flew into the bushes behind him.

Jason struggled and threw the man into the dirt, but he was back up and throwing punches before Jason could move. Courtney shuddered as the dark, wiry man punched Jason and he slumped to the ground. Jason groaned, and she could see dark red blood running through his blond hair.

She took a step toward the bushes where she had seen the gun drop. She struggled to look for the weapon as the fight continued, frantically searching with her hands while her eyes were locked on Jason. The man turned, and Courtney screamed when she recognized Adán—one of the men who had originally kidnapped her.

Adán picked up the branch and swung it at Jason's head again. Jason rolled out of the way, but the stick still connected solidly with his shoulder. He cried out and tried to get up.

"No," Courtney screamed. "Stop it!" She picked up a rock and launched it at Adán.

It hit him in the back, and he turned around, swinging the branch menacingly. Courtney attempted to scramble to the other side of a large boulder, but her movements were pathetically slow.

She looked back at the same time Adán grabbed her leg and yanked her back.

"Please," Courtney sobbed. "Let me go!"

In the next instant, Jason barreled into the smaller man and knocked him off his feet. Adán let go of Courtney as he fell in a heap with Jason. Courtney could see Jason struggling to move while pressing his hand against the gash in his head.

Quick as a cat, Adán was on his feet, holding a gleaming piece of metal.

"Jason, watch out!" Courtney cried as Adán pounced on him. He put Jason in a headlock and lifted his chin. His knife flashed in the sunlight, and Courtney yelled, "No! Don't kill him!"

Adán glared at her, his breath coming in heavy gasps. "You come, or I kill." He pressed the blade into the smooth skin of Jason's neck. Courtney stiffened as a dark splotch of blood appeared near the blade.

She lifted her eyes from the knife to Jason's face. His eyes were full of pain and his skin looked pale. There was blood smeared down the side of his head and onto his tank top. His shoulder was already turning purple from the impact of the branch and Adán's beating.

She searched Jason's eyes for any idea of what to do.

"Run," Jason croaked.

Adán jerked his head back. "No run. I kill."

Courtney believed what the man was telling her in his broken

English. She tried to keep the hysteria from escaping her chest. "What do you want?" she asked Adán.

"You come. No kill." He jerked Jason's head back farther, showing his intentions with the knife. He glared at Courtney. "You come."

She looked at Jason and read the panic in his eyes. She couldn't run, and even if she could, she refused to leave Jason to die because of her cowardice.

Courtney took two steps forward and whispered, "I'll come."

Adán released Jason's head and shoved him to the ground. He put his knife away and stepped on the small of Jason's back with his boot. Jason grunted, but Adán didn't let up. He rummaged in his pockets and pulled out a couple of zip ties. Then he held Jason's hands together and pulled the zip tie snug around his wrists.

Courtney could see that Jason was feeling intense pain from his head injury, and she hoped he would be okay. His head had stopped bleeding so profusely, and he lay still in the dirt—barely conscious. She bent down to check on him, but Adán grabbed her arm.

"You come." He tugged her forward.

Courtney cried out. "My ankle." She motioned frantically to her foot as she tried to keep from falling again.

Adán glanced at her foot and narrowed his eyes, pulling her harder. She hobbled along as best she could, but the pressure brought tears to her eyes. Her body was so overcome with fatigue and pain emanating from various sources that she couldn't focus. She knew she should be devising some plan of escape, but it was all she could do to limp through the rough mountain terrain after Adán.

Just as she thought she might collapse, Adán came to a stop. It took Courtney a second to realize why he had halted the quick pace. A four-wheeler with a camouflage paint job was parked in the trees. Adán pushed her toward it, and she climbed on next to a bunch of marijuana secured with the same type of zip tie he'd used on Jason.

She watched as he wound a zip tie through one of the metal bars on the rack of the four-wheeler. He grabbed her hand, tightened the zip tie around her wrist, and then grinned.

"You stay. No run." He pointed to her hand triumphantly.

Courtney swallowed the saliva she wished she could spit in his face. As if she could run anyway. But he was right—with her hand tethered to the four-wheeler, she was trapped. The thick plastic of the zip tie wasn't something she could wriggle out of—she needed a knife.

Adán hopped onto the four-wheeler and started the engine. He headed back the way they had come and pulled up beside Jason. Adán jumped off, fished around in his pockets, and mumbled something in Spanish that Courtney surmised were cuss words. He narrowed his eyes as he looked at her. She figured he must be out of zip ties.

Adán rubbed his goatee between his fingers and then crouched in front of the four-wheeler. She could hear metal clanking as he worked on something. He stood and carried a chain to the back. On closer inspection, Courtney recognized that it was a winch—Richie had one for their four-wheeler. She watched as he secured the winch to the back and then pulled the heavy hook and attached it to the metal bars on the rack.

He nudged Jason in the side. "Come."

With a moan, Jason rolled over and tried to stand. Adán grabbed his arm and helped him maneuver to the four-wheeler. Courtney could see that Jason's head injury made it hard for him to find his balance, especially with his hands tied behind his back.

He leaned against the four-wheeler, and Adán half-dragged and half-pushed him to a seated position on the back. Then he pulled Jason's hands down until they were close enough that he could hook the wench to the zip tie.

Courtney shifted her body so she could examine how Adán had fastened the hook to the zip tie holding Jason's wrists together. Her right wrist was tethered to one side of the rack, and Jason's wrists were chained to the other side. She wondered how far she could stretch—if she might be able to reach Jason's hands and unhook the wench. She glanced at Adán. She'd have to wait for the right moment.

As Adán approached the front of the four-wheeler, Courtney asked, "Where are you taking us?"

He pulled out his knife and held it in front of her face. "No talk." He motioned to both of them with the blade.

She flinched and pressed her lips into a thin line.

Adán climbed on and gunned the engine. Courtney glanced at

Jason behind her. He grimaced as they lurched forward, and she worried about the extent of his injuries. She put her hand on his leg and squeezed gently, trying to communicate with her eyes. He looked at her with fear in his eyes, and his shoulders slumped.

She wondered if he felt as helpless as she did, tethered to a four-wheeler with a drug criminal acting as chauffeur.

21

PIERSON TRIED to shake off the worry in his gut. He thought about Jason's words, "*Something just isn't right about this case.*" He wondered if Jason decided to do some investigating on his own.

He tried to concentrate on preparing for the info drop, but his mind kept wandering to his partner. Jason was a good kid—a savvy agent. He'd proven his worth since he'd come to Utah.

The files on Jason's desk were in order, as usual. Pierson glanced at the contents of the green folder, the one where Jason stored pertinent evidence to the most pressing case on their docket. His phone rang before he could read past the first page of notes.

"Pierson, this is Branson. I'm out at the Beckhams' place today."

"Yeah, did you find something?"

"Actually, their hired hand just came over and told me there's a car parked by the stables. I went and checked it out. I think it's Edwards's."

"Jason's car?"

"The same. And the hand, name's Richie, thinks it is too, and mentioned that the four-wheeler is gone. He wonders if Edwards took it out across the field."

Pierson swore. "I'm on my way. Let's get a team set up. See if you can find that four-wheeler. My guess is he went into the woods after one of his hunches."

After he hung up the phone, Pierson closed his eyes, whispering a silent prayer that Jason was okay. He couldn't shrug off the worry like he had been for the past couple of hours. Something had definitely gone wrong.

22

THE TRAIL Adán followed through the mountains moved steadily uphill, the terrain growing more uneven and rocky by the second. For the first few minutes, Courtney had struggled not to cry. She swallowed and tried to clear her mind of the frustrations, fear, and doubt about whether she and Jason would make it out of this ordeal alive.

Now she rolled her shoulders back and commanded herself to think of a way to escape. The pine trees grew thick in this part of the woods. There wasn't as much undergrowth as they moved farther from the water source of the creek. Adán wasn't taking them back to the cabin—she at least had that much sense of direction and recognized that they were headed elsewhere.

Think, Courtney, she told herself. Where would he be taking them besides the cabin? Then she remembered the bits of conversation she'd heard that indicated there were other crops of marijuana in these mountains. Was he taking them to a work site where someone in charge would tell him what to do with his prisoners?

She glanced at Jason, wondering what they would do to him if they discovered who he was. As an FBI agent, his life would be worth less than a grain of sand in a scorching desert. She shuddered— there had to be a way out of her predicament. Her captors weren't professional hit men—they were most likely illegal aliens harvesting marijuana in the rugged mountains of Utah. She'd outsmarted them once, and she'd need to do it again to save Jason.

She leaned closer to Jason and squeezed his leg again. He looked at her, and she mouthed the words, *Are you okay?* He frowned and shook his head slowly, as if even that movement caused him pain. The dried blood on his neck and shirt made Courtney's skin crawl.

Focusing on Jason's green eyes, she took note of the size of his pupils. She remembered Sean telling her about the time he got a concussion playing football and how sick it made him. Jason's eyes looked okay, but she wished she could ask him what other injuries he had.

He seemed to be breathing heavily, but maybe that was because his hands were wrenched tightly behind his back chained to an ATV. Every bump in the road seemed amplified to Courtney's bruised body, and she cursed the pitiful shocks on the vehicle. She could only imagine how it felt to someone who had recently had their head bashed in.

She leaned back, trying to reposition herself on the seat. The thick plastic of the zip tie cut into her wrist for the hundredth time, and she winced. She glared at her arm, at the annoying piece of plastic keeping her from trying for freedom. As she stared at her arm, she noticed something about the old four-wheeler.

The rack had rusted out in several spots, leaving jagged pieces of dark orange metal that rattled as they traversed the mountainside. She studied the pipe her hand was attached to with the zip tie. Sliding her wrist down the pipe as far as she could reach, Courtney prayed that her idea would work.

When the four-wheeler hit a bump, the pipe rattled, and she could see the sharp edges of the corroded bar where, with more weather exposure, the rust would finish eating through the metal. She slid her wrist slowly along the bar, grimacing as the plastic bit further into her skin. Adán kept glancing over his shoulder every few minutes, and Courtney concentrated on averting her gaze from his scowl as she continued to inch her arm along the rack.

After several agonizing minutes of moving a centimeter at a time, she scraped the palm of her hand against the rusty spot. Applying pressure to the bar, Courtney pushed down with as much leverage as she could muster. Flakes of orange rust irritated her skin and scattered into the breeze that came down off the mountain.

The bar squeaked, and Courtney jerked her face forward, worried that Adán had heard the noise. She forced herself to take a deep breath, trying to quiet the staccato beats of her heart. Turning her head to the right, she looked at her wrist and the corroded piece of metal.

She concentrated on the trail ahead, trying to anticipate the bumps that jostled all of them. If she could time it right, one of those movements might be enough to cover what she needed to do. She straightened up, extending her arm as far as it would go, lifting the bar slightly.

As the four-wheeler rocked over the next section of uneven terrain, Courtney fell to the side, pushing all her weight into the rusty bar and screaming for effect.

Adán screeched to a halt, and she let the momentum bring her upright, slamming into his back. The force with which she pulled her arm upward shifted the bar, and the metal strained as it broke through more of the rusty underpinnings. The zip tie stopped the movement, and it felt as if her arm would rip from her shoulder. She gasped and didn't let herself look at the metal rack. Instead, she met Adán's cold stare.

"Sorry, I almost fell off," Courtney said.

He narrowed his eyes and grabbed her leg, his fingers clamping like a vise. "No move." He shook his head at her and Jason.

"Sorry. I'm really sorry." Courtney moved away from him, and he released her thigh. Her leg burned where his fingers had dug into the fabric of her capris, and she squeezed her eyes shut, willing the sensation of pain to pass.

She waited until Adán turned back around and shifted into gear, then she glanced at Jason. He gave her a questioning look, and she lifted her chin toward her right hand. His eyes followed the length of her arm and widened when he saw what she was doing.

Her wrist pulsed with pain every time she moved it, and the plastic cut into the raw skin, but she was so close now. Courtney's stunt had broken through the thin line of metal that held the bar in place, but just barely. It looked as if the bars were still connected until they hit another bump and the metal jiggled. She rotated her wrist and pulled it close to the break in the metal. Then she reached with her left hand and pushed down on the bar, at the same time sliding the zip tie loose.

She wanted to cheer as her hand came free, but instead she gripped the bar and turned to look at Jason again. He smiled and mouthed the word, "Go."

Courtney shook her head. She couldn't outrun Adán, and she wasn't going to leave Jason. She chewed on her bottom lip and surveyed the area around them. For probably the past thirty minutes, they had climbed steadily uphill, the engine groaning under the weight of three adults and making slow tracks on the uneven terrain.

It had been years since she had ventured this high up in the mountains because she preferred running to hiking. The tree line had changed dramatically over the past fifteen minutes. The pines clung doggedly to the rocky landscape, their roots snaking in and out of the ground. Courtney wondered how marijuana could survive in these conditions—she didn't see a water source nearby.

A few minutes later, she realized where they were headed. Her dad had always enjoyed hiking, and his favorite spot was the summit of the mountain. She remembered hearing him describe the flat top, almost bare of trees, and how he had a perfect vantage point of the valley below. According to him, once they reached the summit of the mountain, it flattened out considerably before dropping into the next vale. That would be an ideal place to plant his illegal crop, where the sunlight wouldn't be impeded by the towering trees.

She needed to think of something and act quickly. Courtney watched Adán shift into a higher gear and pull the throttle back. The engine reacted to the extra gas with a burst of speed, covering the trail to the next rise. As they pulled around a stand of trees, Courtney gasped. To her right was a steep drop-off to a rocky ravine.

Adán shifted back down into a lower gear and eased off the gas. As Courtney watched bits of earth crumble under the four-wheeler's treads and scatter down the side of the ravine, she thought of another idea.

23

DETECTIVE GARDNER led a team of police officers and FBI agents through the mountains. He was familiar with the vicinity, so he was asked to point out the areas where Jason could have walked within an hour's time earlier that afternoon.

Gardner jabbed the winding blue line that indicated the creek on his map. "Let's first canvass the area leading up to the creek and fan out from there. We only have about two and a half hours of daylight left. Use it wisely."

Several ATVs headed out with Search and Rescue officers and armed FBI agents. One of their own was missing, and they would do all they could to find him. When they found the Beckhams' ATV parked under a group of aspen trees near the entrance to more dense forest, Gardner had a bad feeling. Pierson had told him about the horse-crap "theory" Jason must have been following, and it didn't take long for his officers to find the same evidence.

They headed into the rugged mountain terrain with full force shortly after they found the ATV, calling Jason's name until they were hoarse.

An hour into the search, Gardner' radio crackled. He responded and listened to Officer Branson reporting a piece of evidence. He hopped on an ATV and headed south along the creek bank until the trail forked to the left and began a steady climb up the side of the mountain.

Branson waited for him with a cell phone he had discovered in the dirt just off the trail. The battery was dead, but Gardner had a hunch who the phone belonged to.

Gardner popped the battery out of his own cell phone and swapped it for the one in the white Samsung phone. Then he turned the phone on. He pulled up the list of dialed calls and saw that the last two entered were 9-1-1. He scrolled through the phone book and saw the name Beckham Development.

"Good work." He slapped Branson on the back. "This is definitely Courtney's phone. We need to get this analyzed ASAP. See if it gives us any clues as to who might have abducted her."

"There's a cabin about a half-mile up this ridge. We're checking it out," Branson said and pointed into the woods. "I think you'll want to see what Agent Pierson found there."

"Is it occupied?"

"No, but we're certain Courtney was there."

"Let's go. You lead the way." Gardner hurried back to his ATV and gunned the engine.

24

COURTNEY PEERED down at the steep drop-off to her right. She waited for Adán to glance back at her with his periodic glares and then thought through what she needed to do. Her plan might not work perfectly, but it was the only thing she could think of, and she had to try.

The path, if you could call it that, was narrow, and she watched as bits of dirt and rock cascaded down the side of the ravine. She looked ahead, trying to find the perfect spot to launch her plan into action. Her lungs hurt from holding her breath, and she forced herself to exhale slowly, steadying her nerves.

She bent closer to Jason and fumbled for his hands, locating the spot where he was hooked to the winch.

He shook his head and whispered, "Courtney, what are you doing?"

"Trust me. I'm going to get you free," she murmured. As they climbed the steep embankment, she straightened her shoulders, waiting for the right moment. She unhooked the chain from the zip tie on Jason's wrists, then shoved him off the back of the four-wheeler. He cried out as he rolled in the dirt.

"He fell, he fell!" Courtney yelled.

Adán let go of the gas, braked, and turned to his left to see what had happened. At the same time, Courtney leaned forward, grabbed the throttle on his right side, and wrenched the handlebar toward her.

The four-wheeler lurched forward at full throttle, and Adán yelled and swung at Courtney. The force of his punch almost made her lose her grip, but she held on to the handlebar and the four-wheeler turned sharply toward the side of the cliff. Adán tried to brake, but it was too late. Just as the front tires left the slope, Courtney pushed herself off the back.

She curled into a ball to lessen the impact, but she still landed so hard that it knocked the air from her lungs. After rolling over jagged rocks and sharp sticks, Courtney came to a stop in time to hear a thunderous crash echoing from the ravine.

The painful sensation of her lungs expanding for a breath was all she could concentrate on as the noise receded to the background. She gasped and couldn't seem to get enough air to replenish her lungs. She stared up at the blue sky interrupted by overhanging pine boughs and continued panting for a breath. Then the familiar face of an injured FBI agent appeared over her.

"Courtney, are you okay?" Jason knelt down beside her. "Stop gasping for a second. Give your lungs a chance—they know what to do."

She decided to heed his advice and relaxed against the rocky ground. Her body reacted, and she was able to take a long, ragged breath.

"That's better," Jason said. "How about the rest of you?"

"I'll be all right." Courtney moaned as she sat up. "Your head is bleeding again."

Jason grimaced. "I think I need stitches. Unfortunately, we have bigger problems." His gaze focused on the edge of the cliff. "We'd better see if he's coming after us. It sounds like the engine stopped."

He struggled to stand, and Courtney tried to help him. "We need to get your hands loose."

They hobbled to the side of the ravine and looked down. Courtney cried out when she saw Adán lying under the overturned four-wheeler, his neck twisted grotesquely against a boulder.

Jason stepped back. "Looks like we won't have any more trouble from him."

"I killed him," Courtney sobbed.

"Shh, it's okay," Jason spoke softly. "Don't fall apart on me."

"His name was Adán," Courtney murmured, and she didn't try to stop the tears running down her face.

"You just saved both our lives. I don't want you to worry about Adán right now."

Courtney focused on what Jason was saying. It was true, Adán would have killed Jason. She squeezed her eyes tight, pushing the image of his body from her mind.

"We have time now to get me out of these restraints."

Courtney opened her eyes and glanced at Jason with uncertainty.

"I have a first aid kit in my pack." Jason motioned with his head to the backpack still secured to his shoulders. "There's a pocketknife in it. You'll have to rummage around in there to find it."

"Okay, I can do that." Courtney stepped behind him and unzipped the pack. She located the knife, and within a few minutes was able to saw through the zip ties.

Jason immediately lifted his arms over his head. "Man, my shoulders feel like they've been dislocated." He winced as he continued to reach upward. His wrists bore the same lacerations that Courtney's right hand had suffered.

She watched him stretch, admiring his sculpted triceps and the cords of muscle running across his shoulders. When he turned around, she averted her gaze and concentrated on sawing through the zip tie that was still around her wrist. "I'm sorry I ruined our only source of transportation out of here."

"You saved my life. We'll figure something out."

"Do you think he would've killed you?"

Jason pursed his lips and nodded.

"That's what I thought too. That's why I decided to do something crazy. I figured anything was better than going willingly." She winced as the knife broke through the zip tie on her wrist.

"I'm glad you acted before me. I think your plan turned out much better than the one I was formulating."

"And what was that?"

"Something along the lines of bailing off the back of the ATV and hoping I could put up a good fight with my hands still tied behind my back." He touched his head gingerly. "My head still hurts. I couldn't think straight. I'm worried I might have a concussion."

"I'm worried about the same thing," Courtney said. "Is there something in your first aid kit we can use to fix your head?"

"I have a needle and thread."

He chuckled at the look of horror she gave him. "A butterfly bandage ought to work for now. There are some alcohol wipes in there too."

As she picked pine needles and debris from the wound on his head, Jason clenched his jaw. Courtney swabbed the area with an alcohol wipe. "This is a pretty nasty gash, and there's a lot of dirt around it."

"The bleeding probably got rid of the worst of it." He winced. "Thanks for what you did—putting your life on the line like that."

"Well, my plan wasn't exactly how things turned out." Courtney shuddered as she looked in the direction of the ravine where she knew Adán's body lay. "But at least we're safe now."

"Unfortunately, I think you're wrong—if there's anyone still around, we're gonna be in trouble. I'm sure he was taking us to the next crop they're harvesting—to whoever is in charge."

Courtney felt her chest tighten with fear. "Ramiro."

"Who?"

She finished applying the bandages to Jason's head and sat in the dirt. "Ramiro was the boss when they held me at the cabin. He's the one who talked to my dad—the one I strangled."

"Oh, yeah, I remember now." Jason motioned to his head. "Thanks for fixing me up. We'd better get moving."

"But we're lost," Courtney said. "We're so far away from everything. It'll take us days to hike out of here."

"First of all, my partner is probably already searching for me. I was supposed to be back at the office hours ago." Jason held up his fingers as he spoke, "And second, we might be closer than we think. There has to be a relatively good path to the field of marijuana so they can truck it out. I'm wondering if over that next ridge there might be an old trail that leads to a main road or something."

Courtney followed his gaze. "I think we're close to the summit, and that's probably where they would plant the crop."

"I wish I had my gun." He unstrapped his holster and shoved it in the backpack. "I'm going to have to do a thorough search to find that thing in these woods."

"I saw the general area where it landed," Courtney said. "If we ever get out of here, I can help you find it."

Jason lifted one corner of his mouth in a half smile and slung the pack over his shoulders. "We're going to have to move carefully. There could be more problems if we get too close to the trail. I don't want to run into anybody working the marijuana."

Courtney felt her heart stutter as she thought of the men who had taken her captive. She tried to blink back the tears, but a few escaped down her cheeks. "I'm so scared."

Jason put his arm around her and pulled her close. "It's okay. You've made it this far. We can do this."

She wiped her face with the shirt Jason had insisted she wear and looked at him. "I'm so glad you found me."

"Me too. I'm just sorry we had to take this detour." He gave her shoulder a gentle squeeze. "But we're gonna make it out of this. You'll be safe again."

Part of her felt like she might fall to pieces at any second, but she gazed into Jason's eyes and took strength from the sincerity she saw there. He meant what he said, and she believed him. She was definitely ready to be safe again. Glancing at the trees towering above them, she wondered how long it would take for them to get off the mountain.

25

PIERSON STARED at the bags of evidence and felt a sense of dread as he explained to Gardner what they'd found. "This bloody rope was upstairs under one of the beds. We think Courtney was held in that room."

Gardner examined the other bags and stopped at one holding a large piece of glass. "What's this?"

"It's part of a bowl we found upstairs with blood and hair on the surface." Pierson pointed to the bag. "It appears something in this kidnapping went south. Come upstairs and I'll show you."

Gardner jogged up the stairs after him, and Pierson motioned for him to enter a bedroom busy with activity. "I hope Courtney is still alive and that this blood isn't hers." Pierson studied the dark red stain on the rug and the rumpled sheets on the bed. "We also found blood and dirt in the bathroom."

Gardner shook his head. "Anything else?"

"We've got a forensics team on the way out. We're searching the area. We did discover that this cabin has a landline."

"Good—we'll need to pull a record of all calls made and received here as well." Gardner bent down to examine the phone jack. "How about Internet service?"

"No, and cell service is sketchy. This was where Courtney was held hostage, but it's not the same place the ransom notes were sent from." Pierson frowned. "We definitely have a team of criminals."

"Any word on who was renting the place?"

Pierson tapped his notebook. "We're working on that, but a lot of these cabins are leased to companies who allow their employees to use them for vacation retreats."

"So how does all of this fit into Edwards's disappearance?" Gardner asked.

"Monday morning, he came out to the edge of the woods and found evidence that a horse had been there," Pierson said. "He wanted to check it out, but that's when we got the call for the first info drop that was later canceled. Today was the first chance he's had to come back out here and take a look."

"So the horse and the dog were a red herring." Gardner said.

Pierson tugged at his tie. "I'm betting she was abducted in these woods. They planted the horse and dog to throw us off their tracks."

"Yeah, somebody thought we were getting too close for comfort with our search and left this place," Gardner said.

"We have other men in position for the info drop, but I feel like one of us needs to be there," Pierson said. "Can you head over to Liberty Park?"

"Sure. I'll let you know as soon as we hear anything. Hopefully you'll be in a spot where you can receive my call." Gardner tapped his cell phone. "They've probably planted the directions and account number the old-fashioned way."

"You mean paper?"

"Yeah, maybe they're worried we might trace the text messages."

Pierson walked around the room, absorbing the indicators that Courtney had been there. "That's what we've been working on, but we're keeping an eye on the park just the same."

"I'll keep you updated every half hour," Gardner said.

Pierson nodded and walked back down the stairs. He surveyed the investigation in process. "Jason thought he was just checking out some horse crap. Now I'm wondering if he ran into our kidnappers. The light is fading fast. I hope we can find him before they do."

26

JASON'S HEAD ached something fierce and tramping through the forest didn't help, but he felt an urgency to put some distance between them and the ravine. He didn't share his worry with Courtney because he wasn't sure how much more she could take at the moment.

He knew her swollen ankle pained her with every step, but she wasn't complaining. Perhaps she could sense the urgency without him voicing it. He walked with his arm around her slender waist, trying to guide her away from the hundreds of divots, rocks, and roots littering their path.

They both needed to see a doctor, but hopefully they could last until Pierson found him. He cursed himself for parking behind the stables and not letting Pierson know what he was up to in the first place. Sure, he would have told Jason not to waste his time, but at least Pierson would have known where he was. Jason calculated how long it might have taken for them to start searching for him—he was confident they would be looking for him by now.

He was never late, and this case was too important for his absence to be ignored. Pierson might not have been able to spare any men until after the info drop, but hopefully by now someone would have found his car and concluded where he went.

The crux of the problem was figuring out how far he and Courtney were from the Beckham property and how long it would take searchers to find them. Hopefully, the right people would find them first.

Dusk settled in not long after they started their trek through the woods. Jason led them to a clump of bushes growing next to a stand of pine trees. "We're going to have to camp here for the night."

"Doesn't camping usually include things like a tent, fire, maybe some s'mores?" Courtney said with a smile.

"I have an emergency blanket in the first aid kit and a couple more granola bars," Jason said. "But you did pretty good last night on your own."

Courtney snorted. "Yeah, right. I was so exhausted, I think I pretty much passed out."

Jason laughed at her reaction. "That doesn't sound too bad, the way my head feels right now."

He kicked a few rocks out of the dirt and found a place to sit where he could rest against a tree. Courtney followed suit and watched as he pulled the emergency blanket and a water bottle from his pack. "Do you want another granola bar or an apple?"

Courtney eyed the pack and shook her head. "I'm hungry, but we better save it for morning."

"Good choice. Although I'm hoping we won't be out here too much longer."

He watched her fighting with her emotions again and had the sudden urge to take her hand. He patted her knee instead. "Maybe after we get some rest, things will look better."

"What if they find us during the night?"

Jason didn't have to ask who she meant. "Let's just hope they didn't find Adán yet. They won't know to look for us this far up the mountain, if we're lucky."

Courtney sighed. Jason tried to think of something to get her mind off their predicament.

"So, I feel like I know you—or at least know quite a bit about you because of the investigation."

She looked at him, and her cheeks flushed with color.

"Sorry, that didn't come out right."

"It's okay."

"I just meant that I'd like to get to know *you*, not just the facts on the paper."

She gave him a weak smile. "You probably think I'm just a spoiled little rich girl."

"No, I think there's a lot more to you than money."

Courtney lifted her eyes to his. "Really?"

He smiled at her. "At first, I had to wonder, especially when we investigated all your boyfriends, but I kept seeing things about you that didn't jive with the spoiled sort."

"Like what?"

"I noticed you like to read a lot, and—" He stopped abruptly. He'd almost said he thought it was neat she kept a journal. He felt his face grow warm.

"What?" Courtney scrutinized him.

"Nothing. I still feel bad about that comment I made about your boyfriends."

"Don't be. They were morons. Like I said, I won't be dating again anytime soon."

"Not even if you found the right guy?"

Her head jerked up. She glanced at him and then looked away. "I don't know." She chewed on her bottom lip. "What else did you notice about me—since it sounds like you searched my room?"

He pushed his fingers through the short strands of his hair. "We didn't make a mess of it, though. That's what I noticed—that you're neat and organized."

"And spoiled girls can't be neat and organized?"

He caught the teasing edge in her voice and relaxed. "I guess it's just an overall picture of you that formed in my head. I tend to overanalyze my cases, kind of make my own assumptions about the people we're investigating."

"I'd like to see that picture," Courtney said. "What did you figure out about me?"

He rubbed the back of his neck, hoping she couldn't see the flush of his cheeks in the twilight. He'd been able to distract her from the constant fear, but this wasn't what he had in mind for conversation. He held his chin in his hand and watched the remains of the sunset, thinking about the complicated woman next to him. "I'm still investigating."

"Hey, that's not fair." Courtney pushed his elbow so his hand jerked out from under his chin.

He grabbed her hand before she could make another move. "See, now you're attacking an FBI agent." He grinned. "You're quite different than what everyone else assumed." He released her hand and went back to his thinking position.

Courtney copied his movements and looked at him out of the corner of her eye. "And does it help? These assumptions you make?"

"Sometimes it helps me to see the case in a new light, open up a new possibility that I might not have noticed otherwise."

She loosened the laces on her tennis shoes. "Have you been involved in some pretty big investigations?"

"Yeah, a couple of years ago a team I was on brought down the people who assassinated the Secretary of Defense."

"Secretary Walden?" Courtney's eyes widened. "That was so crazy!"

"That was a pretty intense year for me." Jason massaged his temples, thinking about the Stewart case and how every time they thought they were close to solving it, something unexpected had happened.

"But wasn't that in California?" Courtney asked.

"I worked in the San Diego office. I've actually only been in Utah about six months."

"Do you like it here?"

"Yeah, this area is awesome." He gestured to the mountainside. "You have every form of recreation imaginable within a fifty-mile radius. I went white water rafting a few weeks ago, and I'm looking forward to going snowmobiling in a few more months."

Courtney wrapped her arms around her knees. "It is a beautiful state. But I wonder where I'll end up someday. I've always loved the ocean."

"I miss it." Jason leaned back and thought about the salty taste on his lips when he went running on the beach. "But I've enjoyed the new terrain here." He stretched his arms, trying to free his shoulders from the cramps that continued to radiate through his deltoids.

Courtney touched his tattoo. "You never told me what else this flame stands for . . ."

"I know."

"I'm curious." She tilted her head, looking into his eyes. "It's only fair. You searched my room—the least you could do is tell me about yourself."

"Haven't you ever heard the phrase, 'Life ain't fair?'" he hedged.

Courtney groaned. "Please?"

It was obvious why so many men had fallen for her, Jason thought as he looked into her dark hazel eyes. He remembered the list of descriptive traits he'd written in the green file folder labeled COURTNEY BECKHAM. Beautiful, athletic, fun-loving, resourceful, intelligent, and there was one more word he'd written.

To him, it explained a lot about the type of people she associated with and the activities she was involved in. The word was "insecure." Lots of people were insecure, but he was pretty certain that most people wouldn't choose that word to label the cute and spunky Courtney.

"You're doing it again right now, aren't you?" she asked.

Jason raised his eyebrows. "What?"

"You're analyzing me. I can feel it."

"Okay, I am. I'm trying to figure out why you're so interested in my tattoo."

She tugged on a lock of her hair and twirled it around her finger. "Unless someone rescues us in the next few hours, we're probably not getting out of here until tomorrow. I don't think it's a crime to want to know more about the person you're spending the night with."

Jason shook his head. "You're relentless. That's another word I'm going to add to my file."

"My dad says I'm stubborn." Courtney's smile faltered when she mentioned her father.

"'Determined' is another word for it, and it's a good thing you are, or you might not have escaped."

"You don't think they could find us in the dark, do you?"

Jason frowned. He didn't want to remind her of the reason they were reclining against the rough bark of a pine tree in the middle of the forest. "They wouldn't be able to sneak up on us. There are too many pine needles and twigs scattered everywhere, and they'd be using flashlights."

He watched her lean forward, searching in the darkness that was falling around them, and decided he'd better change the subject again. With a sigh, he murmured, "Passion is like fire."

Courtney jerked her head back to attention. "You're going to tell me?"

Jason flexed his arm. His bicep bulged, and the flame trembled around his muscle. "For some people, that passion burns hot enough to drive them to do things—maybe good, maybe reckless—but that fire can't be ignored." He ran his fingers along the orange-and-black flame of his tattoo. "It reminds me to keep my fire burning on the right course—you know, make something of my life." His voice lowered. "Make my dad proud."

"You're an FBI agent." Courtney touched his hand. "I'd say that's something pretty good. Your dad must be so proud of you."

"I'd like to think he would be." Jason lifted his face to the sky. "He passed away when I was ten."

"I'm so sorry." Courtney wrapped her arms around herself. "That must have been hard, growing up without a dad."

"It was difficult. He was there one day, teaching me how to fish and change the oil, and then gone the next."

"How . . . ?"

Jason's lips twitched. "He was murdered. He was a civil engineer. They think it was a simple breaking and entering gone bad, but the case was never solved."

Courtney stared into the darkness. They sat quietly as the enormity of his words soaked into their surroundings. He could feel the breath of space between their bodies as she leaned against the tree.

She cleared her throat and twisted her hair between her fingers again. "Is that part of what attracted you to the law?"

"Somewhat. Part of me always thought the FBI was invincible." He rubbed the back of his head and grimaced. "Guess we know that's not true."

"I think you're pretty amazing. You found me." Courtney reached for his hand and squeezed it. "I'm so glad you came looking."

Jason's mouth went dry. He looked at her hand resting on his and smiled. "Let's just hope we can find our way out of here tomorrow morning." He interlaced his fingers with hers.

"I hope I can do more than hobble tomorrow morning." She lifted her ankle and rotated it slowly, her eyes crinkling with discomfort as she concentrated on the movement.

"I can carry you if I need to," Jason said. He was aware of the warmth of her hand in his and the steady beat of his heart trying to keep up with the stream of thoughts running through his head about the case, but mostly about Courtney.

"You know I'm not that girl. The one you investigated." Her voice was just above a whisper. "The one who liked to flirt with guys just to get their attention. I haven't been that girl for a while, but I kept putting on the act because I didn't know who else to be."

Jason shifted his back away from a rough section of bark on the tree. "I think I know what you mean. It's hard to find yourself."

"You met my mom—you saw my role model."

He grinned. "Not a hair out of place."

She laughed. "If she could see me now." She released his hand to pull a leaf out of her hair.

He watched Courtney press her lips together, deep in thought. She met his gaze, and he could see a sadness in her eyes.

"I'm still trying to find myself, but it's not just because of what my parents expect," she said. "Did you—when you were investigating my boyfriends, did you look into Felix Haran?"

For a half second, Jason wished he didn't know, but he couldn't lie to her. "Yes, your mom told us about him and that he assaulted you. We investigated him, but he's in Europe right now." He swallowed. "I'm really sorry."

Courtney's shoulders slumped. "You probably think I'm stupid for keeping it a secret."

"No. From a cop's point of view, I wish you would have pressed charges, but I can understand why you didn't." Jason could see Courtney's bottom lip trembling. "You don't have to put on an act for anybody anymore, Courtney. Just be yourself."

She leaned forward and rested her head on her knees. He could see her shoulders shaking with sobs. The pain in her cries gave him a tight feeling in his chest. Jason lifted his hand to pat her back, but he hesitated, unsure how to help her. After a moment, he leaned forward so his face was near hers. "I want to tell you something," he whispered.

Courtney wiped her face on her sleeve and shuddered as another sob went through her. Jason rested his hand on her back and spoke. "I've caught glimpses of the person you really are, and I think there's so much good in you."

She turned to look at him and sniffed. "You do?"

He nodded. "I think I know why you've tried so hard to be someone else." He paused and stared at her dark eyes. "Is it because if you act carefree and happy, it means you won't have to deal with the hurt—the pain you're still carrying from Felix?"

She lifted her head. "And everyone would think I was okay. That was important to me because I didn't want anyone to know, especially Felix, how much he'd hurt me." Courtney sighed, and her breath caught on a hiccuping sob. "He was my first serious boyfriend. I wanted to convince my mom that I was fine, so I've kept dating. Sometimes I would think I had found a guy who could respect me, but every time I end up running again."

"I'm sorry you've been under so much pressure," Jason said.

"You know, you're the first person I've ever told about my secret identity." Courtney's cheeks lifted as she tried to smile.

"Do you feel better?"

Courtney sat up and took a deep breath. "I feel lighter, somehow."

She tugged at another leaf in her hair and sighed. He admired the dark strands of her hair as she swept it across her shoulders. Part of him wanted to reach out and see if it felt as soft as it looked. *What am I thinking?* he asked himself for the hundredth time as he fought with the emotions that kept skittering across his heart every time he looked at Courtney. Maybe it was just the desire he had to protect her.

He frowned, knowing it was more than that. Ever since he'd searched Courtney's bedroom, he'd felt a personal connection to her that couldn't be explained. Why did he have to go and feel something for another victim? He didn't want to get his heart entangled again—like it had with Aubree.

When he'd worked with Aubree Stewart, trying to protect her

and her baby from unknown enemies, the case had become personal. She had been so vulnerable, and he had spent countless hours protecting her, which caused him to let down his guard when it came to his heart.

Courtney turned to look at him. "A Smartie for your thoughts?"

"Smarties?" Jason asked.

"They're one of my favorite treats. You can always keep a roll in your pocket, and no one's the wiser." She patted her pockets. "I don't have any now, but I still want to know what you're thinking about."

Jason sighed. "Too many things—lots on my mind."

"Like?"

He wanted to say, "Like this beautiful, interesting woman sitting next to me." Instead he said, "Like, just how involved your dad is in the drug business."

Her pretty face tightened with worry.

"I'm sorry. It's just that from what you've told me, it's going to be hard to connect him to your case."

"I know. He's doing his best to cover the evidence." She twisted her hair into a thick rope. "But how would he hide the money?"

"I think I have a pretty good idea."

Jason explained that they were investigating Eric for fraud and how they had discovered the fake construction accounts. "He kept trying to blame Cobra, but it didn't add up."

"Poor Cobra. He probably hates my family," Courtney said.

"He's going to be pretty happy to have his name cleared." Jason leaned his head carefully against the tree. "But what about you and your mom? What will you do?"

Courtney let her hair fall between her fingertips and gave him a puzzled look. "What do you mean?"

"All of your dad's assets will be frozen, and his business will probably collapse." Jason threw a rock against a tree, and it echoed in the stillness. "You're looking at being without funds."

"My mom has some of her own money, and I have a savings account and a small trust fund—they can't take those, can they?"

"No, those should be safe."

"I can keep going to school, at least. But I think I'll probably get my own apartment." She flicked bits of dirt from her capris. "I don't think my mom will take kindly to having her lifestyle altered."

"Do you think your mom knew anything about your dad's illegal activities?"

Courtney cleared her throat. "At first I did wonder, but no. Mom would never chance something that might ruin her reputation—she has her limits." She wrapped her arms around herself. "I just wonder what drove my dad to do something so horrible."

"A lot of people in your dad's line of work have had to look elsewhere for jobs since the housing industry pretty much tanked."

"But to do something illegal?" She shook her head. "I guess it shouldn't be a big surprise to me that I don't know my dad as well as I thought I did."

"How's that?" Jason kicked at a rock with his heel and tried to find a comfortable position on the bumpy ground.

"Because his whole life has been centered on work. I'm an only child because that's all he had time for—he doesn't even do much with my mom."

"So, in a way, you grew up without a father too." Jason clasped his hands behind his head.

"No, I wouldn't compare myself to you—that sense of loss," Courtney said. "But I want to do things differently with my own family someday." She looked down. "If I get that chance."

Jason hesitated and then put his arm around her thin shoulders. "You'll get that chance."

Courtney glanced at him, and he could tell she was trying to be brave. He squeezed her to him, and she rested her head against his chest. "It's okay. Everything's gonna be okay now."

27

AFTER IT was too dark to search anymore, Agent Pierson returned to the FBI office and made some phone calls. He was informed that the info drop had been uneventful. Nothing out of the ordinary happened at Liberty Park in Salt Lake City. They searched the area, but instead of getting more intel, Eric received a text:

Get rid of the cops. This is your last chance. The account number will be sent tomorrow at 2 pm.

Pierson and the other officers were frustrated. The info drop had just been a ploy to buy the criminal more time. They had known that might happen but had held out hope the kidnappers might make a fatal mistake when they elected to pass information physically instead of electronically. For some reason, the abductors were trying to drag out the process. It made everyone on the case nervous that something bad had happened to Courtney.

To make matters worse, Eric and Chloe had ordered them off the Beckham property. They continued to monitor all calls and traffic through the area but had been unable to soften the Beckhams toward more police interference.

Pierson called Gardner as soon as he heard about the canceled info drop.

Gardner answered on the first ring. "Found anything new?"

"We found the owner of the cabin. He owns three cabins in the area and leases them out month to month in the summer."

Pierson put his feet up on his desk. "He said this one's been rented all summer, paid for by a woman named Natalie Alexander."

"A woman, huh?" Gardner said.

"We haven't located her yet. But we have located something that just tipped this case into yet another branch." Pierson said. "Our friends at the drug task force will be on site tomorrow morning."

"What did you find? Marijuana?"

"A patch that's been harvested and a lot of work done to cover it up, but my guys could see that movement had been going on in the vicinity and started looking for signs of weed."

"Did they find any growing there?" Gardner asked.

"They didn't find any, just the remains. The patch was only about a half-mile in from the field."

Gardner whistled. "I'm surprised anyone would be gutsy enough to try to grow the stuff that close to the Beckhams' property."

"I know, and the DEA figures they'll probably find more," Pierson said.

"So you're thinking Courtney stumbled upon someone guarding their crop of marijuana?"

"That's what it looks like now, but several things don't add up." Pierson tapped the files on Jason's desk. "This doesn't look good for Jason. It's worth it to them to hold on to Courtney for the ransom, but if they captured him . . ." He shook his head. "We need to find them."

28

WHEN IT was pitch black and Courtney couldn't stop yawning, Jason unfolded the emergency blanket. "It's after ten o'clock. I imagine they'll probably halt the search until first light."

"You're so certain that they're looking for you. I wish I could be that confident."

"My partner won't let me down."

Courtney shivered, and Jason handed her the blanket. "For this to work, we'll have to wrap it around us to keep our body heat in."

She looked at him and then the hard ground. "I'm not much of a camper—my dad was always too busy to take us. I can't believe I'm going to sleep under the bushes for the second night in a row."

"I wish things were different."

Courtney grinned. "No, I'm not complaining. I'm so happy to be away from those creeps. But if anyone had asked me a couple of days ago what I'd be doing now, this would be the furthest thing from my mind."

Jason ran his hand along the ground and dislodged a few rocks. Courtney smoothed out a pile of leaves and settled on the ground, curling into the fetal position. He watched her trying to get comfortable and wished they had made it to safety before nightfall. He lay beside her, pulling the emergency blanket over them. She scooted closer to him, and he handed her the edge of the blanket. "I'm sorry I didn't bring two of these."

"It's okay," she said as she touched his hand. "I think I passed out last night and didn't notice the cold, but tonight I can feel it."

"We're quite a bit higher up than where I found you earlier."

"Do you think they'll find us?" Courtney whispered.

"No, but I'm a light sleeper. I'll wake you if I hear anything."

Jason lay still on the uneven ground. He hoped she couldn't feel his heart racing in his chest as he breathed in her nearness. The forest popped and creaked around them, and the throbbing in his head pushed him toward a fitful sleep.

* * *

Birds chirping in the trees infiltrated Courtney's dreams until she reached the threshold of wakefulness. She held on to her sleep, not wanting to open her eyes and wondering why she felt so tired.

The weight of Jason's arm on her waist brought her back to her senses. Sometime during the night, they had snuggled closer to each other, trying to keep the emergency blanket wrapped tight around them. She could hear the sounds of morning and feel the nip in the air. Her nose felt cold, but the fresh air was invigorating.

Jason hadn't moved, and she figured he must still be sleeping. She lay still and thought about the man next to her. Jason Edwards was definitely an anomaly compared to the guys she'd dated. There was something about the way he examined her with those vivid green eyes of his—as if he could see right through her.

Even if she had felt the urge to flirt with him, she knew it wouldn't work because he was so aware of her. She'd spoken more openly with him than she had to anyone, and he'd understood. But then again, maybe it was just the trauma of being kidnapped and escaping twice that had her feeling like this.

Either way, it was nice to feel safe for the moment, snuggled next to a handsome FBI agent with strong arms wrapped around her.

"Courtney?" he whispered.

"I'm awake," she answered, but her voice sounded groggy.

"Oh." He pulled his arm back slowly. "I'm sorry. I didn't mean to do that."

"No, you're fine." She put her hand on his arm. "I didn't want to move because I thought you were asleep," she said. "And it's pretty cold too."

Jason coughed, and a few seconds passed before he asked, "How's your ankle?"

"I think it's frozen at the moment."

He chuckled, and his breath on her ear sent a pleasant tingle down her back. She flexed her right foot and found that the sharp pains from yesterday had diminished. "Actually, I think the swelling has gone down some."

She rotated her foot slowly. The movement still felt sluggish, but maybe she'd be able to walk.

Jason shifted his body. "I was listening for the sounds of running water—hoping that we were closer to the creek—but we must still be a ways off from where it intersects with this part of the mountains."

He sat up, and Courtney shivered as her heat source moved and the chilly air invaded the emergency blanket. She pushed herself up to a sitting position and examined her ankle. "I think I'll be able to walk better today."

"We'll see when you put some weight on it." Jason glanced at her foot, and his eyes lingered on her before he turned and unzipped his backpack. "Here." He handed her a water bottle.

"Thanks. My mouth feels like it's full of cobwebs." She swished the chilled water around in her mouth and tried to ignore the gurgling demands of her stomach.

"I have one apple and three granola bars left," Jason said. "Is it okay if we save the apple until later?"

Courtney's mouth watered at the thought of crisp apple flesh crunching between her teeth, but she nodded. "I'm okay with eating half a granola bar now. Want to split one?"

"You can eat a whole one." Jason handed the bar to her. "I'm not that hungry yet."

"But you didn't eat last night either," Courtney protested.

"I haven't gone without food as long as you. Go ahead."

"First, I better see if I can stand up."

Jason hopped up and held out his hand, pulling her to her feet. She winced as she distributed her weight on her ankle. He watched her closely, keeping his hand on her arm for balance. She took a few tentative steps. "I think I'll be able to walk."

"I don't want you to overdo it," Jason said.

His hands felt warm against her skin, and she smiled at him. His eyes lit up, and he squeezed her arms gently before releasing her. Courtney gazed around the forest shading them from the morning sun. "Do you think if I wished hard enough, that tree over there would turn into a toilet?'

Jason laughed until his face turned red. Courtney admired his easy smile and laughed with him.

"I'll keep a lookout, but holler if you see or hear anything," he said.

She frowned in the direction of the tree, and with a wave, headed behind a bush. This was why her family didn't camp. As her mother said, there are just some experiences you don't need in life. Courtney smiled. If Chloe could see her now, what would she think?

A few minutes later, she attempted to smooth out her hair and remove the pine needles and twigs that had taken up residence. She wished she had a toothbrush or even some mouthwash—her mouth felt so grimy. Courtney stretched her arms over her head and felt the tender spots of several different muscle aches. Her left side was sore, probably from pulling so hard on the handles of the four-wheeler. She shuddered as she thought of Adán's body at the base of the ravine.

Jason had folded up the emergency blanket and put his backpack on when she returned. He held out the granola bar, and she thought that if her stomach had hands, it would have reached out and grabbed it. "I don't know where I'd be if you hadn't found me yesterday." She took the food hesitantly. "Actually, I'd probably be a prisoner."

"I don't believe that. Look at how resourceful you were in breaking us free."

She unwrapped her breakfast—this one an almond cranberry bar—and broke off a piece for Jason.

"Really, I'll be fine."

"You can at least have a bite. C'mon, I feel weird eating in front of you." She handed him the piece of food.

"Even if you're so hungry your stomach is turning inside out?"

"Hey!" She gave him a playful punch.

He smiled. "I could hear your stomach growling—I think that's what woke me up."

She laughed and took a bite of the granola bar. "Mmm, this tastes so good."

"You know what they say, hunger is the best seasoning." He rubbed his hand over his close-cut hair, and she gasped.

"Look at your wrists." Courtney grabbed hold of his arm and pulled his hand closer to inspect the raw flesh around his wrist. The wound was puffy and red. "Jason, we need to put something on this."

"I'm okay. I think the dirt irritated the cuts overnight."

She ignored him and unzipped the pack strapped to his shoulders. Within a few minutes, she'd disinfected the wounds, applied salve, and wrapped them with bandages.

"Thanks, Court. You're quite the nurse."

She lifted her head at the sound of her nickname.

"Is it okay if I call you that?" He watched her carefully for her reaction.

She smiled. "Sure, I'd like that."

"Everyone kept referring to you as Court—it just kind of came out."

"It's okay." She touched his arm.

He relaxed noticeably and wiggled his fingers. "You can see why I wasn't too shook up when that guy went over the cliff." He pointed at his bandaged head and wrist.

"We make quite a pair with our scrapes, sprains, and bruises." Courtney held out her own bandaged wrists and injured ankle. "Are we ready to hike?"

"I'm pretty certain the creek can't be more than an hour of hiking from here—if we're lucky, we'll run into it sooner." He pointed downhill. "Let's go."

Courtney walked carefully alongside Jason, keeping an eye on the uneven ground to prevent further injuries. Her ankle throbbed, but after fifteen minutes of walking, the movement didn't seem so stiff. She was determined to find a way out of these mountains.

29

AGENT PIERSON was back on the mountain first thing Wednesday morning, combing through the underbrush for any sign of Jason. Several other agents and officers accompanied him, and they followed a pattern to cover as much terrain as possible. Officer Branson sought Pierson out a few hours later and handed him a folded piece of paper.

"What's this?" Pierson asked.

"We've been working on Courtney's cell phone account," Branson said. "We had already analyzed her phone records, but we can't see everything from the web account. When we searched her phone, we looked for things like missed calls."

"Good work. Did you find anything?"

"We found a few missed calls on her cell phone that didn't jive with her usual call list." He motioned to the paper Pierson had unfolded. "We cross-checked the phone records at the house and Beckham Development. There was one number that stood out, received Monday morning."

"And it was this number?" Pierson studied the printout.

"From a place called Tropical Resources. Could be a wrong number, but we're looking into it right now. We're trying to find the location—we found a boutique with that name on the south side of Salt Lake City, but it looks like the place is closed. We're trying to contact the owner." Branson said. "Tropical Resources stood out because there are a handful of calls from this number to Beckham Development, and we could only see this one occurrence to her cell phone, but that was after she'd been kidnapped."

"I hope this leads us to someone who can help us find her."

"Maybe Jason too," Branson offered.

Pierson looked at the mountainside around him. "Yeah, he was definitely on to something when he came out here looking. Let's hope it pays off."

* * *

"We'd better stop and rest." Jason halted their downhill journey next to a large boulder.

"I can keep going." Courtney tried to keep her voice light.

"No, you need to sit down and put your foot up," Jason said. "I know it's still bothering you."

She thought about arguing and pushing forward, but her ankle was protesting and she couldn't ignore it any longer. "Okay, you win."

They drank some water from the nearly depleted supply and rested in the shade of the boulder. Courtney loosened her tennis shoe and slid her foot out with a sigh.

"When we get to the creek, you could soak your ankle. That might help," Jason suggested.

"That's what I did the night this happened. That water is freezing," Courtney said. "How's your head?"

"It's pretty tender. But I feel a lot better this morning." He settled on the ground next to her.

"I'm worried about what will happen when we get back." Courtney swallowed and pushed away the anxiety she felt whenever she thought about the confrontation that awaited her.

"With your dad?"

"Yeah, I'm scared," she said. "But I'm mostly worried that you're not going to have the evidence you need to convict him for producing drugs."

"The DEA will find that other marijuana crop, and even though you said they harvested the first one, there will still be evidence," Jason assured her. "They know what to look for."

"But how does that link back to my dad? I wonder if those men even knew who they were working for."

"Not likely." Jason unearthed a big rock near his foot and ran his fingers along the jagged edges. "Listen, you said your dad received a phone call from Tropical Resources before all this happened, right?"

"Yeah. Can you get records of the calls to my dad's office?"

"That will be easy. What might be hard is connecting that company to your father. A phone call is not enough." Jason took another swig of water. "Is there anything else you can remember about the phone call? Have you ever heard of Tropical Resources before?"

Courtney followed the tufts of clouds dancing through the patches of blue sky above them and inhaled slowly. She tried to remember everything she'd overheard her dad say during the phone call. "Wait a minute. I do remember something. He said 'Natalie.'"

"Who?" Jason asked.

"My dad said, 'Natalie, I told you never to call this number.' If we can find out who Natalie is, then maybe we'll find a connection to my dad."

"It's a start, at least."

Courtney's heart rate increased as she thought about her dad and what he might have been up to lately. Her eyes filled with tears, and she covered her mouth as if that could stop the suspicion from bursting into realization. She had just made another connection about her father.

"What? What is it?" Jason put his hands on her shoulders and turned her to face him.

Courtney shook her head as tears leaked out. Then she whispered, "The murder last year."

"What murder?" Jason looked confused.

"I don't know—a young guy. A runner was murdered in these mountains last year. They couldn't find the killer, and then a few days ago, the police arrested someone for the crime, but that guy didn't do it either."

Courtney let her head hang down, the rocks beneath her blurred from her tears. "My dad has probably been growing marijuana before this year. What if that runner stumbled on a patch of it just like I did? Only they didn't kidnap him, they killed him." Courtney looked at Jason, hoping he would say her idea was far-fetched.

He raised his eyebrows. "It's a possibility."

Her shoulders slumped, and at the same time her throat constricted and angry tears burned her eyes. "Do you think my father is a murderer?"

He looked at her carefully before answering. "It doesn't matter what I think—"

"Yes, it does." Courtney swiped at her eyes and swallowed. "It matters because what you think is probably right."

Jason leaned back and massaged his temples. Courtney could see the lines of stress running across his forehead. She wasn't angry with him; she was scared because so far everything he had thought about her case was right on. She didn't want to think of her father as someone capable of murder. Resting her head in her hands, Courtney took short gasps, trying to push down the certainty of this new realization.

Part of her wanted to scream and deny everything she had learned about her father in the past few days. Instead, she closed her eyes and focused on regaining her composure so they could continue their trek out of the mountains. She didn't realize she was shivering until she felt Jason's arm around her.

"I'm sorry you're going through this," he whispered.

She glanced up at him and could see the concern in his eyes. "I don't know what I'm going to do."

Her lip trembled, and he pulled her to him. "You're going to be okay."

Courtney let him comfort her. She rested her head against his chest and felt it rumble slightly as he continued to speak. "You haven't done anything wrong, so you can just keep doing what you've been doing—going to school. It'll be hard, but you can do it."

They sat that way for a few minutes until she could feel her breathing even out and the panic subside. She tilted her head back so she could look into Jason's eyes. His gaze was intense, and it sent a thrill through her as she realized he sincerely cared about her. She wrapped her arms around his torso and soaked in his strength. "Thank you for this—for everything."

"Happy to help. I'm just sorry you've been dealt such a bad

hand." His voice was husky with emotion. "Are you ready to try walking again?"

She nodded and reluctantly moved away from him. He took her hand and helped her to her feet, but he kept holding it once they began walking. Perhaps that was because Courtney gripped it so tightly, not wanting to let go.

Jason's palms were warm with perspiration, but Courtney still held tight to his hand as they trekked through the mountains. He told himself she was just holding onto him so she wouldn't trip with her weak ankle, but he knew better. His fingers were gripping hers just as tight, and he couldn't ignore the current of electricity flowing between them.

Maybe he shouldn't have hugged her, but he couldn't stop himself. She had looked so fragile, sitting there soaking in the realization that her father was a hardened criminal—maybe even a murderer. And yet, she was so brave, trying to keep it together and swallow back the tears when he could see the emotional turmoil she suffered.

When he held her in his arms, it felt right, like that was where she was supposed to be. He mentally shook his head—his thoughts were headed for a train wreck. Courtney said she wasn't the girl she used to be, and she was ready to stop pretending—but what if that change made under duress didn't last?

He watched her lithe figure as she moved carefully around roots and tree branches in their path, her dark hair falling in thick waves across her shoulders. The wind picked up a few strands and swirled them around her face, and he had to resist the urge to tuck her hair behind her ear.

She turned to him, and he noticed the fullness of her pale pink lips against her creamy skin. Jason smiled when he saw the smudges of dirt across her cheek and the pine needles tangled in her hair. She was still beautiful. He forced himself to look her in the eye and push back thoughts of kissing those lips. "How's the ankle holding up?"

"I'm doing okay. Probably won't be running for a while, but it doesn't hurt as bad as it did yesterday."

"I was hoping the good guys would've found us by now, but I bet they're canvassing the area where we met Adán," Jason said.

"Maybe they'll come this way soon?" Courtney looked hopeful.

"Unfortunately, it'll take some time for them to cover the distance he transported us. I think we're going in the right direction, but I'm not sure." He touched the bandage on his head. "I was kind of out of it."

Courtney chuckled. "And I was preoccupied trying to break through a metal bar."

"I don't think many people would've tried what you did—that was pretty clever." Jason squeezed her hand.

"I'm a resourceful girl."

"There's more to you than most people would suspect." Jason averted his eyes as Courtney looked up.

"Thanks, that means a lot."

"It's true. It's one of the first things I thought when I saw your picture and created my file on you." He noticed a pink flush in her cheeks, and he smiled. Hope flared in his chest even though he continued to push it down. He couldn't help but wonder if Courtney felt something for him as well.

They walked in silence for a while, feeling the warm rays of the sun heating up the forest. Jason surveyed the area around them as they walked, looking for any sign that someone else had traversed this part of the forest. A series of clicks from a black pine beetle echoed above their passage through the dusty path of Scotch pine and blue spruce trees.

"I'm sorry, Jason, but my ankle is really starting to hurt." Courtney stopped and leaned against a tree.

"It's okay. We can rest here." He glanced at his watch. It was nearly two o'clock in the afternoon, and the heat was relentless. He wiped his forehead on his tank top, which was already filthy with the fine dirt that clung to everything in these mountains.

"Wait a minute." He held a finger to his lips and listened. "I can hear running water."

Courtney perked up. "I think I can hear it too."

Jason slung on his backpack and scooped Courtney into his arms. She gave a shriek of protest, but he just laughed. "We made it."

"I can walk."

"It can't be far, and you'll be able to soak your foot." He held her close and half-jogged, following the sound of water. He could see a clump of willows, a bush that usually grew by the water, only twenty-five yards ahead. "There it is."

Courtney held onto his neck, and her nearness increased his heart rate even more. When they reached the water's edge, she cheered and laughed as he carefully set her on the ground. She untied her shoes and put her dirty socks inside them before scooting down the rocky bank.

The stream was probably only eighteen inches deep, but it was cold. He helped her to an area that was nearly four feet across. A giant boulder jutted out of the creek bed, and she perched on it, her feet dangling in the water.

"I'll scout out the area—make sure it's safe to sit for a while. I don't want to be caught unawares." He circled a perimeter of the bubbling water—the noise was usually soothing, but now it kept him on edge because he knew it would be difficult to hear anyone approaching.

There wasn't a sign of another human. He couldn't see any footprints, disturbed vegetation, or vehicle tracks, so he relaxed and headed back to where Courtney rested.

30

ERIC STOOD at the far end of the stables and cast another fur-tive glance about him. He wished he could order all these police officers and FBI agents off his property, but since Agent Edwards went missing, they had refused to leave. Eric griped about their vis-ibility in relation to the kidnapper's threats, but apparently when it was one of their own, they didn't heed warnings.

With the phone pressed to his ear, he stood in the shadow of the stables and listened for the fury in the voice he had come to know so well.

"Why haven't you called before now?" Natalie's voice grated against his ears.

"Why do you think?" Eric snapped. "I'm surrounded by cops, and the FBI keeps asking questions. This is the first chance I had."

"You've made a real mess, and I'm going to have to clean it up."

"No, I'm taking care of everything." Eric kept his voice just above a whisper. "Things are going exactly as planned."

"You call Courtney escaping part of your plan?" Her voice seethed with anger.

"No, but we'll find her. The feds aren't looking for her. They don't know she escaped."

"Maybe you should send another text and delay the transfer."

Eric shook his head. "I can't do that again—it will look too suspicious."

"How will it look when Courtney shows up on your doorstep?"

He glanced around the side of the stables, making sure he was alone. "She won't get that far. The cabin is nearly ten miles from here, and Court's not great with direction. Even if she was, it would take her all day."

"You'd better hope so."

"Ramiro and his guys will find her."

"This is your last chance." Natalie paused, and Eric closed his eyes, fighting back the urge to argue with her. "Don't make me regret working with you."

Eric ended the call and pushed Natalie's threats to the perimeter of his overstressed mind. He walked back through the stables, then stopped, staring out across the open field. The mountains were now crawling with men in blue looking for Agent Edwards. What if they found Courtney before Ramiro could find her?

He hadn't told Natalie about the search, but he'd warned Ramiro to clear out from the cabin. Hopefully the FBI wouldn't cover that much ground in one day, but Eric's muscles cramped with nervous energy every time he thought about the possibility of the feds finding the cabin.

Agent Pierson wasn't sharing details about their search for Agent Edwards. It was possible they'd already found the cabin. Natalie had said it couldn't be traced back to her. Even so, he wasn't going to take any chances. All the men had been ordered to harvest what they could from the upper crop and clear out by tonight.

He pursed his lips. Courtney knew about the marijuana. Once she returned, it would only be a matter of time before the DEA launched a full investigation. It was time to put his plan B into action.

31

"I THINK WE'RE safe to rest here," Jason said as he returned from scouting the area. "I couldn't find any sign that someone has been near this spot recently."

"Come on in, the water's fine," Courtney said and tipped her head back so the sun warmed her face.

He shrugged off the backpack, then tugged his boots off and rolled up his jeans. He retrieved their empty water bottles and waded into the stream to refill them. He handed Courtney a bottle, and she watched as he guzzled a full one and then dipped it back into the water.

The cool liquid tasted better than anything Courtney could imagine, with the late July heat scorching every ounce of fluid from her body. Jason tossed the full bottles onto the pack and glanced at Courtney. "I hope you don't mind, but this heat is killing me, and I think I'm getting sunburned." He tugged at the tank top he wore that was soaked with perspiration and pulled it over his head.

There were definite lines of red and white on his shoulders where the sunburn stopped and started again. Courtney bit her lip and studied him. Jason dunked his shirt into the water, rinsing out the dirt, sweat, and dried blood. She struggled to pull her gaze from the toned muscles of his chest. He turned, and she admired the sinewy muscles of his back. Then she glanced at herself and wrinkled her nose.

"No fair," she said, and Jason whirled around with a grin.

"There you go again with that 'no fair' business."

"I'm way dirtier than you."

"Your feet are clean, though." His eyes danced with laughter.

Courtney waited until he turned around and then eased herself into the creek. The chilly water soaked the edge of her capris and cooled her skin. She leaned against the rock and splashed Jason.

"Hey!" He turned, and she splashed water in his face. He blinked, and then with one wide sweep of his arms, he plowed through the water toward her. The icy stream washed over her.

She gasped and tried to mimic the gesture, but it threw her off balance. Jason laughed and caught her before she fell into the creek. "How's that for fair?"

The water dripped off her face, and she laughed. She held tight to his arms. "I feel better."

"Me too," he said.

There was something in his voice that caught her attention. She looked up at him and couldn't ignore the sparks flying between them. Droplets of water clung to his lashes, the cool green of his eyes inviting her in as she met his gaze.

Rivulets of moisture ran from his hair down his neck. He lowered his head and then hesitated. She leaned closer, her breath catching. He moved his hands to the small of her back and pulled her to him, dipping his head. She closed her eyes as his lips brushed gently against hers.

She reached a hand to the back of his neck and moved her mouth against his, her other hand still gripping his arm. The kiss felt ten times more powerful than anything she'd ever shared with Sean. A spark of energy hung in the air between them when they broke contact. She was close enough to see the flecks of gold in his eyes.

Jason smiled at her and whispered, "No fair. I didn't know you were a water nymph."

She cocked her head to the side. "You were trying to drown me so you could give me mouth to mouth."

He laughed and kissed her cheek. "We'd better get out of this water and put our shoes back on. I'd hate to make a run through the woods barefoot."

Courtney sighed. "It was nice to forget for a minute why we're traipsing through the mountains."

184

Jason lifted her back up on the rock. "I'm happy to help you forget. Anytime."

As she put her socks and shoes back on, Courtney thought that at least one good thing had come from all this mess. The finest member of the force had rescued her with a kiss that had awakened something in her she'd never felt. Maybe this was how it felt when it was real—different with someone besides a shallow football jock or a self-absorbed president-in-training.

She looked up at the sun and squinted. The bright rays sucked out the moisture in her clothing and warmed her skin. Her mind lingered on Jason's gentle kisses and what she had seen in his eyes. Not raw hunger like she was something to be devoured.

Courtney had seen something there that had her heart doing cartwheels. She looked over and noticed him watching her with a crooked smile, and it sent thrills through her. She wanted him to hold her in his arms again so she could revel in that feeling of security.

"You ready?" He wore his wet tank top, and the sun glistened on the droplets of water stuck to his hair.

"Did I mention how glad I am you found me?" Courtney asked as he carried her back across the creek.

"Not as glad as I am." He took her hand as they walked along the rushing water. "I was thinking, when we find our way out of here, we should go get something to eat—you know, real food—not granola bars."

A bubble of laughter escaped her chest, and she squeezed his hand. "Sounds like a plan."

Agent Pierson slammed his hand on the map of the terrain they had been searching. "We should've found him by now."

"The four-wheelers have been everywhere in these mountains," Detective Gardner said. "What tracks we can follow intersect with others so many times, it's like we're going in circles."

"It's time to call in a search from the air," Pierson said.

"I don't know how effective that will be in finding Jason, but I bet they'll get some good sights on where the marijuana is growing, if it hasn't all been harvested."

Pierson circled the area they had searched on the map. Two miles up and down the creek as it wound higher through the mountains, and no sign of Jason. There was plenty of activity in these mountains, though, and he wasn't going to give up the search. He traced the mountain ridge with his finger and paused when he came to a second water source on the map.

"This natural spring here." He jabbed the blue line. "If I were growing weed, I'd go as high up and out of the way as possible where there was a good supply of water."

"I bet that's what the growers figured," Gardner said.

"So that's the area we need to search." Pierson rested his hand on the map. "If they moved Courtney from this cabin, maybe they took her to the next crop, and if they ran into Jason . . ." He coughed, attempting to clear the emotion from his voice. "I'm hoping he's still alive, and I think that's where we should look."

Gardner looked at the map and then at him. "Let's do it."

Pierson punched a number on his phone. "This is Pierson. We need a chopper."

32

JASON GLANCED at his watch again. It was almost seven o'clock, and they hadn't covered nearly as much distance as he would've liked. His head throbbed and his body definitely felt like it'd been tossed off the back of an ATV.

Courtney was a trooper—he knew her ankle must be killing her, but she'd kept on without complaints. With frequent stops to rest and escape the scorching heat, they were still too high up the mountainside. They had maintained a close distance from the stream so they could drink enough water, but food was a problem.

If he wasn't so worried about the wrong people finding Courtney, he might have left her to rest while he went for help. But that wasn't an option. He wouldn't let his guard down, and he constantly worried what might be around the next cluster of trees.

A black fly buzzed around his head and landed on the back of his neck. He slapped at it, and the insect flew away, but the skin on his neck stung, and he knew his sunburn was deep. Courtney's nose had turned pink, but her long hair covered her ears and neck, protecting them from the sun. He stayed as close to her as a shadow while they walked, prepared to catch her in case she stumbled.

"Man, I'll be glad when the sun goes down," he muttered.

"I don't think I've ever hated summer before," Courtney said. "This heat is killing me."

He felt his stomach clench and rumble with hunger. "What I wouldn't give for some ice cream right about now."

"You're not making this any easier, you know." Courtney grinned at him and then stopped and took a long swig from her water bottle.

As he watched her guzzling the water, Jason heard a noise. His first instinct was to take cover, but then he halted. "Do you hear that?"

She swallowed and turned her head toward the sound. She furrowed her brow. "Is that—"

"A helicopter!" Jason whooped and hugged Courtney. "We've got to get out in the open."

"I'm too slow. Run! I'll follow you."

He hesitated for half a second, but as the beat of the helicopter blades drew closer, he took off, leaping over deadwood and sprinting for a piece of open ground. He reached a small clearing just as the helicopter zoomed overhead.

Jason jumped up and down, waving his arms frantically. He could see that the orange and red helicopter was part of the Search and Rescue teams. They were looking for him.

"He's gone," Courtney cried as she stumbled through the brush a few yards away. "He didn't see us."

"Don't worry. He'll do another sweep." Jason dug through his backpack. "I have an idea." He pulled out the silver emergency blanket and spread it on the ground. The sun reflected off the shiny material, and Jason squinted. "This should draw his attention."

"How long do you think it'll take before they come back?"

"I don't know. Let's wait here and rest in the meantime." He finished spreading out the blanket and helped Courtney sit on the edge of it.

He could hear her stomach gurgling, and she gave him a sheepish look. "I'm so tired and hungry."

"I know. Me too," he said. "But once they see us, we could be out of here within a couple hours."

"You really think so?"

"I'm sure they're spread out over these hills with ATVs, and we might be closer than we think to the way out."

Courtney lay back on the ground and looked up at the sky. Then she glanced at Jason. "I wonder how surprised they'll be to find us together."

"I keep wondering what your dad has been doing about the ransom since you escaped."

She gave a mirthless laugh. "I'm sure he's in a frenzy trying to figure something out."

Jason pressed his lips into a tight line.

"What's the matter?" Courtney asked.

"Just thinking of what we talked about earlier."

She pushed herself up onto one elbow and frowned.

"I don't know what my guys have come up with since I've been gone, but there's a good chance we won't have enough probable cause to arrest your dad."

"But we have proof," Courtney said. "I heard him telling Ramiro what to do."

"That's the problem. All we have is what you heard on a phone call where he never identified himself as your father." Jason curled his fingers into a tight ball, and a few of his knuckles popped. "We don't have any solid evidence yet."

"But . . ." Courtney closed her eyes, and Jason could hear her inhale sharply.

He lifted her hand and gave it a gentle squeeze. "We'll find something, though, because he's already under investigation. It might take longer than we'd like to find the evidence we need to arrest him for fraud."

"What about the marijuana? That's got to be worth something."

Jason adjusted the straps of the backpack away from his sunburn. "Even if we can find it, we still can't link it to your dad."

"Maybe when you bring him in for questioning, he'll confess. I can tell him what I heard—that I know everything."

"It's not like TV though. People don't usually confess unless they know we have evidence against them and they think there's a chance for a plea bargain."

Jason touched the bandage on his head. "If we could get a hold of one of the men harvesting the crop, we might find more info, but even then I doubt they know who they're working for."

Courtney picked the leaves off a bush. "Adán's not an option, but Ramiro knows."

"Even though he talked to your dad, he might not have known his real name."

Courtney shook her head. "When I told him my name, he knew who I was. He had to know he was talking to my dad."

"That's good, but only if we can find Ramiro."

She closed her eyes, and Jason knew she was struggling with the hard facts of the case. A woodpecker pounded out a rhythm that reverberated through the trees. Jason felt like every muscle in his body had been pulled in the wrong direction. The skin on his back tingled with the pain of the sunburn as if he had chafed it against the rough bark of the pine trees.

He moved his thumb in a circular pattern along the soft skin of Courtney's hand. The dark lashes that framed her wide eyes fluttered as she lifted them and met his gaze.

He bit the inside of his cheek as he took in the open trust he saw on her face. "I promise you that I will make sure your dad pays for what he's done."

Courtney gripped his hand. "I love my dad. It's hard to think of him this way."

They both tensed when they heard the hum of the chopper blades approaching. Jason stood and waved his arms. Courtney scrambled to her feet and followed his movements. The helicopter passed by, and she cried out. "No!"

"Wait, he's circling back," Jason said. "They must have seen us. Keep waving your arms."

Courtney waved, and they both strained their necks looking upward, hoping that the chopper would come back into view. Then the drone of the helicopter grew louder and they cheered when they saw it appear above them and hover in the sky.

Jason hollered and jumped in the air. Courtney shrieked and hugged him. "They found us!"

A few seconds later, the chopper buzzed off in another direction.

"Wait," Courtney cried. "Why did he leave?"

"Because there's nowhere for him to land. He's marked our spot and reported it, so now help is on the way." Jason still held on to Courtney, and he couldn't stop smiling. They would soon be heading out of these mountains.

She gripped his arms, keeping the weight off her foot, and frowned. "So, what now?"

"It's probably best if we stay put." Jason grinned. "At least we have good company."

When Courtney heard the familiar rumble of an engine, her heart jumped into her throat. She grabbed Jason's hand and saw a flicker of worry in his eyes, but then his jaw tightened and the emotion was gone.

"You stay here," he whispered. "I'm going to see if it's someone on our side."

"I'm scared." She didn't let go of him as he moved to stand.

"It's okay. I'll keep out of sight until I make sure they're our guys." He put his arm around her and held her tight. "I won't let anything happen to you."

He wadded up the emergency blanket. "Go sit near the trees so you're not out in the open. I'll be fast."

She watched as he edged down the side of the mountain, adjacent to the tree trunks and getting closer to the approaching four-wheelers. It was all she could do to keep breathing—the adrenaline pumping through her veins made it hard to ignore the urge to run.

The ATV ground to a stop as Agent Pierson answered his radio.

"We found the marijuana, and people were making a run for it," the chopper pilot reported. "They're probably not far from where I sighted the other two. Put your guys on alert."

"Okay, men. Weapons ready, but look twice before you shoot," Pierson barked. "The weed patch has been spotted from the sky, and there are reports of at least six individuals fleeing the scene. We still don't know if one of them could be Edwards."

He scanned the line of trees in front of him. The helicopter pilot said there were two people near what looked like an emergency blanket, and they were signaling for help. The pilot said one of the two was a blond male. That had sounded like Jason, but who was with him?

He radioed back down the mountainside to Detective Gardner. "Any news from our kidnappers?"

"Nope, nothing, and it's been over thirty-six hours since the last contact," Gardner said. "I think something's happened to her."

"Let's hope not."

Neither said what they were thinking—that if they didn't hear from the kidnappers soon, it meant Courtney Beckham was probably dead.

Pierson engaged the ATV again to continue up the mountainside at a steady uphill pace. They had thirty-five Search and Rescue officers combing the hillsides for any sign of Jason or Courtney. He prayed they would both be found alive.

Jason took careful steps through the trees, wincing as each twig snapped and leaves crackled under his boots. He heard the sound of motors ascending the hill, the noise growing louder as he approached. He saw a clump of bushes and ducked behind them to wait until the men driving appeared.

From the sound of it, there were at least three ATVs traversing the slope of the hillside. Jason's heartbeat quickened in anticipation—it was likely Search and Rescue officers in a group. As the first one appeared around a pine tree, Jason felt the air whoosh out of his lungs in relief. It was a police officer, and as he approached, Jason saw the second ATV close behind.

When he saw Pierson following, he wanted to jump out of the bushes and cheer, but he didn't want to be taken down in friendly fire. He eased slowly from the bushes and took a few steps forward. Another FBI agent saw him first, and Jason put his hands up in the air as the agent grabbed for his gun. He noticed a fourth ATV making its way up the mountain behind the others.

"Hold your weapons. It's Edwards," Pierson barked as he jumped from the four-wheeler. "Jason, are you injured?"

He motioned to his bandaged head. "I've felt better." He grinned. "But I have great news."

A shot rang out, and everyone turned in the direction of the sound. They watched as an officer about thirty yards away slumped over and fell off his ATV.

"Take cover!" Pierson yelled.

Everyone dove for the ground as another shot fired. Jason

scrambled to the nearest ATV and peered around the side. He could see two men running through the trees. Jason looked for Pierson and then jumped on the ATV.

"Edwards, stay down," Pierson shouted.

"I have to get Courtney!" Jason said. "She's still up there." He gunned the engine and drove up the incline he'd just walked down.

"You found her?" Pierson called, but Jason didn't answer. His thoughts were focused on what might happen to Courtney if those men found her first. He knew it would only take two or three minutes to get to her, but the machine seemed to crawl up the steep mountainside and he couldn't calm his racing heart.

The large pine tree Courtney had been sitting beside came into view, and he shouted, "Court, stay down. I'm coming for you." As the words left his mouth, he saw one of the Latinos break from the cover of trees. He ran straight for Jason, but he wasn't quick enough.

Before the man could react, Jason leaped from the ATV to tackle him. The impact of their bodies hitting at full speed made Jason's head spin, but the thought of Courtney kept him moving. He rolled over and popped back up to a standing position. The man moved to get up, and Jason kicked him in the ribs. The man grunted and muttered something in Spanish.

Jason nudged him over onto his belly. "Keep your hands where I can see them." He pressed his boot into the small of the man's back.

Glancing around the trees, he looked for the second man he had seen earlier. As he did, he heard a rustling in the trees and turned to see Courtney emerge.

"Are you okay?" He rushed to her side as Pierson and another agent appeared with weapons drawn.

Courtney burst into tears and buried her head in Jason's chest.

"I've got you now," he whispered and held her close.

He watched as Pierson secured the other man in handcuffs. Pierson shook his head and gave Jason a broad smile. "You have some explaining to do."

Jason chuckled. "I think I have some overtime pay coming." He glanced at Courtney and cleared his throat. "Did you find the shooter? This man wasn't armed."

"It's a good thing, too, or you might not be standing here,"

Pierson said. "What were you thinking, going after him unarmed?"

"I lost my piece, and I couldn't let them take Courtney again," Jason answered.

She looked up at him. "Thank you. I don't have any more escape tactics left."

"I don't know if my guys got the shooter, so we'll tread carefully," Pierson said. "Let's hope Swensen is okay."

"Is that who went down?" Jason asked.

"Yeah, but it looked like a through-and-through near his shoulder. I need to get back down there." Pierson directed his gaze at Courtney, still trembling in Jason's embrace. "How in the world did you end up with her?"

Jason quirked an eyebrow at Pierson. "This girl's got spunk. She's escaped twice now."

"Let's get off this mountain and get you two some medical attention," Pierson said. He nudged the handcuffed man. "Is this one of your kidnappers?"

"I don't recognize him," Courtney said. "I've never seen him before. He must have been one of the other workers."

"Do you know how many men were involved?" Pierson asked.

"I'm not sure. I only ever saw three of them—they were all Latino." She lowered her head. "One of them is dead."

Pierson's eyebrows rose, but then he patted Courtney's arm. "It's okay. You can explain everything later. Let's go. You can ride with Branson."

Courtney seemed reluctant to ride with the other FBI agent, but she went quietly. Jason wanted to keep holding her and not let go until he was certain she would be safe.

Another agent pulled up beside them. "We've got the shooter in custody, and Swensen is stable enough to transport to medical," he said. His eyes widened when he saw both Courtney and Jason.

"Good. You can haul this one down." Pierson jerked his thumb at the handcuffed man.

"Let's hope he's not as resourceful as you," Jason murmured to Courtney as they watched the agents put the man on the other ATV.

Jason winked, and she smiled as they began their ride out of the mountains.

33

EVEN THOUGH the hospital had much better accommodations than camping in the woods, Courtney didn't want to stay. When the doctor expressed concern that she might be suffering from dehydration and needed an IV, she refused to be admitted to a room.

"I don't want to stay in the hospital—I'd rather wear dirty clothes than a hospital gown. Can't I just have an IV while I answer questions?" she asked Agent Pierson.

He shrugged as he looked at Jason. "We can make it work. I've called your mom, and she's on her way here with clean clothes."

"Oh, thank you." Courtney relaxed and allowed the nurse to insert the IV. Then she stiffened. "What about my dad?"

"We haven't been able to reach him. Your mother said he was doing some work at the office and she'd keep trying to get in touch with him."

Courtney opened her mouth to speak, but she saw Jason shake his head and glance at the doctor. "We're starving—for Courtney, I think that would be in the literal sense," he said.

"Let me get you something to eat," Pierson said and turned to the doctor. "What can she have?"

"She's fine to eat anything." The doctor looked at Courtney. "Just take it easy so your system doesn't flip out."

She took that as a warning to eat slowly so she wouldn't throw up. "I'd like a turkey sandwich with avocado, if that's okay."

Pierson nodded. "I'll see what I can do. What would you like, Jason?"

"A nice juicy steak, double cheeseburger and fries—oh, and mashed potatoes to go with that steak, and how about some ice cream—"

"I think you're over budget, buddy." Pierson slapped him on the back.

Jason winced. "The sunburn."

"Oops," Pierson said. "I'll be back soon."

After Pierson left the room, Courtney watched as Jason tried his best not to flinch while the doctor worked on cleaning his head wound.

"This probably needed stitches, but I think we're past that now," the doctor said. "You'll have a scar."

"I'll add it to my battle wounds," Jason said.

With his dirty tank top and jeans, he looked as grimy as Courtney felt. His arms were covered in scratches and dirt, but he was still something to be admired, and that's what she was doing. Jason looked up and smiled at her. "Smartie for your thoughts?"

With a laugh, Courtney covered her cheeks, feeling the warmth creeping up her face. "We should've added Smarties to our order, I guess."

Jason chuckled and rubbed his stomach. "I'm thinking about eating." Then he gave her a serious look. "I'm also thinking about you. I don't think you should tell your mom anything yet." Jason glanced at the nurse and back at Courtney. "It might help us get the evidence we need if someone doesn't know what you found out."

Courtney wrapped her arms around her torso and processed his words. She had a hundred questions she wanted to ask her mom, to see if Chloe knew anything about her father's activities, but Jason was right—they could wait. "Good idea."

When Pierson brought back the food, Courtney tried to eat slowly, remembering the doctor's words of caution. The food tasted so good, she wanted to eat the whole sandwich, but her stomach felt like it had shrunk to the size of a pea. While she chewed, she watched Jason wolf down his cheeseburger and complain about the lack of steak. Her mom showed up just as she was finishing off the last bites of a giant chocolate chip cookie.

"Courtney!" Chloe cried out when she saw her daughter.

196

"Mom." Her voice caught, and they spent several moments hugging and wiping away happy tears.

"You poor thing!" Chloe exclaimed. She examined Courtney's face and then noticed the brace on her foot. "And your ankle too? Honey, are you sure you don't want to stay at the hospital?"

"No. I just want to go home and sleep in my own bed," Courtney said. "I feel like I could sleep for three days straight."

"I have a thousand questions to ask you, but that FBI agent told me it'll have to wait until he talks to you," Chloe said. "But sweetie, I have to know. Did the men who took you—did they hurt you?"

Courtney could hear the unspoken question in what her mom had said. Tears welled up in her eyes again. She could feel Jason watching her. She hadn't told him the details of what Ramiro had tried to do. A tear escaped down her cheek, but she straightened her shoulders. "I'm okay, Mom. I got away."

"Thank goodness." Chloe hugged her again. "I'm so sorry this happened to you." Then she perked up. "You know what I'm going to do? I'm going to make you an appointment with my massage therapist." She touched Courtney's cheek. "You could probably use a facial too."

"Thanks, Mom." Courtney felt tears sting her eyes. No matter their differences, she loved her mother.

"How about a pedicure? Oh, and look at your poor hands— what happened to your wrists?"

"It's a long story," Courtney murmured. "I don't want to think about it right now."

"Of course. I wanted to take you home with me right now, but they said they need to get your statement and you could be here for a while. So I'll just wait with you."

"Actually, if you don't mind, I can bring Courtney home when we're finished," Jason said.

"But I've been going out of my mind for the past four days," Chloe said. "I want to see my daughter."

"Mom, it's okay." Courtney grasped her hand. "I'm right here, and I'm not going anywhere."

"I want to wait for you." Chloe pressed her lips into a thin line.

"You can wait," Jason said. "But we might need to go over to the office as soon as Courtney gets her IV out so we can get the information we need to solve her case."

"That's fine. I'll do whatever I need to, but I don't want to leave you, honey." She hugged Courtney again.

"Thanks, Mom. I'm glad you're here." Courtney hesitated, her eyes flicking to Jason's and then back to her mom. "Where's Dad?"

"I don't know where your father is—this isn't like him at all," Chloe said. "He's had his phone right next to him the entire time in case new information came in."

Eric watched his phone light up again with another incoming call and ground his teeth. Ramiro and a few other workers took off with the bagged plants as soon as they saw the helicopter, but the rest of the crop was lost.

When Ramiro reported the helicopter sighting, Eric figured Courtney had been found. He had missed Chloe's first call and listened to her emotional message telling him their daughter was headed to the hospital.

Now he was scrambling to figure out what to do. He had worked too hard to have everything come apart like the frayed edges of rope that Ramiro used to hold his daughter hostage.

"I can't believe how much damage your daughter has caused." The petite Latino woman next to him drummed her red fingernails on the desktop. "Our entire operation is at risk. Do you know how much this will set us back?"

"Yes, I know, Natalie," Eric said. "But I can't stall any longer or someone might get suspicious."

"Are you certain she doesn't have any information that could tie Tropical Resources to her abduction?"

"Ramiro said she never had any idea who was behind everything." Eric paced in front of the black desk accented with gold trim, the centerpiece of the office in Natalie's home. "She knew about the marijuana, but there's no way they can trace anything back to us."

Natalie stood and put a hand on Eric's arm. "You're pacing." She moved her hand to his chest and tipped her head back. "There's no need to be nervous." She snaked her hand behind his neck and stood on tiptoe to place a sensuous kiss on his mouth.

Eric returned her kiss, then pulled away. "Not now. I'd better call Chloe back and find out where they've taken Courtney."

Natalie traced a long fingernail down the front of his shirt. "Remember—no matter what questions come up, we're safe. They'll never have enough evidence to pin anything on us as long as we stick together."

Eric nodded. "I guess you'll take care of Ramiro?"

"It's already in process." Natalie gave him a deadly smile.

A few moments later, Eric eased into his shiny Jaguar and leaned his head back against the leather seat. He massaged his temples and thought about the path he'd taken. The past few years, life had been good, with plenty of money continuing to roll in. Natalie had always assured him they'd never be caught, but this time he didn't know if he could trust her. They might have taken too many risks.

Eric pursed his lips. He had to be ready for anything and, at the same time, keep Natalie calm. He regretted ever letting her get her hooks into him, but it was too late for regrets.

* * *

"Mrs. Beckham?" Agent Pierson poked his head into the room. "I'd like you to try to reach your husband again."

"I'll hurry back." Chloe squeezed Courtney's hand before following Pierson from the room. Courtney gave her a weak smile and then sighed as the door closed.

"Tired?" Jason asked as she slumped against the chair.

"Completely exhausted," she said. "By the way, I saw you." She pointed a finger at him.

He gave her an innocent look. "What?"

"I bet your sides hurt from trying so hard not to laugh at my mom."

"Who, me? Laughing?"

Courtney threw a wadded-up napkin at him.

Jason shied away from the lumpy missile. "Really, I'm jealous. I wish I could get some pampering. You heard Pierson? He said, 'Take care of that head. We need you thinking straight tomorrow.'"

Courtney couldn't help but laugh. "I could see if my mom would schedule you in for a pedicure too."

Jason shuddered. "No, thanks."

After they cleaned up, Pierson told them the hospital had allowed them to use her room for questioning so they wouldn't have to go to the FBI office. Since Courtney was still hooked up to an IV and the doctor wanted to monitor both Jason and Courtney for another hour, the hospital was the best place to debrief.

Courtney told Pierson everything she'd already told Jason. Then she and Jason answered questions for over an hour as they tried to gather the facts they needed to prove her father's involvement in her kidnapping.

Courtney felt grimy and exhausted, but she agreed to meet with a sketch artist to describe Ramiro's features so they could start circulating his picture. It unnerved her more than she wanted to admit as she watched his diabolical face appear on the paper before her.

"I don't want to see my father. What if he suspects that I know about him?" Courtney struggled to keep her lip from trembling.

Pierson ran his tongue over his teeth. "Jason said he told you that we were investigating your father before, right?"

Courtney nodded.

"We're going to place him under arrest tonight."

"But I thought you said there wasn't enough evidence."

"There isn't for the drug operation, but we have enough to bring him in for fraud." Agent Pierson turned his cell phone over in his hands. "We've held off while we gathered more information because we didn't want to have evidence thrown out on a technicality. But in light of everything, I think we should move."

"How soon can you arrest him?" Courtney asked.

"As soon as we find him," Pierson said. "Makes me wonder what he's up to right now. We've already had someone go by his office, and there was no one there."

Courtney felt her insides clench with nerves.

"I think he'll end up here soon. That means you're probably still going to see him. I know it will be hard, but you need to pretend like you don't know," Pierson said.

"I don't think I'm that talented an actress," Courtney said. "I'm so angry at him, and scared at the same time."

"Then just cry," Jason said. "Don't hold anything back. That should hide the anger."

Courtney ran her fingers through her hair and swallowed. "I'll try, but wouldn't it be better for me to confront him? Maybe he'd confess."

"If I hadn't spent so much time with your father lately, I would agree," Pierson said. "That man has nerves of steel."

"That's true," Jason said. "I was right there asking questions about how Tika's hoofprints came to be on the edge of that pasture, and your dad didn't even break a sweat."

"But I heard his voice on the phone," Courtney protested. "I know what he told Ramiro."

"Which isn't hard evidence, and your dad is smart enough to lie his way right out of it. Then what would you do?" Pierson asked. "It's basically your word against his at this point, and that's not enough."

She hung her head and murmured, "I don't want to pretend. I wish we could just get this over with."

"The DEA has their guys on the mountain right now investigating the crop we found, and tomorrow they'll keep looking for more evidence," Pierson said. "Unfortunately, we haven't been able to locate any other workers, so I'm guessing this Ramiro guy has skipped town."

"So my dad is the only link to the crime?" Courtney asked.

"For now. We'll see what tomorrow brings." Pierson put a hand on the door. "I'll warn you before your dad comes in."

After Pierson left the room, Jason took Courtney's hand and gave it a gentle squeeze. "I want you to be careful and remember what I said about not letting on to your mom about your dad."

She licked her lips and swallowed. "I wish I could tell her, but it's probably for the best. She's going to totally freak once she finds out."

Jason crouched in front of her. "You'll be able to help her when that time comes. You're stronger than you think, Court."

She felt tears sting her eyes. "I don't feel strong."

Jason leaned forward and brushed a strand of hair away from her face. "Every officer on this case is shaking his head right now and wondering how in the world a beauty queen survived being held captive by pot farmers and then escaped twice."

Courtney lifted the edge of her mouth in a half smile.

"But I'm not surprised. I knew you were stronger than you

appeared." Jason squeezed her hand. He cleared his throat, and Courtney thought she detected a bit of nervousness in his demeanor. She put her other hand on top of his and looked at him expectantly.

Jason smiled. "As soon as this is over and you're no longer the victim with me as the investigating agent, I'd like to take you someplace nice for dinner."

Courtney hugged him. "I'd like that."

34

ERIC TOOK a deep breath before he walked into the hospital. He saw Chloe pacing in the waiting area, and he wrinkled his nose at the antiseptic smell of the facility. His wife cried out as he approached.

"Eric! Where have you been?"

"I'm sorry. I drove straight here as soon as I heard your message. I had to deliver some documents for the Highland project, and I missed your call." He put his arms around her. "How's Court?"

"The poor thing—she looks awful. The police are questioning her now." Chloe wrung her hands. "I'm so worried for her, but they wouldn't let her leave until they took her statement."

"That's ridiculous," Eric bellowed. "I'm going to see her."

Chloe grabbed his arm. "They told me to wait here, and they'll bring her down when they're finished."

"They can't keep us from our daughter. She can answer questions later." Eric shrugged off Chloe's hand and walked down the hall. He spotted an FBI agent standing outside a set of double doors.

"Where's my daughter?" Eric barked as he approached.

"Mr. Beckham, your daughter was injured. Let me check with the doctor to see if she's ready for a visitor." The agent moved to open the door, but it swung wide as Agent Pierson walked through.

"I'm not a visitor. I'm her father," Eric said.

Pierson put a hand on Eric's arm. "Just wait a couple more minutes. I know it's hard, but Courtney's been through a lot, and I think they're taking her IV out now."

"An IV?" Eric frowned. "What happened to her?"

"She was dehydrated and weak—even though she drank water from the creek, she's had hardly anything to eat in three days." Pierson sucked in his bottom lip and shook his head. "Your daughter is lucky to be alive. She's a fighter."

"I want to see her now," Eric demanded.

"Wait here." Pierson's tone left no room for argument.

After Pierson left, Eric fidgeted outside the door. He willed his heart to take on a steady rhythm and pushed his palms against each other. He tried not to think about what Courtney was telling the officers or the cause of her injuries.

With a concentrated effort, he rubbed his hand across his forehead, smoothing out the worry lines. Everything would be fine once he got his little girl home—away from the intrusive authorities.

* * *

Pierson ducked into Courtney's room, and she looked up as he entered. "Your dad is here and is demanding to see you. He seems pretty worried about you."

"I'll bet he's worried." She held out her battered wrists and turned her bruised face toward Pierson. "Think he'll like what he sees?"

"C'mon, it's time to put your game face on," Jason said. "You can do this."

"I'll go get him before he lets himself in," Pierson said. "I'm sorry about this. We're still working on the new charges to be added to his arrest warrant, but it should come through shortly."

Courtney closed her eyes and pushed back the memories of Ramiro's leering face—the man that her own father had worked with to grow marijuana. With a shudder, she opened her eyes and leaned back in the chair to wait for her dad.

The door opened slowly, and Courtney heard an intake of breath before her father spoke. "Sweets, I'm so sorry this happened."

She looked up, and her chin wobbled as tears fell down her cheeks. She took comfort in knowing her dad wouldn't realize she cried hot tears of anger instead of happiness to see him.

He knelt beside her and gave her a hug. Chloe entered the room and joined the embrace.

"What happened?" Eric took her hand and surveyed the bandaged wrists and the abrasions covering her arms.

"It was awful," Courtney whispered. "They beat me up, didn't feed me, tied me up. My body is so sore."

"They didn't even feed you?" Eric's face turned red, and he narrowed his eyes.

Courtney watched him, wondering how much he knew about the conditions of her kidnapping.

"We've been so worried for you," Eric said. "We searched everywhere, and then when the ransom note came in . . ." He ducked his head and wiped at his eyes.

It was all Courtney could do to keep from beating her fists against her father's chest. The fake tears were too much. He knew exactly what had befallen her, and he had let it happen. "I don't want to talk about it anymore," Courtney whispered. "I'm so tired."

"That's okay, dear," Chloe said. "Let's get you home so you can rest."

Courtney glanced over her parents' heads at Jason. He pointed at his watch and gave her the sign for five more minutes.

"I need to use the bathroom."

"That's fine, Sweets," Eric said. "Let me help you." He took her hand to pull her to her feet.

"No." Courtney withdrew her hand but stopped herself when she saw the surprise on his face. "I'm okay. It's just that everything hurts, so I'd rather not be touched right now."

She knew her excuse sounded weak, but it was all she could come up with. She retreated to the bathroom, locked the door, and turned on the water to hide the sound of the sob she could no longer hold back.

The anxiety was too much—she couldn't stand for her father to touch her with hands that only days ago she thought were filled with love. But now she knew better. She knew what he was capable of and didn't want to be in the same room with him. A few more tears escaped her red-rimmed eyes as she looked in the mirror and wondered what had happened to her family. The prestigious Beckhams had fallen.

* * *

Jason waited in a tense kind of silence with Courtney's parents while she was in the bathroom. Eric had begun asking questions, but Jason had put on a show of being in pain—wincing as he tried to sit up straight. He held the side of his head and sank back onto the recliner with a murmured apology.

Now he felt each second tick by as Courtney holed up in the bathroom to escape. What was taking Pierson and Gardner so long?

Chloe knocked on the bathroom door. "Court, are you okay in there?"

"Yes, I'll be out in a minute." Her response was muffled by the door.

If they didn't hurry, she'd have no choice but to come out of the bathroom and face Eric again. The door to the hallway squeaked, and Jason relaxed as he watched Pierson and Detective Gardner walk through.

"Mr. Beckham, could you come with me for a moment?" Gardner said. "There's something I need to ask you."

"Can't it wait? I'm here to take my daughter home."

"I'm sorry, but it can't wait." Pierson's tone was firm. "Now, if you'll please step outside."

Eric gave an angry huff and followed the two officers. Chloe cast a worried look at Jason, but he didn't acknowledge the question in her eyes. Just before the door swung shut, Jason heard Pierson say, "Eric Beckham, you're under arrest . . ."

Chloe gasped and bolted for the door.

35

BEFORE THEY could take him away, Eric pulled Agent Pierson aside. He had to think of something. He struggled with how he could protect his daughter but keep the authorities from finding out about his involvement with the marijuana crop the choppers had found earlier that day. He looked at Agent Pierson and took a shallow breath. "Is it normal for kidnapping victims to experience psychological trauma?"

Pierson's head snapped up. "What do you mean?"

"I mean that Courtney isn't herself. I've never seen her act this way before." He glanced back at the hospital door. "I think she may be confused."

"The doctor checked her out and said she's fine," Pierson said.

"When Courtney was in her early teens, she had trouble with nightmares," Eric said. "She had trouble separating the dreams from reality."

"What are you suggesting?"

"I'm saying that she's unreliable. Whenever she was under stress, the nightmares would take over. She'd slip from reality and struggle to piece together what was real and what happened in her dreams."

Pierson rubbed his chin. "I don't think she dreamed any of this. Her injuries are concurrent with her story, and Agent Edwards was witness to the latter events."

"I still think it would be a good idea for her to have a psychiatric evaluation," Eric said.

"We'll worry about that later," Pierson said. "Right now, you have some explaining to do."

* * *

Jason had never been so happy to see someone hauled into the station as when he witnessed Eric Beckham being escorted from the hospital. Pierson told Jason that he and Gardner took Eric in and gave him the offer of making a statement, but he lawyered up.

By the time Jason reported to work Thursday morning with the remnants of a headache, word had been leaked to the press about the millionaire developer arrested for fraud on the heels of his daughter's rescue.

Pierson met Jason in his office. "The men we picked up in the mountains don't know anything. They're all illegals. A couple said they worked for Ramiro, but they couldn't tell us more."

Jason jiggled the mouse by his computer. "I didn't expect much."

"Me neither, but there is something you won't expect."

"What's that?"

Pierson pressed his lips into a thin line. "Eric said he wants to talk to us."

"About what?"

"He said he'd figured out something the judge should know."

Jason narrowed his eyes. "More like, he had time to figure out a new lie, with someone else to blame." A night in lockup had probably helped Eric think of a slew of deceptive points he would be eager to share, especially if it might help with his bail hearing tomorrow.

Pierson rolled his eyes. "I know, but I figure we may as well listen. He might incriminate himself—you never know."

Jason shook his head. "We're in for more trouble."

They met with Eric and his lawyer in the stark white interrogation room with the flimsy table Jason hated. It was forever unbalanced, and the constant tipping and squeaking annoyed him even on a good day.

Pierson loved the room because he felt it put their suspects off-kilter, just like the uneven table legs. Jason tried not to glare at Eric as they scooted their chairs closer to the table.

"My client is ready to share some information about his case with you." The young lawyer was impeccably dressed and sat ramrod straight in the uncomfortable chair.

"Do you mind if we record this?" Pierson asked as he pressed the button.

Eric waved his hand before his lawyer could respond. "That's fine. I wanted to say that I think you guys are barking up the wrong tree again."

Jason found it hard to resist shaking his head at the expert criminal in front of him.

Eric looked each of them in the eye and then swallowed. "I think my daughter is behind this fraudulent activity."

"What?" Jason blurted out before he could stop himself.

Eric scratched his head. "It's the only thing that makes sense. You guys cleared Cobra—she was the only other person with access who was smart enough to do something like this."

"Except for the obvious person—yourself." Jason couldn't keep the venom from his voice. He saw Pierson give him a look that he knew meant "put the fire out."

Pierson folded his arms and leaned back against the chair. "Tell me your theory."

"I don't know what happened up there in those mountains, but I think Courtney is trying very hard to cover her tracks." Eric clasped his hands together. "She's a whiz at the computer. She put together our accounting system—it would be simple for her to mess with it."

"How does that have anything to do with her kidnapping?" Pierson asked.

Eric lifted his hands in a helpless gesture. With a glance at his attorney, he continued, "I'm still trying to figure that out, but I wonder if she was trying to extort more money from me to finish off whatever she's been doing."

"That doesn't make any sense," Jason said. "Are you forgetting that I was with your daughter when she was captured for the second time?"

"I found something last month when I was double-checking the accounts. There was a new company listed called Tropical Resources."

Jason's spine stiffened, but he kept his gaze steady on Eric.

"I think Court set it up."

Pierson held up his hand. "Mr. Beckham, are you accusing your daughter of channeling illegal funds through your company?"

"You've seen the accounts—she had access to everything. Have you checked her trust fund?"

"Our investigation has been thorough, and the evidence clearly points to you," Pierson said. "We have acquired a search warrant for your home, and they should be finished with that shortly."

Jason watched as Eric's eyes shifted back and forth between them. "My daughter is more intelligent than she lets on. Have someone check her accounts. You'll probably find evidence of a cover company. That money had to have gone somewhere."

"Courtney isn't capable of that," Jason said.

"So, she got to you too, huh?" Eric shook his head.

Jason felt the heat flame across his face.

"She's using you," Eric spat. "She's using you the same way she uses every guy she comes in contact with. Once she gets what she wants, she'll drop you." He shook his head. "Didn't you learn anything from all the boyfriends you investigated?"

Jason bit back the retort forming on his tongue. Courtney wasn't like that, but he couldn't prove it until they examined her financials.

Pierson intervened. "Mr. Beckham, we'll check into Courtney's accounts, but if we find something, it will not exonerate you."

"I think that's all my client has to offer at this time," the lawyer spoke up. Eric glanced at him and nodded.

"Remember that I warned you," Eric said.

Jason stood and left the room, seething with anger and frustration. Pierson stayed to arrange Eric's court appointment for the following afternoon. When he reached his office, Jason gripped the green folder containing the information he had gathered about Courtney Beckham.

"Guess we'll have to look into this," Pierson said as he entered the office.

"You're not going to waste time on his lies, are you?"

"Do we have a choice?" Pierson asked.

"And what do you think we're going to find?"

"I'm betting we'll find something, but whether or not Courtney has anything to do with this—"

"No. There's no way," Jason snapped.

"Hey, buddy." Pierson slapped his back. "Remember, we're on the same side here."

A few hours later, with the information Eric had given them and help from the techs, they were able to analyze Courtney's accounts. Eric's name was on all but two of her accounts, so they were able to search her trust fund, savings account, and a checking account.

What they found left Jason's mind reeling. "How did he do this?" he asked Pierson.

"I don't know, but it doesn't look good." Pierson rubbed the back of his neck. "We're going to have to bring her in for questioning."

"After all she's been through?" Jason said.

"I'm sorry." Pierson rolled his pencil back and forth on the desk and glanced at Jason. "Do you want to call her and see if she'll stop by?"

It was easy to set up the appointment with Courtney. She figured they wanted to ask her more questions about her father's illegal activity. It shredded the fibers holding Jason's heart together to have to do this to her.

He tried to ignore it, but a small particle of doubt crept into his mind. What if she had manipulated him to get what she wanted? Were those kisses just some kind of sick "get out of jail free" card? He clenched his jaw in anger and punched the back of his office chair.

✳ ✳ ✳

Later that day, Courtney came into the office, smiling despite the yellowed bruises on her face. Her ankle was improving, but her heart beat double time when she saw Jason.

"Hi, Court," Jason said. "Would you like to come into my office? Agent Pierson's waiting."

She put her hand on his arm as they walked down the hall. "Did you find the evidence you need on my father?"

Jason stopped at the open doorway. He opened his mouth to answer, then glanced at his partner.

Agent Pierson looked uncomfortable. "Why don't you have a seat?"

Courtney furrowed her brow and looked at Jason, but he averted his eyes.

"As you know, we found your cell phone and analyzed every call incoming and outgoing." Pierson tapped his fingers on the table. "When we searched the incoming calls to your phone, we found one irregular number. It belonged to a company called Tropical Resources."

"On *my* phone?" She glanced at her phone peeking out from a pocket in her purse. The police had returned it to her late last night. "Why would someone call me from that number? Jason and I figured it was the cover company my dad used for his drug business."

Pierson cleared his throat. "After talking with your father, we wondered if perhaps it wasn't an irregular number . . . if you might know more about Tropical Resources . . ."

"What? You think I knew it was my father?" She glanced at Jason, but he didn't say anything. She saw him clench his jaw—a familiar movement that meant he was angry. The muscles in his neck were pulled tight, and he didn't meet her eyes.

Pierson continued, "Not your father, but maybe someone else who worked with him. We're wondering if you know someone at Tropical Resources, since we haven't been able to find anyone associated with the company."

For a moment, Courtney was speechless. She scrutinized Pierson's face to see if he was serious, and she felt sick to her stomach. "You're really asking me this?"

Pierson frowned and looked down at the table, then back at Courtney. "We interviewed your father, and he told us that you set up Tropical Resources because you were stealing from him—that you were running the fraudulent accounts."

Courtney felt as if she'd been punched. She pushed her chair back and faced Jason. "What is going on here, Jason?"

The look on his face told her that there was trouble. "Court, we've analyzed the accounts you hold jointly with your father, and your trust fund." He paused, and Courtney noticed he wasn't making eye contact with her. "There are deposits that match up exactly to the bookkeeping at the office. An entire line of clients we couldn't account for was linked to your fund."

"But I've had that trust fund for years—my dad set it up when I was a toddler," Courtney said. "Everything is automated. I've never even made a deposit."

"What do you mean?" Jason asked.

"I mean that Dad set it up so a certain amount was directly deposited from my parents' bank account every month. I have a separate savings account where I make transactions."

"Can you tell us how much money is in your trust fund?" Pierson asked.

"Around two hundred grand," she said.

Jason leaned forward. "Your account balance today is over four million dollars."

"What?" Courtney sat up in her chair. "No, this can't be happening." She twisted her hair into a long rope. "Don't you see? He must suspect something, so he's trying to discredit me before you even have a chance to investigate him. Why else would he risk bringing up Tropical Resources?"

"I'm sorry," Pierson said. "But we can't ignore the financial activity in your account."

She ran her hands over her face. "How does this have anything to do with my kidnapping?"

Again Pierson cleared his throat—a sign that he was uncomfortable. "Your father said you set the whole thing up to get the ransom money."

"I can't believe you brought me down here to ask me questions because my father—who not only is a liar and a criminal but also allowed his own daughter to be held hostage while he harvested drugs—told you some bogus story." Courtney's eyes filled with tears, and she felt the warmth of Jason's hand covering hers. She looked up at him. "You don't believe him, do you?"

"No—I—we have to," he stuttered.

"Jason, you saw me. You saw what Adán did to me." Her voice rose in pitch, and she felt her chin wobbling. "You think that was an act?"

"Try not to be upset," Pierson said. "At this point, all we have is your word against your father's, and he's raised some doubts about the psychological trauma you've experienced."

"What?" Courtney's head snapped up. She could feel the anger flare in her chest. "This is insane! I can't believe you would put stock in anything he's told you."

"If we had some hard evidence, we wouldn't even bother with the questions," Jason said. "But your dad has retained a lawyer, and we have to be careful so we don't mess up this case."

Courtney glared at both FBI agents before her. "You want hard evidence?" she spat. "I'll give you evidence." She shoved her chair back and stood, her body trembling with rage. "I'll prove my dad is lying." She walked to the door.

Jason jumped up and reached for her arm. "Wait."

She pulled her arm from his reach. "I can't believe you would have me come down here to answer these false accusations from my father!"

"Court, I'm sorry," Jason said. "But until we find something definitive that ties your dad to this case, we have to examine the evidence against you."

"If I'm not under arrest, I'm leaving." She walked out of the office and winced as she put pressure on her ankle. Ignoring the pain, she hurried to her car. She fumbled with her key fob and opened her door just as Jason caught up with her.

"Please don't leave like this," he pleaded. "Let me help you."

Trying to hide the choking sobs taking over her body, she slammed her car door in his face. He knocked on the window, but she ignored him, turning the key in the ignition and then peeling out of the parking lot.

She wiped her eyes as she sped up the street from the FBI office. *I've got to get control of myself and figure this out*, she thought as she revved the engine and headed out of town. Her phone rang, but she ignored it. Talking to Jason right now was not a good idea.

None of it made sense. She couldn't rely on anyone. Her mother didn't know what was really going on. The charges against her father's fraudulent activity had Chloe hanging on to her financial sanity by the tips of her manicured nails.

Twenty minutes later, a hip-hop tune played from the passenger seat where she'd dropped her cell phone. Courtney picked it up and answered the call in disbelief.

"Sean?"

"Court, are you okay?"

"I—uh—not really," she said and shook her head with frustration.

It seemed like months instead of days since she'd last seen Sean. Their breakup had seemed so final when she was with Jason, trekking through the mountains. She realized it would take some explaining for Sean to realize she was no longer interested in him—at all.

"I can't believe you were kidnapped. If you would've been with me, this never would have happened."

Courtney shook her head. What had she ever seen in this guy? "Don't you remember? We broke up."

"That was temporary."

"Not for me, it wasn't." She kept her voice even.

"C'mon, Court, this isn't the time to play hard to get." Sean's voice sounded gruff.

"I'm going to take some time off to heal. I'm not ready for a relationship right now, and we're really not compatible."

"What? We're great together—"

"Sean, don't you get it? I don't want to see you anymore." She ended the call before he could say anything. She wouldn't make the mistake of answering his ringtone again.

A minute later, her phone jangled with an incoming text. With a groan, she stopped her car next to the entrance to the canyon. The text was from Sean:

I'm sorry. You must be pretty messed up from everything that happened. Call me if you want to talk. I miss you.

Courtney deleted the message and tossed the phone back on the seat. She gripped the steering wheel and looked out the window at the mountains ahead. Her usual place of escape was no longer an option, but by habit, her car had seemed to drive itself there.

She pushed back against the headrest and refused to allow the tears of betrayal to leak from her eyes. The part of her that knew Jason was just doing his job argued with the other half that felt betrayed by his questions. The time they had spent together trying to escape the mountains may have given her a false sense of trust. She couldn't ignore the feelings she had for him, but perhaps he could. She thought he believed her, but now she wasn't so sure, and she was alone. There had to be some way to prove her innocence.

She turned her car around and tried to think of a safer place to blow off steam. With her injured ankle, she couldn't run out her frustrations, and she'd never been the type to sit quietly and mull things over. She did her best thinking when she was on the move.

She smiled when she saw a sign for Interstate 80. A long drive with the top down could do wonders for problem-solving.

36

AFTER ABOUT thirty minutes of fast driving and racing thoughts, Courtney remembered something. At the time, it hadn't seemed that extraordinary, but now with hindsight as her perfect lens, she could see what she had missed. Now if she could get Jason to believe her.

Courtney felt a sense of relief over the new information she had remembered. After making a couple of different calls to her bank, she was able to confirm her suspicions. It might not be hard evidence to prove that her father had kidnapped her, but it was enough to discredit the allegations he'd made against her for fraud and turn the pointing finger back at him.

Her mind raced with ideas of how she could prove her father was connected to Tropical Resources. If only she knew where to find the woman he had been calling that day—Natalie. As she drove down the freeway, she wondered how far her father was willing to go to protect that woman.

She was brought back to the slow speed of reality by the ringing of her phone. She checked the caller ID and recognized Jason's number. As the phone rang, she tried to decide if she was ready to talk to him. Just before it went to her message service, she answered.

Jason spoke before she could finish saying hello. "Please, don't hang up."

She swallowed and listened to the beat of silence. She wanted to tell him everything she'd just found out, but she didn't know if she could trust him. "I don't know if I want to talk to you."

"Court, don't push me away. I'm trying to help you. I know you're innocent."

"How do you know?"

"I told you about my gut instincts, remember?" he said. "Well, they were spot on about you. Every time I investigated something new, I felt like I was being pulled in your direction, like I had to save you."

"But no one else seems to have your gut instincts." Courtney tried to keep the emotion from her voice and tamp down the hope that rose in her chest.

"I'm not changing my mind about you," he said. "I have to do my job, even if I don't like some parts of it."

"I'm glad you think I'm innocent, but that doesn't help me."

"Actually, I think I have an idea of how we can clear your name and nail your father."

Courtney swallowed and considered her options. "I'm listening."

"Can we meet somewhere?" Jason asked. "I'd like to talk to you in person."

"You're not going to try to arrest me, are you?"

"Okay, I deserved that." Jason lowered his voice. "No, there's no real evidence against you."

"When do you want to meet?" Courtney slowed her car to take the next exit. She had driven nearly an hour from the city.

"Anytime. What works for you?" Jason asked.

"Tell me where, and I'll meet you there in an hour."

He gave her the address of a diner not far from his office.

"I know the place. See you soon," she said.

"Thanks. I promise I'll make things better," Jason said before ending the call.

The intense heat diminished as the sun inched toward the horizon. Courtney shielded her eyes against the glare as she pulled her Mini Cooper in front of the diner where Jason waited on the outdoor patio.

He stood when he saw her and took a step forward. "Court, I'm so sorry."

"It's okay. I understand." She allowed him to help her with her chair.

"But still, I want you to know that I didn't want to ask you those questions." He sat across from her. "Your dad is a pretty convincing liar. I'll admit, I let some doubt creep in, but after I had some time to think . . ." He shook his head. "Like I said, I'm really sorry. I never should've doubted."

"You aren't the only one my dad has fooled," Courtney said. "We're all learning."

After the waitress took their orders, Courtney decided to launch into the information she'd found. She took a sip of ice water, trying to think how to explain herself. "I went for a drive to clear my head, and I thought of something to explain my father's accusations."

"His allegations are pretty thin—but we haven't come up with evidence to disprove him."

"Well, I have evidence now."

Jason lifted his eyebrows. "You do?"

Courtney took his eagerness to signify that he did want to clear her name. She leaned forward and spoke in a soft voice. "I told you that I don't put in or take out any money from my trust fund, but I do have a checking account linked to it, should I ever need to do that. When I turned twenty-one, the bank helped me set it up."

She paused as a noisy group entered the patio and passed by them. The sun moved in and out of shadows from the few puffy clouds hanging near the horizon, and Courtney cocked her head to keep the brilliant light from her eyes.

"About six months ago, I couldn't remember the password for the account linked to my trust fund. I had to call the bank and get instructions to set up a new one. I set it up, but the next month when I tried to check the balance, my password didn't work again."

"I'm listening," Jason said.

"Anyway, I thought about that, and I remembered that you can see the last failed login attempt on the computer—it never goes away."

"So you think your dad changed the password?"

"Yes, and that's the part where you come in. You guys are the FBI—have your computer experts check. You won't see any deposits coming from my password."

"And what is your password?" He grabbed a notepad and pen from his back pocket.

"Running girl 6.2." Courtney watched him write it down. "I haven't done anything with my account, but someone has, and that someone is my dad. He must not have realized that when he changed the password to my trust fund, it would affect my account, which is linked to it."

"Did you ask your dad about the password?" Jason asked.

"Yes, he told me he was looking at switching banks and wanted me to set up a new account at a different bank."

The waitress brought their food, and Courtney's mouth watered at the sight of the juicy bacon cheeseburger. Jason picked up his hamburger and eyed it reverently. "Remember I told you we'd get some decent food once we got off that mountain?" He smiled and took a huge bite.

Courtney laughed.

"Did you notice any strange behavior from your dad around that time?" Jason asked.

She bit into her hamburger and recalled how hungry she had been on the mountain. Chewing slowly, she tried to analyze her father's actions a few months ago.

"Just before all this happened, I was thinking that I hadn't seen my parents spend very much time together. Dad had been sleeping at the office a few nights a week. Now I wonder if he was with Natalie."

Jason frowned, and they ate in silence for a few moments. He polished off his hamburger and rubbed his stomach with an exaggerated sigh. Then he studied his notepad. "We've searched your dad's office and your home, but we can't find anything to link him to Tropical Resources."

"I don't understand why he would call my phone."

"That's what I've been trying to figure out." Jason slurped around an ice cube in his drink. "It looks like whatever business was going on at the physical location of Tropical Resources was just a cover—the place has been vacated, and the phone is disconnected. The call to your phone came on Monday, after you escaped. I think your father, or whoever he worked with, was preparing to set you up."

"You mean Natalie? Do you think she placed the call?" Courtney asked.

Jason nodded. "I think that landline was useful for sending out red herrings. Usually, cell phones don't register a name on the caller ID—just a number—so those instances where the screen read 'Tropical Resources' are significant."

"We can't let my dad get away with this." Courtney could hear the anger in her voice. "You mentioned you had a plan?"

"It shouldn't be too risky, but considering the latest tactic your dad has taken, you'll need to be careful." His eyes searched her face for agreement.

"What do you need me to do?"

Jason crumpled his napkin and threw it into the garbage can behind Courtney. "If you could get your hands on the cell phone he's been using to make calls to the people who kidnapped you—you could confront him about it."

"Do you think he'd confess?"

"I don't know. I have an idea," Jason said, "but it's going to take some undercover work on your part."

She dipped her onion ring in fry sauce. Nibbling slowly so she could savor the salty goodness, she considered what Jason was asking her to do. "You want me to search for the phone?"

He nodded. "Or one of them. I'm betting there are a few different phones. Your dad has one; someone else has one that sent the ransom notes via text. He was too smart to make any calls in the area in case we could trace them."

"Ramiro used the landline at the cabin to talk to my dad, but he took my picture with a cell phone."

"We know the ransom note wasn't sent from there," Jason said.

"Maybe that was because the cell reception was bad," Courtney said. "He must have gone somewhere else to send it."

"Natalie would be my guess. That might have even been her phone. Unless your dad has another partner, she would have sent the texts for the ransom notes."

"But we have no idea where she is."

"That will have to come later." Jason tapped his notepad. "All we need is one of those phones."

"How do we know my father has another cell phone?"

"How else would he have contacted Ramiro?" Jason said. "He's too smart to have called from a landline or anything traceable. We had his cell phone hooked up to our equipment to record and trace everything."

"You're right."

"The key is to find the phone your father used and then hope it will give us some leverage on him. My hope is that we'll be able to encourage him to rat on the person he's working with."

Courtney took another drink of water. "Do you think the phone is enough?"

"By itself it isn't, but that's where my plan comes into play." Jason squeezed her hand. "Are you up for this?"

"If it means putting an end to all these lies and accusations, I'm up for anything." She gripped the edge of the table with her other hand to keep it from shaking.

Jason rubbed his chin and stared off into the distance. Then he refocused on Courtney. "Here's what I think your father has been doing to keep that phone hidden. I think he was keeping it at the office, so when we searched his office, he moved the phone to your home. Once he knew the office was secure, he moved it back in time to avoid the search of your home."

His green eyes flickered with excitement, and Courtney felt a rush of adrenaline. "I know where the safe is in our house, and there's one at the office, but Sandra has access to that and I think Cobra might as well."

"So that means he has another hiding place."

"Or did he always keep the phone with him?" Courtney asked.

"I think that'd be too risky. We need to think like your father—he's been one step ahead of us this entire time."

"Basically, you're saying we need to think like a criminal."

"I'm sorry, Court."

"It's okay," she murmured. "We're going to stop him this time."

"Here's the thing—we'll keep an eye on you, but you'll have to do this part unaided by the FBI. What I want you to do isn't exactly under our search protocol. We would need to have justifiable cause to get another search warrant for either location. We might be able to do that, but not in enough time. Besides, it's important that *you* find the phone."

Courtney felt a buzz of positive energy. "I can do it—whatever you need. Just tell me what to do."

"That's my girl," Jason said. "Your dad's bail hearing is tomorrow at 12:30. Depending on what the judge decides, he could be out a few hours later."

"That soon?" Courtney said.

"Yes. I bet the judge will require cash for the bail amount, but your dad's lawyer probably expects that too, so I'm sure they're getting funds together now."

"My mom has been on the phone a lot today—she was still on it when I left, and I heard her talking about cashing out her accounts."

Jason shook his head. "I wish we could keep him locked up, but finding his phone and confronting him might be the only way to link him to your kidnapping and the marijuana operation."

"So what should I do first?" Courtney asked.

"You'll want to start by searching his home office. If you don't find the phone there, maybe you can think of a place we could've missed in our search. I'm betting we won't have much time, so hopefully you'll have a chance to check out the house tonight."

"I can be fast," Courtney said. "And I'm familiar with my dad's office at work. I can go there tomorrow."

"Good. Now let's put this plan into action."

37

THE NEXT morning, Courtney put on her game face and headed downstairs. Last night when she'd come home, she'd found the house empty. She knew Chloe had gone to visit Eric, probably to figure out how much cash she needed to post bail so he would be released as soon as possible.

Courtney had performed a cursory search of the office but didn't want to risk being found there if her mother returned suddenly. She also didn't want to talk to her mom, so she went to bed early to avoid any discussion.

That morning she would have to face Chloe and continue the charade of worry for her father. She took a deep breath as her foot hit the last stair. Jason believed she was stronger than she appeared. She held on to that belief as she stepped lightly across the hardwood floors—the same place where a criminal had tread so many times before. Her mother was in the kitchen pulling the crust off a piece of toast.

"Hi, honey. How was your meeting with the FBI yesterday?" Chloe dropped her toast onto the china saucer. "I'm sorry I missed you."

"Me too. I wanted to talk to you last night. I was gone longer than I thought and then you weren't here when I got back," Courtney said.

"I know. I tried calling and texting you, but you must have gone to bed early."

Courtney yawned. "Yeah, I don't know how long it'll take me to feel normal again."

"Did that nice FBI agent find out anything else?"

Her reference to Jason brought some heat to Courtney's cheeks. "They just asked me a bunch more questions about what happened."

"How many different ways do they want you to tell the story?" Chloe sounded exasperated. "They have all the information. I wish they'd quit wasting time asking you the same questions and find those men who took you."

"It's okay." Courtney sat next to her mom in the breakfast nook, ignoring the flare of anger it brought to her chest when she heard the reference to her kidnappers—if only Chloe knew her own husband was responsible. Instead, Courtney pasted on a smile. "I know they're doing all they can."

Courtney picked a few stems off the strawberries sitting in a bowl on the table. It was important to act normal. She cleared her throat before asking her next question. "Aren't you going to the spa? Or have your accounts already been frozen?"

"No, sweetie. I have my own money, but your father's hearing is just after noon." Chloe's eyes filled with tears. "I need to get ready and be there early to support him. I understand if you aren't feeling up to it after everything you've been through."

Courtney shook her head. "I don't. I just don't have the energy."

Chloe seemed to consider that, and she put an arm around her daughter. "Make sure you take care of yourself."

Courtney hugged her. "I need a long bath and a long nap—my body is still sore from everything."

"Then why don't you come to the spa with me later today?" Chloe's face lit up at her own suggestion.

Courtney frowned. "I don't want to talk to anyone right now. I just need to rest. Please, will you go? I hate to see you worrying over me."

"I don't want to leave you alone after all you've been through," Chloe said. "I can come right back after your father's hearing. The lawyer said it will probably only take an hour."

"You're going to be stressed after all that. Why don't you keep your regular appointment and stop by the spa on your way home?"

Courtney forced her smile to look bright. "I feel guilty for the trauma you've been through because of me. It would make me feel better to know you could have some time to relax."

"I'm the one who feels guilty. I wish there was some way I could go back in time and undo all this mess."

"I wish that were possible." Courtney motioned to her bruised face. But even as she spoke the words, she knew it was better this way—to know who her father really was. "But since it's not, we have to go on living, and that starts with you going to the spa today."

"Are you sure that's what you want?" Chloe looked at her nails, which were in need of a manicure, and then back at Courtney. "It makes me nervous, being away from you."

"Yes, I'm sure." Courtney gave her mom a hug. "Nothing's going to happen to me. Jason said the police are monitoring the house and the woods for any other activity. So you should go."

"Maybe I will. I'll call to check on you after the hearing." Chloe rolled her shoulders back. "I want you to know that I've asked your father to stay at a hotel for a few nights." Chloe watched for Courtney's reaction. "Yes, I'm angry with him."

Courtney tried to cover the surprise that must have registered on her face. "Do you think he's guilty?"

"I'm not sure." Chloe pursed her lips. "I'm sure he's done some things that aren't exactly by the book, but I didn't think he'd gone so far as to commit federal crimes."

"It'll all get sorted out," Courtney offered.

"The lawyer said if they charge him with fraud on a federal level, he'll have to serve every single day of his sentence—no getting out early for good behavior."

"That's terrible." Courtney squeezed her mother's hand. She felt the loss of her father deepen, the pressure around her heart tighten with sorrow. Prison was a certainty for her father—it was just a question of how long he would stay there. She eyed the clock. "I'd better let you get ready."

It was nearly ten. "Oh dear, I'll have to hurry. I don't want to talk to any reporters, so I'm going to get there early and sneak in the back."

"Good luck." Courtney watched her mom hurry from the kitchen and released the breath she'd been holding. She slid down in her chair and looked out the window.

The horse pasture looked dry and uninviting with the late summer heat wilting the last bit of green from the grass. She didn't feel like her performance had been Oscar worthy, but at least her mom had been too preoccupied to notice.

She had to find that phone, and the best way to do that was if her mom was busy elsewhere. There was no way she could keep up the act if she had to face her father again. Chloe definitely wouldn't want Courtney going out on her own, so her plan was to be back before her mother returned.

Courtney spent thirty minutes slowly eating a piece of whole wheat toast and a banana in an effort to kill time before Chloe left. She didn't want to give any indication of her plans to her mother. After she heard the garage door close, she left the kitchen and jogged up the stairs to her room. She opened the bag Jason had given her and carefully taped the wire to her chest like he instructed. It would monitor every bit of conversation she might have with her father.

She pulled on a pair of denim capris and a turquoise shirt and checked to make sure the wire was firmly in place. She brushed her hair back into a ponytail and let a few dark tendrils hang loose around her face.

"I hope you guys can hear me. I'm on the move," Courtney said. She couldn't see the van from her window, but Jason had said that they would get into position to follow her as soon as they saw Chloe leave the property.

Courtney crept into her parents' bedroom. She smiled at herself. No one was home, so there was no need to be sneaky, but she couldn't ignore the fact that she *was* being sneaky by snooping through the house.

The search was fruitless, as she expected it to be. Jason had encouraged her to think like her father. Where would he hide a cell phone? She walked back downstairs and entered her father's office. It was too clean and orderly to hide much. She approached the safe built into the back wall. The phone could be inside the safe, but

Jason had assured her it was not there when the house had been searched a few days before.

The most likely place was the offices of Beckham Development, since it had first been searched almost a week ago. There had been ample time for Eric to hide the phone there before his home was searched.

Remembering Jason's instructions, Courtney slung a large purse over her shoulder and stuffed a manila folder with a few sheets of paper inside. She checked to be sure her cell phone had plenty of room to take several pictures, if needed, and tucked it in her back pocket.

Courtney took one last look through the office, grabbed an apple, and headed out to her car. It was almost noon, and she didn't want to cut the time too close to when her father would be released on bail.

As she began the descent through Big Cottonwood Canyon, she checked in with Jason. She told him what she learned from her mother—that Eric would be out of jail once bail had been posted.

"Be careful, Court," he warned. "I don't want you alone with your dad at the office. If you're right, that will be the first place he goes, and it'll take us a few minutes to get inside if you need us."

She drove faster than her usual pace, which was already over the speed limit, trying to outfly the butterflies in her stomach.

The office looked mostly deserted since her father's arrest, but Courtney knew she would have to deal with Corbin Whittier. He had too much stake in the company to quit.

She drove around the building slowly until she spotted Cobra's bright red Dodge Ram pickup in the back parking lot. Clenching her steering wheel, she continued to drive around to the front of the building. Cobra must have wanted to avoid everyone—she knew he usually parked out front.

Courtney lowered her head toward the wire under her shirt and said, "Cobra's here, but maybe I can get into the office without him seeing me."

She parked her car and sat still, trying to calm her nerves. With trembling fingers, she dug through her purse for her peppermint lip gloss. She applied it and smiled at her rearview mirror. *Just act normal, Court*, she told herself.

The only problem was she didn't know what normal was anymore. The Courtney Beckham who had walked into her dad's offices a week ago no longer existed. She'd experienced a crash course in self-awareness, forced to look at herself closer than she ever had and admit she didn't like what she'd seen. Courtney had committed to leave the old girl with all her false pretenses behind. She didn't want to repeat past mistakes, but it was hard not to let the façade fall back into place.

As she walked toward the door, she hoped maybe she could sneak past Cobra's office. The door swung open silently, and she stood for a few seconds in the plush waiting area.

The receptionist's desk was empty. Courtney heard that Sandra had been mortified to be questioned by the police and was taking some time off until things cooled down. She wondered if Sandra had joined the ranks of those who believed her father's lies.

She hurried down the hallway, grateful to see Cobra's door closed. She hesitated before opening her father's office door, then pushed the key in the lock and walked inside.

His office was decorated simply, with leather furniture. The expensive paintings that used to hang on the walls had been replaced with blueprints of buildings they had constructed and pictures of completed projects. At the time he sold the paintings, Eric's reasons had seemed valid.

"These don't instill confidence in our future clients," he had told her. "I need something to show them what we're capable of."

Gazing about the office now, Courtney wondered if her father had been forced to sell the paintings to keep afloat before he'd started raising marijuana. She'd learned that much of his business income in the past two years was fraudulent.

The massive cherrywood desk was the focal point of the room, and Courtney sat in her father's chair and tugged at the drawers. Jason had instructed her to look for anything that might lead them to his partner. Courtney searched through a leather binder with dozens of business cards people had given her father. She didn't think she'd be lucky enough to find a business card for Natalie.

Unfortunately, her dad couldn't be labeled as "old school" when it came to his business. Most of his information was on the computer the FBI had seized. She opened another drawer and pulled out a notebook. She flipped through the pages, trying to decipher the notes her father had scrawled throughout. After a few minutes, she sighed. There wasn't anything useful in the notebook, so she put it back in the drawer.

A search of the potted plants in the office only left Courtney feeling embarrassed. She knew her father would have a more sophisticated hiding place, but she was beginning to think the phone wasn't in his office. She glanced at the clock—she'd already been there for nearly twenty minutes. It was time to move on.

She pulled open another filing cabinet and tried to see if a cell phone might be hidden under the hanging files. The sound of a key turning in the lock sent ice through her veins. There wasn't time to hide, so she pulled out the file she'd brought with her and tucked it into the filing cabinet.

"Hi, Court," a familiar voice greeted her.

"Oh!" She jumped and then felt the heat race up her cheeks as she looked at Cobra. "You scared me."

"Sorry, didn't mean to sneak up on you. I heard something and thought I should check it out."

She forced a smile. "It's okay. I'll probably be jumpy for the rest of my life."

"I'm sorry you had to go through that mess." Cobra shook his head. "What are you looking for?"

Courtney turned back to the filing cabinet, willing herself to act normal. "Just some of my personal things." She pretended to flip through a few files. "Here it is."

She pulled out the file and waved it at Cobra. "This has my résumé and letters of recommendation. Since I'm not working here anymore, I figure my dad won't need them." She turned back around to close the filing drawer.

"You mean he fired you?" She could hear him approach tentatively.

"No, I quit." Courtney turned to face him, sure he could see the anger glinting in her eyes.

"Hey, I'm sorry about all that." He rocked back on his heels. "I believe you, you know."

"You do?"

Cobra raised his eyebrows and nodded.

She smiled. "Of course you do—you got a taste of the real Eric Beckham, didn't you?"

He rubbed his hand over the stubble on his chin. "I'm salvaging what clients I can, and then I'll be out of here."

"I'm sorry my dad tried to pin the blame on you too."

"You don't need to worry about me." He touched her arm, and Courtney willed herself to stand still.

She had an idea. She looked into Cobra's eyes, trying to decide what to do.

"What is it?"

Battling within herself, she tried to think of what Jason would advise. She straightened her shoulders. "Maybe you can help me."

"With what?"

"Do you know where my dad might keep sensitive documents besides the office safe?"

Cobra gave her a funny look. "What are you planning to do?"

"It's probably better if you don't ask questions."

"I don't think there's much left that the cops haven't looked through."

"I know." Courtney leaned against the wall and scuffed her toe on the carpet. "But I need to know where my dad might put something." She hesitated again. "Something that he needed quick access to but didn't want anyone else to see."

Cobra looked at the door and then back at Courtney. "What are you up to?"

"I just need to check some things out for myself." She shook her head when Cobra opened his mouth to speak. She lifted her chin. "I'm hoping it might help reveal the truth."

"There is one place where your dad used to go to zone out," Cobra said. "You probably know it."

"The upstairs lounge?"

"Yep, I caught him there more than once, just staring out the window."

"Thanks, Cobra." She patted his arm. "I hope things work out for you—with your new company and all."

He smiled. "I hope you get your life straightened out too." He turned to head back to his office and then paused. "I'm still bummed I got gypped on that date we had planned."

"Yeah, I would've much rather gone boating than get kidnapped." Courtney laughed. She watched as a hopeful emotion flickered across his face. "But a lot of me has changed from all this—I don't think it would work between us."

Cobra raised his eyebrows. "Really? That's too bad, but considering everything, it's probably for the best."

"That's a nice way of putting it. Get back to work." She waved him down the hall. Courtney waited until he'd closed his door, then walked back to the front lobby and glanced at the parking lot. No one else was here, and she figured she'd better hurry before that status changed.

As she climbed the stairs, Courtney hoped Cobra was right about the lounge. The upper level of Beckham Development was used mostly for storage, but it did have one nice room. She had seen her dad occasionally venture out of his own busy office to enjoy the view from the second-story window.

The air conditioner kicked on as she opened the door, and she stood for a second, enjoying the cool blast. The room was small, with only a love seat and a few chairs, all facing the large window that overlooked the valley. The mountains appeared dry and wilted this time of day with the sun baking out every last ounce of moisture. But maybe that was just her memory of hiking through them with a sprained ankle coloring reality.

She lifted the couch cushions and pushed her hand down the sides, but then she stopped. Think like a criminal. She remembered what Jason had said. A criminal would have a plan for smooth action to get the phone in and out quickly. Lifting the couch cushions would draw too much attention.

She put her hands on her hips and surveyed the room. The olive green chair that Cobra had probably seen her father sit in faced the large window across the valley. With a frown, she looked out the window and stiffened. She felt her heart bang against her chest erratically as she watched her father climb out of his silver Jaguar.

A glance at her watch heightened her anxiety, and the muscles in her neck constricted. It was only one thirty, and her father was already there. He must have come straight from jail to get there so fast, and if he was after the phone, that meant it was in the building somewhere.

She only had a few minutes left before he saw her car out front. When he did, he would come looking for her, and she wanted to be on her way out of the building.

She'd already made a quick search of the room, and the elusive cell phone was nowhere to be found. Courtney knelt on the carpet next to the chair and ran her hand along the edge. She checked to see if there might be a hole in the lining underneath—that would be a great place to hide something. Her fingers traced along the lip of the microfiber upholstery, and her hand brushed against something that hung down from the bottom corner of the chair.

The sound of Velcro coming loose seemed to reverberate in the empty room, and Courtney cringed as she pulled at the flat leather bag she had found. It was dark brown and looked like a bank bag with a zipper, only it had a wide strip of Velcro attached to the back.

Adrenaline surged through her body as she realized what she had found. She unzipped the bag and pulled a slim cell phone from the interior. There was no time to look at it now. She stuffed it in her purse, zipped the bag, and slapped the bag back into place.

She jumped to her feet and hurried from the room, wincing at the pain in her ankle. The sound of her short gasps of breath reminded her that she needed to calm down, but it was all she could do to resist the urge to sprint from the building. She had just rounded the corner from the staircase when she saw her father coming down the hall.

"What are you doing here?" His neck was covered in red splotches, testament to the agitated state he must be in.

"I see you got released." Courtney narrowed her eyes. "How much was bail?"

Eric grimaced. "Two hundred and fifty thousand dollars, cash. Your mother paid it, but she's not happy with me. You didn't answer me. What are you doing here?"

"I came to get my stuff," Courtney said. "Since I won't be

working here anymore, I didn't want it to get thrown out."

"What do you mean, you won't be working here anymore?" Eric demanded.

"I'm not going to waste time talking to you," Courtney said. "I have things to do." She brushed past him.

"Court, wait," he said. "You don't understand."

She ignored him and hurried down the hall and out the front doors. Before he could react to her rude behavior, she jumped in the car.

With trembling hands, she shifted into gear and sped out of the parking lot. She dialed Jason's number on her cell phone. He could hear through the wire, but she needed to hear his response. "It won't be long now," she said when he answered. "My dad came into the office while I was there."

"That was fast. We picked up the chitchat."

"I bet he was there to get the same thing I was."

"So you found it?" Jason's voice lifted in excitement.

"Yes." She glanced at her bag and frowned when she thought about what she had to do next.

"Okay, remember what I told you," Jason said. "For this to work, our timing has to be perfect."

They went over the final details of the plan once more, and Courtney hung up. The next number she called was her mother. Now that she had found her dad's phone, she needed to be sure her mom wouldn't come home before the plan was executed.

"Hi, Mom. How did the hearing go?"

"It was terrible." Courtney could hear tears in Chloe's voice. "As soon as I paid the money, I left. Your father was in a hurry to get somewhere too."

Courtney didn't mention that she knew where Eric had gone. She sped through town as she listened to her mom talk about how humiliating it was to bail her own husband out of jail.

"I'm so sorry. At least this part is over."

"Are you okay? Do you need me to come home?" The worry was apparent in Chloe's voice. "I don't think I'm up to going to the spa today after all."

Courtney's heart lurched. She had to keep her mom away from

the house. "I'm fine. Are you sure you don't want to go? A massage would probably do you good."

"No, I think I'll just hurry home. I didn't want to leave you alone too long anyway. I'm on my way back from the courthouse."

Courtney infused brightness into her voice. "Okay, but I was just wondering if you could get me something while you're out."

"Sure, what do you need?" Chloe said.

"I wondered if you could stop at the bookstore and pick me up a few books. I need something to take my mind off the stress." Courtney tapped the steering wheel, her hands trembling with nerves.

"I can do that for you, honey. What would you like?"

"I was hoping you could get me the new novels by Stephanie Black and Jeffrey Savage, and also the new one in that series by Tristi Pinkston." Courtney decided to ask for one more title to keep her mom busy. "Oh, and I can't find my copy of *Gone with the Wind*, and it's one of my favorites. Could you pick that up too?"

"Are you sure you'll be okay? That will probably take me an extra forty-five minutes."

"I'm sure," Courtney said. "And Mom, why don't you get a book too? Then we can sit out on the deck like old times and read together."

A few beats of silence ensued before her mother responded in a tear-filled voice, "I'd like that very much."

"I love you. I want you to know that."

"I love you too, Court."

Courtney ended the call and blinked back the moisture in her eyes. She hoped she was doing the right thing. The chain of events she was setting in motion would put her mother's world into upheaval. But maybe she'd underestimated Chloe.

The past couple of days had shown a different side of the self-absorbed woman to whom she'd grown accustomed. Her feelings were tender because she believed her mother loved her. Courtney only hoped her mom would still feel that way after everything was over.

The tires of her car screeched as she turned past the front of her house and continued on to the stables. She eased behind the large building into the spot Jason told her he had parked a few days before. Then she shoved the car into park and moved at a fast trot into the house. Glancing at her watch, Courtney began timing. She had roughly twenty minutes to get everything ready.

The absence of a familiar yipping urged her forward with her plans. All she needed to do to keep the fear at bay was to remember what her father had done to Pepper, to her, and probably the man who was murdered in the mountains last year. She forced herself into action even as her chest constricted with worry.

In her bedroom, she knelt by the bed and pulled out the bag she had stashed there earlier. She opened her purse and stared at the incriminating evidence. Her hands shook as she pulled out the black cell phone and examined it. Then she plugged the phone into the device Jason had provided for her. It only took a few minutes to download all of the phone's memory, but Courtney found herself racing back and forth to her window to see if her father had arrived.

There was a chance he would just check to see that the bag holding the phone was in place and leave it there. But Jason figured Eric had been biding his time to contact Ramiro, so he would need the phone. When he opened the bag and found the phone missing, Courtney knew he would come to the house next.

She scrolled through the call records until she found her own cell phone number. Her throat tightened, and she was overcome by the level of betrayal to which her dad had stooped.

The device beeped, and she unplugged the phone and pushed the bag back under her bed. Her cell rang, and Courtney nearly shrieked. Her nerves were wound so tight that her body held a current of tension just waiting to be released. She sank onto the bed when she saw it was Jason.

"Will your mom be gone long enough?"

"Yes," Courtney said. "I'm really scared."

"You can do this. Gardner is already in place. When he sees your father, he'll text you."

"Okay."

"It's almost over, Court," Jason said. "Hang in there."

She ended the call and shoved her phone back in her pocket. It was difficult not knowing what her father was capable of doing. There was a good chance he would suspect she had taken the phone and confront her first thing. She was prepared for that scenario, but it would be better if they could stick with the plan.

She glanced at herself in the mirror before leaving her bedroom. Her cheeks were pink and her dark eyes were bright with the adrenaline coursing through her bloodstream. With a firm gaze, she smoothed the dark strands of her hair into place and left her room.

38

ERIC RAN upstairs to the lounge, his pulse pounding, causing an ache that encompassed his head. He walked in and casually lounged in his favorite chair. He waited to be sure he was alone.

When he lowered his hand over the side, as he had so many times before, and felt the leather bag, he sighed with relief. With one swift movement and a rip of Velcro that seemed amplified in the quiet surroundings of his once-busy office building, he held the bag in his hands.

He glanced again at the doorway and unzipped the bag, reached in to retrieve the cell phone, and felt nothing. A shock radiated from his stomach up to his throat, and he gasped for air. Had the FBI found it?

In a panic, he jumped up and headed for the door, but then stopped. If the FBI had found his phone, wouldn't he be under arrest right now for kidnapping? He pressed his lips together. His phone was safe.

Perhaps in all the confusion, he forgot the last place he'd left the phone. It had been difficult keeping ahead of the search warrants and questions. He had always been good at paying attention to detail, but the past few days had taxed his abilities.

He slumped back in the chair. He had traveled back and forth so many times with that phone. He must have lost track. It must still be at home in his safe. It would be difficult with Courtney and Chloe there, but he had to make that call to Natalie. It might already be too

238

late. At the thought, Eric gripped the arms of the chair so tightly his fingers turned white. Natalie had threatened before—he could only hope he hadn't run out of time.

He allowed himself a moment to rest his head in his hands and breathe slowly. If anything happened to the operation now, he would have nothing left. Eric stood again and straightened his shoulders. It would only take him twenty-five minutes to get home, and if he was careful, he could find a way to make the call in the next hour and salvage what was left of his mortgaged life.

Courtney's phone vibrated with an incoming text. She opened the message from Detective Gardner.

He's driving fast. Be ready.

Part of her wanted to curl up in a ball and hide in her closet, but she forced herself to keep moving and didn't allow panic to take over.

She hurried down the stairs and looked toward the hidden camera Jason said would be set up on the bookshelf in her dad's office. She adjusted her shirt, checking that the wire was still in place, and then exited the room.

There was a bathroom just off from the kitchen and only a few paces from the office. Courtney stepped into the bathroom but left the door open. A sliver of light shone on the green ceramic tiles. She stood in the darkness with only the beating of her heart to keep her company.

The minutes ticked by in painful seconds, and Courtney tried to listen over the blood pulsing in her ears. She heard the alarm beep— someone had entered the house. Her breath caught in her throat.

She strained for the sound of her father's footsteps and was soon rewarded with the familiar clip of his Italian leather shoes on the hardwood floor. He headed directly for his office, and Courtney counted to thirty before easing out of the bathroom.

She stood outside the office door—her father had left it open just a crack, as usual—and listened for her signal. Perspiration beaded on the back of her neck as she waited. Then, the sound of the safe swinging open, with the slight squeak in the upper hinge, set her into motion.

Slipping quietly into the room, she eyed the crouched figure of her father next to the safe. Courtney pulled the phone out of her pocket. "Looking for this?"

Eric whirled around. His eyes bulged, and he gasped. She watched his Adam's apple bob up and down as he tried to regain his composure.

"No, I misplaced some files."

"Maybe they're back at your office, since you like to play musical hiding places."

"What are you talking about?" Eric stood next to his desk and tried to keep from staring at the phone in her hand.

She kept the phone in sight and narrowed her eyes. "That was pretty tricky how you moved stuff from your office to here and then moved it back to the office before they searched our house."

"I don't know what you're talking about, Courtney. What do you want?"

She smiled—she had him now. "You're lying, Dad. You never call me Courtney unless something is wrong." She pushed a button on the phone, bringing up a list of numbers. "Did you know that this number calls the cabin where my own father had me held hostage for a fake ransom?"

Eric stiffened, and she could see the tendons of his neck standing out tight against the flesh.

"Daddy, how could you let this happen to me?" Courtney cried. "Do you know what Ramiro tried to do to me?"

"I told him not to touch you." His voice was even and menacing.

"Well, he didn't listen!"

A flicker of pain flashed through his eyes. "What did they do to you?"

Courtney motioned to the fading bruises on her face. "Besides this? Ramiro would've done a whole lot more if I hadn't escaped." She struggled to maintain control of her emotions. "Finding out my own father was behind everything gave me the courage to get out of there."

"How did you find out?"

"It doesn't matter. I know everything, so you can stop lying."

Eric shook his head, but Courtney continued. "I could've died out there, but I guess that might have been a better plan so you could have my trust fund money too, right?"

"No, you don't understand. I never meant for you to get hurt." Eric shook his head and took a step toward her with his hands outstretched.

Courtney stepped back. "Another lie. If you never meant for me to get hurt, you should've told Ramiro to let me go instead of keeping me there until he finished harvesting your drugs!"

Eric pushed a hand through his hair. "Look, it wasn't my choice to make."

"Whose was it, Natalie's?" Courtney hissed.

His eyes narrowed, and a strange emotion passed over his face.

Courtney swallowed as she tried to gauge her father's reaction. Jason had assured her that she wouldn't get hurt, but now she was beginning to question the safety of her actions. The code word for her distress signal tickled the back of her tongue. If she said the word "lightning," the police would be inside the house in ninety seconds to help her. But her father hadn't told her enough yet.

"I deserve the truth," Courtney spoke slowly. "Especially after what you've put me through—trying to place the blame on me and anyone else who gets in your way."

Eric stared at her, then stepped back and sat in the leather office chair. "I'm sorry." He rested his head in his hands.

Courtney realized she'd been holding her breath. She gripped the edge of the bookcase and took a few steadying mouthfuls of air. She watched him for a moment and shook her head. "Sorry that you've been cheating on Mom and trafficking drugs? Or sorry that you had your own daughter kidnapped and beaten to protect those assets?"

"It's not like that, Court." Eric looked at her and pursed his lips. "There's a lot you don't understand."

"Well, perhaps you should enlighten me."

"It's safer for you if you don't know."

Courtney held her tongue against her father's lies. He thought because he'd fooled her once, he could do it again. "I'm not stupid, Dad. You always thought that just because I got Mom's looks, I didn't get any of your brains."

"You're right. I underestimated you, and you've shown me that today," Eric said. "But I'm trying to make things right."

Courtney flipped her hair back and straightened her shoulders. "By accusing me?"

He sighed and shook his head. "I accused you because I was trying to buy some time—the same with Cobra. While they were investigating you, I was hoping I'd get a chance to contact Natalie. The plan was that if she didn't hear from me by this afternoon, she would salvage what she could from my crop and break all ties with me." Eric's frown deepened. "I'm not supposed to tell anyone, but if I don't tell you now, everything will be lost."

Courtney's fingers turned white from gripping the edge of the bookshelf. "What are you talking about?"

"I've been working as an informant with the drug task force in Salt Lake City."

She shook her head. "I don't know how you come up with these stories so quickly. Actually, I do—you're a good liar."

"I'm not lying." Eric put his elbows on the desk and pushed himself upright. "I'm not saying I didn't mess up. I did, and I got caught."

"But why? Why would you get involved in the first place?"

"When the housing industry tanked, I had to mortgage everything to stay afloat." He pinched the bridge of his nose and exhaled slowly. "We were going to lose everything—the house, the stables, our land. I was trying to pay off those debts so we could stay in the house." He lifted his eyebrows and met Courtney's glare. "I'm sorry. At the time, I felt there was no other way. Business wasn't going to pick up any time soon."

"Jason says you've been growing marijuana for at least three years."

"He's right. Last year I got caught," Eric said. "The drug task force offered me a deal. If I would turn informant and work with them to bring down Natalie and her operation, I wouldn't have to go to prison—federal prison."

"You expect me to believe that you had me kidnapped to protect your undercover operation?"

"That's exactly what you should believe, because it's true." Eric stood and walked around the side of the desk. "If anything went wrong, the whole operation would go south, and all my efforts would be wasted. I might already be too late. That's why I needed my phone."

Courtney took another step back, gripping the phone tightly.

Eric's shoulders slumped. "I'm not going to take it from you, and I'm not going to hurt you, Court. I hate myself for putting you through this, but there was no other way. I needed that phone because I agreed to call my contact only through a burner cell—I've bought several, and I throw them away so everything's untraceable."

Courtney held the phone with her finger and thumb. "With this, I have the evidence I need to get you convicted."

Eric nodded. "First, look up the name Greg in my phone. If you call that number, the person who answers will be the head of the DEA."

Courtney felt worry and anger spinning out of control. Her father was lying, wasn't he?

"I understand why you don't want to believe me—I've had to lie to you so many times, but this is the truth." Eric's eyes glistened with moisture. "It was about the money at first, and I'm sorry it took getting caught to make me see. But you have to believe me—now it's about bringing down this drug operation. Natalie isn't the head honcho, and if she gets away . . ." He hesitated, and fear flickered across his face. "You and your mother could be in danger if she suspects anything."

"Natalie won't stop, will she?" Courtney asked. "She was the one driving this—the one who decided to hold me for ransom. Did she send the texts?"

"Yes, and she's the key to bringing down this operation." Eric swiped his hand against the stubble on his chin. "Remember the man who was murdered up the canyon last year?"

Courtney swallowed, and her throat felt dry with fear.

"Natalie was behind it," Eric muttered. "She ordered him killed before I had a chance to come up with another plan. I promised myself I was going to stop her."

The doorbell rang, and he flinched. "Who is that? Did those FBI agents help you find my phone?"

"It's too late, Dad."

"Court, if you won't help me escape, at least call Greg. Tell him they're arresting me and that Natalie will be gone by tonight—we can't let her leave." He took two steps toward her. "Please believe me. I'm so close to making things right, but if Natalie leaves town . . ." He bit his lower lip and bowed his head. "She wouldn't give me the chance to rat her out. She's ruthless. She threatened to break all ties, but she wouldn't leave me breathing."

Courtney felt her throat tighten as she struggled for words. She stared at the phone in her hand and made a snap decision. She scrolled through the handful of numbers stored in the phone book until she came to the one attached to Greg's name. She pushed "call," and while the phone rang, she put it on speaker.

After three rings, Greg answered, his speech clipped and hurried. "Eric, I've been keeping tabs on you. Are we still under wraps?"

Eric glanced at Courtney. "Yes, but I hope we're not too late. We need to move now."

Courtney gasped and then grabbed the wire taped to her chest. She struggled to remove the tiny microphone on the end as the conversation continued.

"Were you able to get the intel we needed from Natalie?" Greg asked.

Courtney looked up and saw Eric watching her.

"Not all of it." He grimaced. "Look, the situation with my daughter went south, and she's here now—she found my cell phone, and the FBI is knocking on my door."

"Can you make it out?" Greg asked.

Eric didn't answer. He raised his head to meet Courtney's gaze.

With her hand still covering the wire, she nodded. "Take my car. It's parked by the stables." She tossed him her key ring. "Go out the side entrance. I told Jason to just come in if I didn't answer the door within five minutes."

Eric grasped the keys, and his eyes crinkled with a half smile. "Thanks for giving me a second chance. I won't let you down." He reached for the phone, and Courtney handed it over with trembling fingers. "I'm coming, Greg."

"Good. Meet me at the 600 South location behind *la panadería* and d—" Eric switched off the speaker function and rushed out the door with the phone pressed to his ear. Courtney counted to ten and took several deep breaths. Her head argued with her heart over the decision she had just made.

She heard the front door open and swallowed hard as she approached the office doorway. Jason wouldn't believe her father, but she did. Hopefully, she'd given him enough of a head start to finish what he started. Smoothing the wire back down inside her shirt, she hurried out to meet the FBI. Jason stood in the entryway with Agent Pierson and Detective Gardner.

"Court, are you okay? We lost our connection," Jason whispered. He stepped forward, scrutinizing her face as he put a protective arm around her.

Courtney nodded and looked away. "He's in the office." She pointed down the hall and then led the way, her insides coiling with dread. She stopped in front of the office and swung the door open wide. Jason stepped through, followed by Agent Pierson and Detective Gardner. "Eric Beckham," Pierson barked. "You're under arrest for the kidnapping of your daughter—"

"Where is he?" Gardner shouted.

Jason stood in the doorway to the office, surveying the room. He turned around slowly to face Courtney. "What happened?"

At first, she'd thought she could feign alarm at her father's disappearance, but when she met Jason's eyes, she knew he would see through her lies. She leaned toward him and murmured, "Jason, I need to talk to you."

"Where is your dad?"

"He just left."

"Do you have the phone?"

Courtney could see the other men listening to their exchange. "No, I gave it back to him."

"Did he threaten you? We were coming. We could've helped you."

"No, I let him go."

A flush of anger crept up his face. "What happened to your wire?"

"I disabled it." Courtney reached out and covered his tight fist with her hand. "I need to talk to you alone."

Agent Pierson narrowed his eyes. "What's going on here? Where's Beckham?"

Jason exhaled. "I need to talk to Court for a few minutes."

Detective Gardner swore. "Whatever she has to say, she can say it right here."

Courtney flinched, and Jason spun around. "Beckham left. We need to locate him. Now get out of the house before Mrs. Beckham gets home."

Gardner glared at Jason, and Agent Pierson didn't look happy either, but they both walked out of the office. Jason held on to Courtney's hand and followed them to the front door. He put his other hand on Pierson's shoulder. "I'm sorry about this, but I'm going to figure it out."

"As long as you know what you're doing," Pierson said.

"Just give me five minutes." Jason gave him a sharp nod and stepped back as they closed the front door.

Courtney looked out the front window and scanned the driveway. She felt a sigh of relief escape that her mother hadn't come home yet. She sat on the sofa and studied the intricate pattern of the Oriental rug covering the hardwood floor, allowing the swirls of blues and reds to blur and wishing that this part of her life would do the same.

Jason sat beside her and gathered her in his arms.

"It'll be okay. I heard what he was telling you. But we can't just let him go without verifying his story," he said as he stroked her hair.

Courtney couldn't stop the flow of tears. "I messed everything up, and now Natalie might escape before my dad gets the intel he needs."

"What?" Jason straightened and lifted her chin. "You don't believe him, do you?"

"I didn't at first, but then he had me look up a number on his phone and call a man named Greg. He's the cop my dad's been working with—the head of the DEA."

Jason shook his head. "No way. Your dad is a good liar, and he's smart. He probably had you call one of his drug buddies."

"No, you heard him. He said the DEA caught him growing marijuana last year and they offered him a deal. If he helped them, he wouldn't have to go to prison."

246

"If they really did flip him." Jason popped his knuckles. "He must be in over his head." Jason's head snapped up when he heard the front door open. Pierson dashed inside. "Branson just reported seeing Courtney's vehicle going ninety down the canyon."

They both looked at Courtney, and her shoulders slumped. "It's my dad."

"We'll have to put out an APB on your car," Jason said.

"Actually, I think I know where he was headed." Courtney stood. "Greg said something about the 600 South location and a panadería—doesn't that mean 'bakery' in Spanish?"

"What else did your dad tell you that we weren't privileged to hear?" Pierson asked with a hard look at the tip of wire sticking out of her shirt.

"He said that if Natalie didn't hear from him by this afternoon, she'd cut all ties with him and leave the area."

Jason pulled out his phone and looked at Pierson. "Courtney believes Eric."

"I don't care," Pierson said. "Let's get him before he skips town with this Natalie character."

"Wait!" Courtney put her hand over Jason's phone. "What if going after him compromises his plan to get Natalie?"

Jason carefully removed her hand from his phone. "We have to take that risk. I'm going to make a few calls and do some checking on the way."

"I'm going with you."

"No," Pierson said.

Courtney frowned and faced Jason. "I gave you the information because I believe my dad and I trust you."

"We can't take her with us," Pierson said.

Jason hesitated and looked from Pierson to Courtney. The door opened again, and Detective Gardner burst into the room. "We need to leave now!"

"We've got it under control. We know where Beckham is headed," Jason said.

"And we *are* leaving. Now." Pierson moved for the door, casting a troubled look over his shoulder at Courtney.

"I can either drive myself—my dad left his Jag here—or I can come with you."

Pierson's shoulders tensed, and he paused with his hand on the doorknob. "Hurry up."

Jason raised his eyebrows toward Courtney, and she allowed the corners of her mouth to lift as she followed them out of the house.

She rode in the back of the black Crown Victoria, followed by Gardner and Branson in their patrol car. Her insides tightened as she listened to Jason calling the DEA. With a little effort, he was able to reach the secretary of the head of the department—a man named Greg Rhodes—but only connected to his voice mail.

Pierson scrolled through Google Maps on his laptop, trying to decipher the exact location Eric was headed. "I'm not finding any panaderías or bakeries along 600 South."

"Maybe they were referring to something else," Jason said.

"My Spanish is pretty basic. I could be wrong."

"There's a trailer park next to the remains of an industrial plant at the end of town. There's been an ongoing investigation around the building. It's a hot spot." Pierson brought up an image of the area. "And it's just off 600 South."

"That's it," Jason said. "The bakery probably refers to where they're storing the drugs getting ready to be shipped out."

"Let's call in some backup," Pierson said.

"Shouldn't you try to get hold of Greg again?" Courtney asked. She was torn with anguish between the possibility of messing up her dad's operation and the chance of catching both him and Natalie in a last-ditch effort to escape.

"Your dad had a head start. Whatever he needed to do—he's had time," Jason said. "I'm sure he figured we'd come after him."

Twenty-five minutes later, they rounded a corner, and a large warehouse constructed with aluminum siding and steel beams loomed before them. Courtney curled her fingers into her palms. Jason turned in his seat to make eye contact with her.

"I want you to stay here." He held up his hand. "Don't argue. I'm sure these people have guns, and I don't want you to get hurt."

"Okay," Courtney said. "But please be careful, and don't shoot my dad."

"I'll be careful," he answered without making any promises about her dad's safety.

Pierson pulled across the street from the warehouse, and Courtney glanced out her window to see several other police cars and unmarked vehicles fanning out around the building. At the same time, bodies started spilling out of the warehouse, running in all directions.

"Looks like the anthill's gonna explode," Pierson said as he jumped out of the car.

Jason followed with his gun drawn. Courtney could hear a voice on a loud speaker ordering, "Stop. Put your weapons down."

Then the shooting started. Courtney ducked when she heard the reverberations of several guns going off at once. She peered around her seat and saw four Latino men firing guns at the officers.

Two Latinos collapsed under fire, and the other two threw down their weapons and put their hands up. Courtney opened the door of the car halfway so she could hear bits of the orders Pierson and Jason barked at the two men.

"Down! Get down!" Jason yelled.

The two men lay flat on the ground, and Jason and Pierson cuffed them. Courtney counted seven men in handcuffs prostrate on the ground. A dozen officers and agents weaved around the building, looking for more criminals.

"The building is surrounded," Detective Gardner's voice boomed through the loudspeaker. "Eric Beckham and Natalie Alexander, throw down your weapons and come out with your hands up."

Crouching down, Courtney slid from the car and surveyed the area. If her father had tricked her, she'd never forgive him, or herself. She ventured to the side of the car. She wanted to see if her father came out of the building.

The police officers began to collect the Latino men cuffed on the ground and herd them toward the patrol cars. Jason didn't relax his stance, and Pierson also kept his weapon trained on the front of the building. Courtney wondered how many people might still be inside. Jason wanted her to stay put, but when Courtney looked around at the men captured, it seemed like the real danger was over.

The area was quiet—only the static between transmissions

filtered through the air. Courtney felt her heartbeat thrumming in her chest as it worked to maintain a natural rhythm apart from the adrenaline rush of the past twenty minutes.

She glanced around her again and then fixed her gaze on Jason. His muscles tensed, and he motioned toward Pierson, pointing at the front of the building. Courtney gasped as she saw her father inching slowly through the front entrance.

"I need to see your hands." This time Pierson's voice was amplified by the loudspeaker.

Someone pushed Eric out the front door of the warehouse. The light caught a flash of silver pressing against his skull, and then Courtney saw a woman. The gleam of her black hair shone in the sunlight, and her red lips curved into an evil smile as she continued pushing Eric forward.

Natalie pushed the gun against his temple and shouted, "Whatever he's told you is a lie. He's been running this operation for six years, and I'm happy to kill him for you."

"Put the gun down. We'll take you into custody and get to the bottom of this," Pierson said.

Courtney watched the exchange, knowing that Pierson was lying. This woman wouldn't be getting any special treatment—unless he believed what she was saying.

Natalie sneered. "I walk out of here or Mr. Beckham dies now." She pushed her gun against his head, and Eric winced. Then his face took on another emotion.

"Shoot her. I'm ready to meet my maker."

"No, Dad!" Courtney jumped up and ran toward Jason and the other officers forming a perimeter of fire power around the building. "Don't let her do this."

Natalie turned her head toward Courtney and smiled. She jerked the gun forward so it pointed at Courtney. Natalie's finger flexed on the trigger.

"No, Court! Get down!" Jason tackled her to the ground. Courtney screamed as she heard the shot slice through the air above them and then several shots fired in return. She lifted her head and watched as a bright red stain billowed onto the lemon-colored silk of Natalie's blouse. Eric scrambled down the steps toward the officers.

Courtney watched in horror as Natalie reached her long, manicured nails toward the silver gun lying next to her. The blood had soaked the front of her blouse and ran down the caramel-colored skin of her arm.

"Get down!" Pierson hollered.

Natalie's fingers curled around the grip, and she flicked her wrist and fired.

Eric turned to look behind him as the bullet struck his back.

"No!" Courtney screamed.

Natalie shuddered as several shots rang out simultaneously, slamming into her body.

Jason rolled Courtney toward him, cradling her from the bloody scene. She pushed against his arms. "My dad—I have to see if he's all right."

"No, you're not moving until we have the area secured." Jason held her tight. "I told you to stay in the car."

A sob raked her throat, and Courtney covered her mouth as her shoulders shook with cries.

"Shh. I'm sorry," Jason said. "I don't want you to get hurt. That was too close."

"But my dad." Courtney could barely speak through her tears. "Is he alive?"

"I don't know yet."

Jason rubbed her arms and held her while the other officers and agents secured the area. A few minutes later, Pierson hollered, "All clear."

Jason helped Courtney stand, and she leaned into him, not wanting to view the carnage before her but not able to resist looking for her dad's still form lying on the asphalt. She watched as two EMTs approached. A few minutes later, they strapped him to a gurney. Courtney could see the dark stain of blood shimmering in the late summer heat. Her stomach rolled, and she put her hands on her knees and threw up.

By the time Jason had helped her clean up, the ambulance with her father inside had already left the scene.

39

JASON ACCOMPANIED Courtney to the hospital, where they learned Eric had lost a lot of blood. The doctors informed them that Eric was in surgery and things were looking good. He was listed in critical condition, and Courtney hoped he would survive being shot by one of the top drug dealers in North America. Natalie didn't fare as well. She was shot four times and died on the scene.

A few hours later, one of the doctors informed them that the surgery went well and that Eric should make a full recovery. Officer Branson had been sent to tell Chloe what had happened, and he brought her to the hospital. She arrived when Eric was still in recovery, and Courtney held her mother as she cried, and shed a few more tears alongside her.

The fatigue and stress from the past week overtook Courtney's best efforts to stay awake, and she struggled to keep her eyes open.

"Let me take you home." Jason put his arm around her. "The doctor said your dad probably won't be fully awake until tomorrow. You need a good night's rest."

"He's right," Chloe said. "I'll let you know when your dad wakes up."

Courtney stifled a yawn. "What will happen to him?"

"I got in touch with the mysterious Greg at the DEA." Jason led her toward the hospital exit. "Turns out he tried to send a message to the FBI through the office of the US Attorney to tell us to back off

Eric Beckham. He was trying to protect your father and his investigation, but we didn't get the message in time."

"I'm glad Dad was telling the truth," Courtney said.

"Your dad will still have to pay some hefty fines and do community service, but apparently he's been a valuable asset to the DEA, and he fulfilled his end of the deal to keep himself out of prison."

"I'm sorry I let him go without talking to you first," Courtney said.

Jason shook his head. "You went with your gut, and I'm not going to argue with that. Everything worked out."

"But Natalie is dead."

He frowned. "It would have been nice to take her alive, but I doubt she would've offered us much more than what your father has told the DEA."

✱ ✱ ✱

When they reached the Beckham residence, Jason hurried to help Courtney out of the car but then paused near the front walkway. "Your dad will still have a lot of work to do on this case, but I think it's obvious what's most important to him."

"And what's that?"

Jason tucked a strand of hair behind her ear. "You." His eyes focused on hers. "I want to kiss you, but I'm on duty."

Courtney felt her cheeks flush. "What about a hug?"

"I think that would be okay," he whispered and then embraced her.

Courtney rested her head on his chest and breathed in the fresh citrus scent of his cologne.

He pulled one of her hands from around his back and examined her wrist. "Still sore?"

Courtney shrugged and moved a hand up to touch his hairline near the bandage. "I'm sure it's not as bad as your head. Are you going to take some time off now?"

Jason grinned. "Probably not just yet, but a good night's rest will do wonders for this." He tapped his head.

Courtney held on to his hand. "I hope you feel better soon."

"I'll be fine," Jason said. "But will you be okay?"

"I—uh, I'll manage." Courtney forced herself to smile.

"I'll be on my way then, but I'll give you a call as soon as I can."

"Thanks, Jason. I couldn't have done this without you."

"Actually, that's what I was going to say to you." He lifted a strand of hair away from her face. "You were smart and incredibly brave about this whole thing." He kissed her forehead and held her close for another moment before squeezing her hand good-bye.

Courtney watched him walk toward his car and allowed herself a small smile at the warmth she felt from his embrace. Then she went up to her room and took a hot bath, trying to think about the new direction her life would take as a result of everything that had transpired in only a week's time.

As she soaked in the Jacuzzi tub, she thought about the person she was last week compared to who she was now. She was ready to face her fears head on and quit pretending. But would her resolve last? Courtney wondered if Jason would still be interested in her once the case was officially over. Maybe the feelings they had would fizzle out once the constant adrenaline rush ended.

She brought her fingers to her lips and thought about Jason wanting to kiss her again. He had said he knew there was more to her than just a pretty face. He was the first person she had ever spent time with who acted like he really wanted to get to know her. The first person to find out what was inside her decorated shell.

She let the water out and stood in the steamy bathroom, feeling the droplets cool on her skin. Maybe their relationship wouldn't last, but if Jason wasn't in her future, then at least she had something to measure by. None of the guys she had dated fell into his league, and she wouldn't make the mistake of dating outside that league again.

40

IT WAS mid-August when Jason headed out to the Beckham residence again. Over the past two weeks, he had worked doggedly on the information Eric had given them that had spiderwebbed into several new cases. Jason had called and texted Courtney several times but hadn't been able to see her since the day her father was shot. Eric's surgery went well, and after nearly a week in the hospital, he was released but kept under protective surveillance.

Jason hadn't been able to see Courtney, in part, because she had accompanied her mom to their house in Park City to escape the hungry news reporters and to rest. They left as soon as Eric was in recovery from his surgery and the doctors had confirmed that he would be okay. Chloe wanted to give Eric time to clear his things out of their home in Big Cottonwood Canyon. Before Eric was shot and the truth came out, they had decided to separate for a while. Chloe found out about his affair with Natalie, and she hadn't decided if she was willing to take him back or not. In the meantime, he'd be staying at an apartment closer to his business.

Now that Courtney and Chloe were back, Courtney was preparing to start school in a week. Jason was anxious to see her before he got mired down in another case. He'd called earlier that morning, wanting to visit her.

"Meet me by the stables," Courtney said. "I think it's best if you steer clear of my mom for now—she's pretty sick of anyone associated with law enforcement, but we can go for a horseback ride, if you'd like."

"That sounds great. Can I take you out to dinner afterward?"

"Um—sure."

He didn't understand the hesitation in her voice. Had she hooked back up with her old boyfriend? As he replayed their exchange, he didn't feel so confident about seeing her again. His heartbeat accelerated as he pulled up beside the stables. He grabbed the sack off the passenger seat and shut the door quietly.

Courtney must have been waiting for him because she rounded the corner of the building and motioned for him to come inside. "I've got the horses ready."

Jason hurried after her. "I'm sorry. I should've been here earlier to help you saddle them up."

"Now you sound like Richie—I'm quite capable when it comes to my horses."

Her dark hair fell across her shoulders as she moved around Tika to tighten the cinch. Jason wanted so much to pull her into an embrace. "It sure is good to see you."

Courtney stopped what she was doing and looked at him. Some emotion he didn't recognize flickered across her face, and then she smiled. "You too. The past couple of weeks have been an absolute nightmare."

Jason set his sack on the ground and walked closer to her. He could see the way her hands shook as she fussed with the horse's saddle. He touched her arm. "Is everything okay?"

She turned to him, and in that moment, he felt her nearness and how much he'd missed her. He watched her shoulders rise and fall as she took a deep breath.

"I don't know what's going to happen to me—my life's kind of a mess right now," she said. "I keep thinking about my dad and how he failed me and my mom in so many ways. I feel so much anger toward him, even though I know he was working to bring Natalie down in the end."

"I would feel the same way," Jason said.

"Part of me still worries that my dad was only trying to keep himself out of prison—not really working for the greater good of bringing down the drug operation."

Jason swallowed and squeezed her hand.

Courtney let her shoulders slump. "Then I start to think about the changes I'm trying to make . . ." She looked at the ground. "I just want to do something good with my life."

"You're a lot stronger than your father, Court." Jason touched her cheek. "So much stronger than you think—I wish I could get you to believe that."

Courtney lowered her eyes. "I'm sorry. It's just so hard."

"I know, but I'm here to help you. I'm not going to let you do this alone," Jason said.

She glanced at him and then back down. "I don't want you to feel that way—like I'm some pity case because you brought down my father."

Jason's fingers grazed her cheek. "Court, do you really think that's why I'm here right now?"

Her bottom lip trembled. "I don't know." She shrugged. "I figured it's just a matter of time before you feel like this case is officially closed, and then you'll move on."

With one finger, he tipped her chin up and looked into her eyes. "I'm not going anywhere unless it's to follow you."

Her eyes sparkled with moisture. "Really?"

He pulled her close. "I'm here right now, and I won't leave unless you tell me to."

A few tears escaped down her cheek. "Oh, Jason. I don't deserve you."

He wiped the tears away with his thumb and leaned closer to her. "You deserve a lot more happiness than you've had lately, and if you'll give me a chance, I'd like to be there to see you smile."

She put her arms around his neck and leaned toward him. Their eyes met, and Jason closed the distance between their lips. He kissed her and held her close. "I brought you something," he murmured.

She leaned back and lifted her eyebrows. "What, more granola bars?"

He chuckled and moved to grab the sack near his feet. He opened it and handed her a jumbo-sized bag of Smarties. "I'm hoping these will buy me a ticket to hear what you're thinking a lot more often."

Courtney took the bag, and her eyes filled with tears again. She shook her head slowly. "Why me? You could have any girl. You know, a buff FBI agent with a killer smile like yours."

"Because you're not just any girl, Court." He traced a finger down the side of her cheek. He kissed her again. Her soft lips caressed his, and then he rested his forehead against hers. "And I'm hoping this fall I can go hiking in these mountains just for fun."

Courtney groaned. "I said I never wanted to go hiking again."

"Well, I guess we could take an ATV." Jason laughed at the look on her face. "Okay, how about we just roast some marshmallows on a campfire?"

"I think I could handle that."

Jason squeezed her tight and ran his fingers through her silky hair.

"Ready to go?" Courtney asked. She stepped back and pulled herself up on Tika. Jason followed suit on the Appaloosa she'd readied for him. He gave the reins a light whip, and they rode at an easy pace toward the water trough at the edge of the pasture.

"So do you think you'll be staying in Utah, then?" Courtney asked.

"I do. I've grown attached to certain things about this place." Jason smiled.

They stopped at the water trough and let the horses have another drink. The sun was nearing its descent behind the mountains, and though the air still felt prickly with heat, the temperature was dropping steadily.

"I may have to do some traveling to hunt down some of the people associated with Tropical Resources."

"Still haven't found them all?"

"No, but we're working on some leads."

Courtney patted Tika's neck and then sat up straight in the saddle. "Do you think you'll ever be able to find all of them?"

"No, but we'll keep chipping away. Right now, there's so much intel to sort through, it's hard to know where to begin."

"Kind of like how I feel about my life," she murmured.

"In the meantime, there's other stuff to work on." He smiled at Courtney. "And maybe there'll be more time for fun stuff, like dating a beautiful girl."

"I think I'll have some openings in my schedule for dating the right guy."

They rode out across the same field where he'd found the first signs that Courtney could be nearby, and Jason's heart thumped with appreciation. Life was moving at a speed to keep him running, but he felt more confident about his destination now. Courtney urged her mare forward, and Jason followed her movements with a smile. He hoped that finding her was a sign of good things to come.

BOOK CLUB QUESTIONS

1. What would you have done if you found yourself in Courtney's situation?

2. What kind of character development did you notice in Courtney throughout the course of the novel? What things do you think she learned from her experiences?

3. How do you think Jason contributed to Courtney's self-awareness and subsequent changes?

4. Do you think offering a criminal a chance to become an informant in order to bring down more criminals is worth the risk? Sometimes informants are offered deals or reduced sentencing for information. What do you think about this practice in law enforcement?

5. Red herrings and foreshadowing are used in novels to keep the pace of the story speeding forward. Did you notice these elements in *Caller ID*?

6. The illegal growth and distribution of marijuana is a widespread problem across the United States. Were you aware of this crime, where drugs are grown mere miles from residential areas?

7. When Courtney is accused of having something to do with her own kidnapping, Jason is bound by his job to question her. How might you react in a similar situation if you were Courtney? If you were Jason?

ABOUT THE AUTHOR

RACHELLE J. CHRISTENSEN was born and raised in a small farming town in Idaho. She now resides in Utah and is a stay-at-home mom of four cute kids—two girls and two boys. She has an amazing husband, three cats, and five chickens. She loves reading, running, singing, and playing the piano. Rachelle also likes to think she has time to garden, can fruits and vegetables, sew, start too many craft projects, and teach her kids piano.

She graduated cum laude from Utah State University with a bachelor's degree in psychology and a minor in music. She loves dark chocolate, peanut butter, and graham crackers—together.

Rachelle's first suspense novel, *Wrong Number*, was selected as the 2011 LUW Outstanding Book of the Year and was a Whitney Finalist. She is currently at work on her next novel. You can stop by her blog at www.rachellewrites.blogspot.com or visit her website, www.rachellechristensen.com, to find out more. She loves to hear from her readers and can be reached at rachellethewriter@gmail.com.